14

DOG DAYS

DOG DAYS

Wendy Corsi Staub

SEVERN HOUSE

First world edition published in Great Britain and the USA in 2024
by Severn House, an imprint of Canongate Books Ltd,
14 High Street, Edinburgh EH1 1TE.

severnhouse.com

British Library Cataloguing-in-Publication Data
A CIP catalogue record for this title is available from the British Library.

ISBN-13: 978-1-4483-1248-1 (cased)
ISBN-13: 978-1-4483-1249-8 (e-book)

All Severn House titles are printed on acid-free paper.

MIX
Paper from
responsible sources
FSC® C013056

Typeset by Palimpsest Book Production Ltd., Falkirk,
Stirlingshire, Scotland.
Printed and bound in Great Britain by TJ Books,
Padstow, Cornwall.

For Mark, Morgan and Brody, the Guys . . .
For James and Chas, the Hosts with the Most . . .
And for Mr Manchops and Delta, the Dogs.

In loving memory of Dash, Krypto, and Nicky the Cream.

ONE

'nd I miss my bed, and I miss running through the sprinklers, and I miss swimming in the lake,' seven-year-old Max ticks off on his fingers. 'And digging for pirate treasure in the back yard, and riding my scooter, and . . .'

Seated beside him in the back seat of the big black luxury sedan transporting them to O'Hare airport, Bella Jordan checks her watch. She hadn't expected much traffic this early on a Sunday morning, but they're crawling along the expressway, an hour into a fifteen-mile trip.

Returning her gaze to the string of brake lights ahead, she reminds herself that their flight doesn't take off for another two hours. They have their boarding passes, and they aren't checking bags.

It'll be fine. Of course, it will. In three hours, they'll land in Buffalo, and an hour after that, they'll be home in Lily Dale. Except . . .

This is mid-August, the height of vacation season. O'Hare will be crowded, and it's massive. How is she going to hustle one small boy and two heavy carry-ons from the car to – and through – security to the gate to the plane?

At times like this, she isn't just anxious, she's wistful, imagining how different things would be, should be, if Sam were here.

'Mom? What do you miss the most?'

Startled, she looks at Max. Lately, he's known so many things he couldn't have known. Maybe he really is—

'You miss Chance and Spidey the most, right, Mom?'

Oh. Max wasn't reading her thoughts, asking what she misses most about his daddy. Of course not.

'I do miss the cats,' she assures him, 'but we haven't even been gone two full days.'

They'd flown to Chicago Friday evening to attend her mother-in-law Millicent's whirlwind wedding, which had capped off a whirlwind courtship. Bella had never seen it coming, but Max had predicted back in June that his grandmother's new friend, George, would soon become his step-grandfather.

Bella reminds herself yet again that her son isn't psychic, no matter what her friends back in Lily Dale would have her believe. He's just an ordinary, homesick little boy.

One who sometimes knows things he has no way of knowing.

One who looks more and more like his late daddy every day.

While Bella is a blue-eyed brunette, Max's brown hair is the same sandy shade as Sam's, with a distinct cowlick in the same exact spot as Sam's. Max wears glasses, as his father did. His eyes are the same gold-flecked brown as Sam's, with the same earnest expression Sam so frequently wore – when he wasn't grinning. Max has the same grin, minus the front tooth he lost a few weeks back.

He's growing up, Sam. If only you could see him.

If only I could see you.

Max is back to counting on his fingers. 'I miss Valley View . . .'

That would be the Victorian guesthouse they've called home – and Bella has managed – since last summer.

'And Jiffy . . .'

Jiffy Arden, Max's best friend.

'And Jelly.'

Jiffy's puppy.

'Mom, can I have—'

'No.'

'But I didn't even finish asking.'

'I know what you were going to say, and you know the answer.'

And neither of us is psychic.

'But puppies are so cute and fun and I really really *really* wish I had one.'

Bella sighs. 'We aren't talking about puppies, though. We're talking about things we miss about home.'

'Oh. Right. I miss playing *Ninja Zombie Battle* on Jiffy's Playbox. Can I have—'

'No.'

'But—'

'Max, video games are a special treat. You can play them when you visit Jiffy. And at this time of year, it's much more fun to be outside in the fresh air, isn't it?'

'Oh! I miss fresh air! Chicago air isn't fresh. And I miss the playground.'

'You did get to go to the playground across the street from Grandma's apartment, yesterday morning before the wedding,' Bella reminds him.

'Yes, but the air was too hot and stinky. And I like the rusty metal kind of swings with the chains that pinch your fingers, like at home.'

'You told George you liked these better.'

'I didn't want him to feel bad because he was practicing to be my new grandpa and it was nice of him to take me.'

'It was,' Bella agrees, though she suspects the groom had been as eager as Max had been to escape the flurry of wedding planners, caterers, florists, musicians and salon staffers.

She, too, longed to flee, because the pre-nuptial chaos reminded her of her own wedding day well over a decade ago, and because Sam should have been there yesterday, for his mother's.

'And you really do think he'd be OK with my marrying George?' Millicent had whispered to Bella, her maid of honor, as they waited in the church vestibule for the organ music to begin.

Bella had assured her that as much as Sam had loved his father, he'd always worried about his mother, long before she was widowed. Bella had never met Thierry Jordan, but she knows he wasn't home a lot, due to business travel and late nights at the office. Sam always said his mother played a far bigger role in raising him, which was why he was so determined to be a hands-on father himself.

'Children need their dads as much as they need their moms,' he'd told Bella when Max was born. 'I don't ever want him to need me and I'm not there. I don't want to miss a thing.'

Yesterday, Bella had swallowed a lump in her throat and assured her mother-in-law, 'Sam would want you to be happy. Not lonely and living alone for the rest of your life. Remember what George said when you two got engaged? That everyone deserves a second chance at love? I know Sam would have felt that with all his heart.'

Millicent looked closely at her, and said, 'I believe he would have – and not just for me, Bella, but for—'

The first strains of the Wedding March had cut off whatever she was going to say. But Bella is pretty sure she knows what it was, and that it's not something she'd want to discuss with Sam's mother. Or with anyone, really. Not yet. Not—

'You know who else I miss, Mom? Dr Drew. I'll bet you miss him even more,' Max adds slyly.

Drew Bailey isn't merely the veterinarian who'd saved Chance and Spidey's lives. Nor is he merely a trusted friend and confidant. He's become . . . well, important.

Very.

'I do miss Drew,' she admits, remembering that she hadn't responded to his most recent text. He's been running Valley View in her absence, and they'd gone back and forth earlier this morning when he'd reached out to ask her how to handle a last-minute reservation cancellation for a guest who'd had an unexpected death in the family.

She pulls her phone from her pocket and rereads the latest message, which had popped up just as she and Max were leaving for the airport.

Are there extra cushions for the chairs by the firepit? It was chilly so I lit it for the guests, and storm came in overnight. Sorry.

Bella writes back, *No extras, but no worries. They'll dry. But how's the roof in the rain?*

Leaky but holding up, he responds.

Like many things around Valley View, the roof needs a costly repair that the owner has been trying to put off as long as possible.

Everything else OK? she asks Drew.

He replies with a thumbs-up emoji, and she smiles.

Good. Can't wait to get home to . . .

She'd like to conclude the sentence with a heartfelt *you,* but it seems like too much.

Instead, she writes, *cool weather. Heatwave here all weekend.*

Her thumb hovers over the Send button. Is she really going to make this about the weather?

No. She deletes everything after *home,* adds a period, and sends the message.

Wobbly dots appear, meaning he's typing something. The dots disappear. She waits, wondering if he, too, is trying to figure out how to say what they never say – not in text, or on the phone, or in person.

The dots reappear, and then, *Checked your flight again. Still on time. Safe travels.*

He isn't the most effusive man in the world. But it's clear he's been thinking about her, and he misses her, too.

Thanks! See you soon, she responds, and adds a heart emoji before returning the phone to her pocket.

'And I miss Odelia, and Luther, and Misty,' Max is saying.

Odelia Lauder lives next door to Valley View; Luther Ragland is her retired law-enforcement significant other; Misty Starr is Jiffy's mom.

'I even kind of miss Miss Feeney. Hey, I said *miss-Miss*. That's funny, isn't it?'

'Mmm hmm.'

'Do you miss-Miss Feeney, too, Mom?'

'Sure.'

Though Pandora Feeney is the kind of neighbor who pops over to mention that the flowerbeds need watering or the grass needs mowing. She tends to borrow books Bella has yet to read, and to offer spoilers for the ones Bella's about to finish. She often rummages through Bella's fridge, critiquing the contents while helping herself.

No matter how her intrusions – er, visits – unfold, at some point she always, always pauses to address someone Bella can't see, or hear.

Pandora Feeney talks to dead people.

She isn't the only one.

Lily Dale, founded in the nineteenth century by spiritualists, remains populated by psychic mediums to this day. During the busy summer season, there's a full slate of daily programming, with lectures, presentations, group readings, and classes on everything from levitation to psychometry. The mediums provide spirit messages, psychic visions about the future, physical healing, spiritual counseling, information. It often seems to be delivered by their 'guides', immortal beings they believe are with them throughout their lives – lives being plural, as in reincarnation.

As a former science teacher, Bella is grounded in facts, evidence and logic.

OK, she's also a widow who'd give anything to connect with her late husband. But if it were possible to communicate from the Other Side, Sam would have come through to her by now.

Her Lily Dale friends are convinced that with open-mindedness and mediumship training, everyone is capable of interacting with the spirit world.

They're also convinced that Bella *has* heard from Sam.

Granted, a few rather . . . *unusual* things have happened since her arrival. But in retrospect, she always – well, almost always – finds a logical explanation.

At first, she simply assumed that her mind – or the mediums

– might be playing tricks on her. But now, more than a year into living in the Dale and nearly two into widowhood, she's more confident in her own perception and the mediums' integrity. Now, she attributes these so-called mysterious occurrences – most of them, anyway – to electromagnetic energy, sensory phenomenology, mere coincidence . . .

There are no coincidences.

That's an oft-repeated motto in Lily Dale, where such things are invariably attributed to *Spirit*, as the locals refer to the dearly departed.

In Lily Dale, when you stumble across a hidden compartment in an old house and find the tourmaline necklace your husband was planning to give you for the Christmas he didn't live to see . . .

In Lily Dale, that's your husband reaching out from beyond the grave. In Bella's mind, it's . . .

Well, she doesn't know what it *is*, but she's pretty sure it isn't Sam, sending gifts and messages from the Other Side. Because if he were capable of that, wouldn't he just . . . appear? Especially knowing Bella as he does . . .

Did.

Sam is past tense. Sam is dead.

There's no such thing as dead is another oft-repeated local credo in Lily Dale, where souls that have departed the earthly plane reportedly pop in to offer wisdom, warnings, and the occasional prank. Bella has grown accustomed to her medium friends interrupting the conversation at hand to address invisible visitors from a family ancestor to Winston Churchill.

In the moment, it's often believable, but in retrospect . . .

Yeah, not so much.

'Mom! Duck!' Max shouts.

Bella, hearing a roar overhead, throws herself over his small body before realizing that it's just a low-flying 747 coming in for a landing.

Max wriggles from her grasp. 'Whoa! That was a close call! Wait till I tell Jiffy! I bet he never almost got squished by a giant airplane!'

Max is no slouch in the creative imagination department, but Jiffy Arden is the kind of kid who can spin an everyday garter snake sighting into a narrow escape from a Burmese python's death grip. He is also, according to Odelia, one of the Dale's most gifted young mediums.

Up front, Barb, the driver, announces, 'We'll be at the terminal in three minutes, folks.'

'Three?' Max asks. 'Not four? Not two?'

'Three.' She points to the dashboard clock. 'You'll see.'

'How do you know?'

'I do this a lot,' Barb says with a smile.

She's a gray-haired woman who'd retired from a long career as an accountant only to find that she hated being at home with her retired husband puttering around. Earlier, she'd told Bella that working for the car service had saved her marriage.

'Too much togetherness, if you know what I mean,' she'd said.

Bella pretended that she did, imagining a life in which that might be an actual *thing*. Imagining herself, always home with too much time on her hands, sick of Sam, also always home and underfoot.

Exactly three minutes later, they're double parked in the passenger drop-off zone in front of the terminal. Barb pops the trunk.

'I'll get your bags. Make sure you don't forget anything.'

Bella pats her pocket to make sure she has her cell phone. She has a habit of putting it down and losing track of it – which is one thing when you're at home, and quite another when you're in a cab and about to board a plane.

She remembers to check her purse, too, for the envelope Millicent had handed her this morning.

'George has college funds for all of his grandkids.'

'And you set one up for Max when he was born,' Bella reminded her.

'But I haven't contributed since then. Take this check, Bella. I know Sam was listed as the co-owner at the time, but since you're his heir, you shouldn't have any problem depositing it. It's made out in your name, see?'

She'd gasped when she'd seen the amount.

'Two hundred thousand dollars? Millicent, you don't have to—'

'I want to. *We* want to,' she'd amended. 'George has been telling me how quickly tuition is rising these days. I had no idea what it costs to get an education.'

'But this . . . this is too much money to just give away!'

'To my grandson? Don't be silly. Anyway, George and I are getting up there in years, and we can't take it with us. This should be enough for Max to go wherever he chooses, even a decade from now.'

Max – in college. It's so hard to imagine, but Millicent had warned her that the day will come sooner than she thinks.

'I just hope I'm here to see it,' Millicent had said.

'Of course you will be.'

'You never know.'

No, you never do. Bella had never considered that Max's dad wouldn't be here for that – for any of it.

Oh, Sam. You're missing everything.

She unbuckles Max's seatbelt, makes sure his sneaker laces are tied, tells him not to budge until she goes around to the curb side, and gets out of the car.

Whoa. Even at this early hour, the sun beats down with searing heat.

The place is a madhouse – cars and cabs maneuvering for space, passengers hauling luggage, people shouting, horns honking, security guards blowing whistles, jackhammers vibrating in a construction zone that blocks off a good-sized section of road and walkway.

Bella hurries to open the door for Max, gripping his hand tightly as he climbs out.

'You know what else I miss about Lily Dale?' he asks. 'It's not hot. Sometimes it's even cold. And snowy.'

'Not in August.'

Though you never know. Given the volatile weather patterns along the eastern edge of Lake Erie, July is reportedly the only month of the year when snow is pretty much guaranteed not to fall in Western New York.

'Well, at least it's never as hot as . . .'

The rest of Max's sentence is drowned out by a blast of whistle and a security guard shouting at a driver behind them, 'Hey! This is passenger drop-offs only!'

Barb pulls the rolling bag over with the duffel balanced on top. 'Got everything?'

'Yes, thank you so much.' Bella fumbles in her purse with one hand, still gripping her son with the other and wondering how she's going to wrangle Max and the bags through this chaos. 'Hang on, and just let me find my wallet.'

'No need, Mrs Jordan. Your in-laws took care of everything. I'm all set.'

Her in-laws. She smiles. They'd been so generous, sending her and Max to the airport in a limo instead of—

'Mom! I forgot my . . .'

Again, Max's words are lost in the blast of a whistle and a shout.

'Hey! Hey, what are you doing?' the guard bellows. 'I said, this is passenger drop-offs only! Get back in your car!'

'What did you forget, Max?' Bella asks.

He's slack-jawed, gaping at something behind her.

She whirls, expecting to see another low-flying jet. Finding nothing out of the ordinary, she turns back to him.

'Come on, Max, we have to hurry. What did you forget? Is it in the car, or at Grandma's?'

Barb leans into the back seat. 'It's his backpack. I've got it.'

'Mom! *Look!* It's the golden car!'

Again, Bella turns to follow Max's gaze.

A uniformed security guard is standing beside the open driver's side door of the car pulled up behind theirs. It's an older model Subaru, with dingy metallic paint and a dented fender.

'Sir, you need to get back behind the wheel and move this vehicle immediately!' the guard shouts.

Bella tells Max, 'They're just parked in the wrong spot, sweetie. It's OK. There are rules about—'

'Hey, Mom! Look at the guy!' Max is urgent now, clutching her arm.

'He's a policeman, Max. He's just trying to—'

'Not that guy! The guy in the golden car!'

Bella looks. As the Subaru slowly rolls past them, the driver's face is clearly visible behind the windshield. He's looking right at them. He's . . .

He can't be. It's impossible.

But it's not, because he *is*. He's . . .

'Daddy!' Max shouts.

'Sam!' Bella breathes.

And then he's gone.

TWO

Lily Dale: 1 Mile.

Spotting the sign, Bella exhales for perhaps the first time since Chicago.

Max, asleep in the back seat, doesn't stir as she turns off Route 60 onto Dale Drive.

Slowing her speed, Bella removes one hand from the steering wheel to press the tight knot of exhaustion between her shoulder blades. The long day is almost behind her.

They're in the country now, passing small homes and open fields as the road traces Cassadaga Lake's grassy shoreline. The water shimmers in the setting sun. A cool breeze wafts through the open window, scented with wildflowers and summery suppers on backyard grills.

Bella's stomach rumbles. She'd skipped breakfast in the flurry to get to the airport and should have been home in time for lunch. But five minutes before the flight was scheduled to board, the gate attendant announced an hour-long delay. That turned into two, and then four hours. When they finally boarded, the plane was held at the gate for a round of thunderstorms, courtesy of the fierce midwestern heatwave.

Then came the endless taxiing crawl along the runway, followed by a short, turbulent flight over the Great Lakes. In Buffalo, they were greeted by a refreshing temperature drop and a Thruway traffic jam for tonight's headline concert at the massive Erie County Fair.

Bella rounds the last bend in the road, and the entrance to Lily Dale comes into view. It consists of a pair of brick pillars, a small windowed hut where an attendant collects the daily gate fee, and a painted blue sign that reads: *The World's Largest Center for the Religion of Spiritualism.*

If Bella had noticed the sign on that first night, a year ago last June, she'd have kept right on driving. Recently widowed, having lost her job *and* suburban New York City apartment, she'd been headed for Chicago with Max, longing to make a fresh start somewhere, *anywhere* else, when Lily Dale had popped up in her path.

More specifically, a stray cat had, quite literally, popped up on the highway in front of the car and refused to budge.

Cats, Bella has since learned from her Lily Dale friends, reputedly show up where and when we need them to, whether we know it or not.

'They're mystical creatures,' Odelia Lauder likes to say.

Mysterious, maybe. But mystical? Certainly not *magical* – even though the pregnant tabby on the highway in Western New York was identical to the one that had perched on Bella's doorstep four hundred miles away the night before.

That night, Bella had assured Max it wasn't the *same* cat because that would have been impossible. And because she hadn't yet been to – or even heard of – Lily Dale.

Nor had she ever heard of Summer Pines Campground but, according to a roadside billboard, it was nearby, and would be a convenient place to stop for the night after they got the cat to a vet.

At Lakeview Animal Hospital, Drew Bailey identified the pet owner as Valley View's then-innkeeper, Leona Gatto. He was tending to a sick patient and informed Bella that she'd have to return the cat to Lily Dale. He also informed her that there was no such thing as Summer Pines in the area – which, she later discovered, was absolutely true.

Had she imagined the billboard? She never did figure that out. All she knows is that when she and Max reached the Dale, they had nowhere else to go, so spending the stormy night in a cozy, vacant guesthouse was pretty appealing.

She had no idea, of course, that Leona had died in an accident that had been no accident, or that the quaint Victorian cottage community was populated by spiritualists.

She'd agreed to stay on to help out at Valley View for a few days that had become weeks, months, a year.

'Welcome home!' Roxy, the teenaged attendant, greets Bella as she pulls up to the small gatehouse. 'How was the wedding? Was it totally romantic? Did Millicent wear a white gown with a veil?'

'It was beautiful. She wore a cream-colored suit.'

'A *suit*? A bride in a *suit*?' Roxy makes a face. 'When I get married, I'm going to have a silk gown with real diamonds sewn on the neckline, and a train that reaches all the way down the aisle, and my bouquet is going to be all lilies. And I know what my first dance with my husband is going to be. What was Millicent's song for her first dance with her husband?'

It had been a small wedding – just family, in the private room at a restaurant. No dance floor, but one of George's teenaged grandsons had brought a speaker, and they had danced, Millicent and George.

'It was "Almost Paradise". It's from an old movie – *Footloose*.'

How sweet they'd been together – Millicent and George, newly husband and wife, wrapped in each other's arms, her head on his shoulder.

After that, Millicent had whispered something to George's grandson, then clinked a glass and made a toast to her groom.

'For all the years I've been alone, I've thought the only happily ever after I'd experience would be in those romance novels I love to read,' she'd said. 'I never thought I'd end up like one of those heroines. I never imagined my hero would come along and sweep me off my feet. But that's exactly what happened when you walked into my life, George. I'm dedicating this next song to you.'

It was also from the movie *Footloose*: 'Holding Out for a Hero'. Everyone had laughed, and they'd all gotten up and danced. What a joyful time they'd had. Bella smiles, remembering.

'I never heard of that movie or the song,' Roxy tells her. 'My first song with my groom at my wedding is going to be "Love Story". It's a Taylor Swift one.'

'Sounds like you've got the whole thing planned out.'

'Pretty much. Now all I need is someone to marry.'

'At sixteen? Roxy—'

'I'm seventeen! But don't worry, I don't want to get married *now*. I'm going to college next year, and then law school. Or medical school. Or I might be a movie director. But I want to meet a nice guy to hang out with, like you did. I mean, Drew Bailey is super cute. And those puppies!'

Max stirs to life in the back seat. 'Puppies?'

'What puppies?' Bella asks.

'The ones Drew has at Valley View! Pandora told me about them, and I went over last night to see them.'

'There are puppies at Valley View?' Max is wide awake now. 'Are they a surprise for me, Mom?'

'They're certainly a surprise for *me*. We'd better get home. See you later, Roxy.'

'Bye, Bella! Bye, Max!'

'I can't wait to see the puppies,' Max says as they move on. 'How many are there?'

'That's a good question.'

'I have another good question, Mom. How many puppies can I keep?'

'They're just visiting with Dr Drew, Max.'

'Well, he knows I want a puppy.'

Everyone knows Max wants a puppy.

Someday, Bella intends to make that happen. Not this day, on the heels of an emotional wedding, an exhausting trip and, oh, yes, that inexplicable airport encounter with her dead husband.

The Dale is luminous with streetlights and lamplit windows, yards aglow with solar lanterns, fairylight strings and fireflies flitting in the trees. Every parking spot is taken along the narrow, rutted streets, but there are no pedestrians or porch-sitters tonight. Residents and visitors alike must be gathered in the auditorium for a mainstage event featuring The Specter Inspectors, a pair of television reality show ghost hunters who checked into Valley View's only suite this morning and are scheduled to stay until midweek.

Bella turns down Cottage Row, a leafy lakeside lane lined with nineteenth-century homes. At the far end, Valley View's mansard roof looms in the night sky.

Most of the cottages they pass are well-kept, with colorful gardens. Some feature as many yard ornaments as flowers: statues, fountains, gnomes, birdbaths, bird feeders, birdhouses.

Nearly all have wooden shingles advertising the occupants' metaphysical specialties.

Reverend Doris Henderson, Shamanic Healer

Misty Starr, Psychic Consultant

Odelia Lauder, Registered Medium.

At Valley View, all but one of the guest parking spots is occupied, and the signpost reads *Vacancy* – unheard of between late June and Labor Day. She'd asked Drew to change it from *No Vacancy* after this morning's cancellation.

She'd also instructed him to refund the guests' deposit, though it goes against official policy, and to extend their condolences along with a discount code for a future visit.

Can you afford to do that? he'd texted her. *You're already losing money.*

They canceled because they had a death in the family, she responded. *Maybe they'll come back someday seeking comfort.*

And contact, he returned.

Well yes, that goes without saying. People travel to Lily Dale from around the world, hoping the mediums can reconnect them with loved ones on the Other Side.

Drew's pickup truck sits in one of the two spaces marked *Reserved for Owner*. Bella pulls into the other.

Twilight shadows mask the faded, peeling patches in Valley View's lavender-gray paint pallet, and areas of disrepair amid the scallop-shingled gables and gingerbread trim. Bella knows where to look for them, but in this moment, she sees only a glorious, floodlit Queen Anne mansion, welcoming her home.

Max jumps out of the back seat and races toward the porch steps. 'Hey, Dr Drew! We're back! Where are the puppies?'

About to remind him to take his backpack and close the car door, Bella thinks better of it. He's so excited to be home, and she needs a moment to breathe and digest the day before seeing Drew, and . . . puppies?

He hadn't mentioned any furry tagalongs when he'd offered to stay at Valley View this weekend, but she isn't surprised. Lakeshore Animal Hospital is also a rescue, taking in homeless strays along with ailing patients. Drew and his veterinary technician, Janet, do their best to find foster homes for them, but it isn't easy on short notice.

She wonders where he's keeping the puppies, with a houseful of guests. He's been sleeping on the pullout sofa in the back parlor, though she'd offered him her own second-floor quarters. Every bedroom in the house has a themed décor and name to match, and hers is the Rose Room, with pink floral wallpaper and bedding.

'Too feminine?' she'd asked when he quickly turned it down.

'No, just too . . .'

When he'd hesitated, she was certain he'd been about to say too intimate, sleeping in her bed even when she was halfway across the country.

'Too inconvenient,' he said instead. 'For you. That's your only private space in the house. You don't need me . . . you know. Invading it.'

Invading? No way. And . . .

You don't need me?

He's wrong about that.

She grabs Max's bag and her own, and steps out of the car.

The night is cool and still.

No, not cool. It's bone-chilling.

Nor is it still.

Hearing a melodious tinkling, Bella turns toward the delicate blue glass angel wind chimes in the porch eaves. A long-ago gift from Sam, they're swaying gently in the breeze, only . . .

There is no breeze.

Bella scans the graceful flowering shrubs along the property line, then the maple trees above the three-story house. Not an arching bow or fluttering leaf to be seen. But there's movement in a lamplit second-floor window. A feline silhouette appears – Chance, looking out into the night.

Bella has often commented that she's a 'watchcat', ever vigilant and protective of Valley View and her family – feline, and human. Maybe she, too, senses that something strange is going on out here.

Shifting her gaze to her left, Bella notes that many houses along the Row have wind chimes and pinwheel ornaments, but none are stirring.

To her right, the road curves around the wooded dead end toward Friendship Park. All is still back there beyond the trees. The fishing pier, bandstand and small beach will have been deserted at sundown.

Bella shivers, goosebumps prickling her bare limbs.

'Sam?' she whispers, scanning the landscape again, expecting to see him lurking behind a tree trunk or in the shadows beyond the lamppost's beam.

Impossible. She'd been with her husband when the doctor gave him the death sentence on that gray September day; had held his hand in the hospital as he wasted away; had watched the coffin being lowered into the yawning grave as wet December snow fell into the mud.

Yet she holds her breath, waiting for him to appear; not wanting him to appear; *willing* him to appear.

She'll count to three.

One . . . two . . .

No, she'll count to ten. She closes her eyes. When she opens them, he'll be here, and she'll believe it, all of it, the whole Lily Dale 'dead isn't dead' credo.

. . . seven . . . eight . . . nine . . .

'Bella?'

She gasps.

But it isn't Sam.

Drew Bailey has just stepped out onto the porch.

He's tall, with brown hair like Sam, but that's where the resemblance ends. He isn't clean-shaven – ever. And clothes, to him, are a rugged afterthought – work boots with the laces undone, worn jeans, and a chambray shirt. The sleeves are shoved up to reveal strong forearms and a wind-up watch that had once belonged to his grandfather.

He quickly descends the steps. 'You're back.'

'I'm back.'

He hugs her, and she breathes in soap and mint and . . . *Drew*. He's warm, familiar, solid . . .

Real.

'Everything OK?' he asks.

She hesitates, glancing at the wind chimes, now still and silent. And at the cat in the upstairs window. Just a silhouette, but Bella can feel those green eyes fixed on her, as if she knows . . . something.

But that's impossible. It's all impossible.

She returns her attention to Drew with a firm, 'Yes. Everything's great now that we're home.'

THREE

S tepping over the threshold, Bella is struck by the contrast between Valley View and her weekend accommodations.

Millicent's penthouse is filled with gleaming glass, metal, and stone. The contemporary layout is all rectangular edges; the modern light fixtures are stark and bright. The décor is white, white and more white.

Here, the palate is warm and eclectic – amber brocade wallpaper, carved mahogany woodwork, richly patterned fabrics, lace curtains, jewel-toned stained-glass window panels. Golden light spills from ochre globes on wall sconces and the bronze Victorian chandelier suspended from a scrolled plaster medallion.

And while Millicent's place smells as sterile as it looks – not that there's anything wrong with cleanliness – Valley View is wonderfully fragrant, a mixture of old wood, honeysuckle from the vase on the console, and . . .

'Do I smell Italian food?' Bella asks Drew as he sets down the bags and closes the door behind them.

'There's a lasagna in the oven. I figured you'd be hungry.'

'You made a lasagna?'

'I *bought* a lasagna. And it should be ready in . . .' He checks his watch. 'Ten minutes.'

'You're amazing. Thank you. Max will be thrilled. He loves lasagna.'

'So I hear. He's upstairs looking for Chance and Spidey, so . . .' He clears his throat. 'Listen, Bella, I had an unexpected rescue yesterday.'

It's what he does. He rescues animals.

Something he'd recently told her comes back to her now. 'If ever there was a woman who didn't need rescuing, it's you.'

It had been exactly what she'd needed to hear in that moment.

In this one, she asks, 'Aren't all of your rescues unexpected?'

'Some more than others.'

'We're talking about the puppies?' she asks, helping herself to a handful of M&Ms from the crystal bowl on the registration desk.

'Yes. You know, it never ceases to amaze me how quickly word gets out around here about—'

'Everything,' Bella says. 'It's just like any small town, I guess. You can't keep a secret.'

'I wasn't trying to. I just didn't want to worry you about anything here on a weekend when you were supposed to be relaxing and having fun.'

Relaxing and *fun* don't entirely describe the last forty-eight hours. Certainly not the last twelve or so.

'Anyway, I'd have brought them to my place,' Drew goes on, 'but Janet is staying there with the kittens.'

'There are kittens?'

'There are *always* kittens. Two nursing litters at the moment, and a pair of orphans, and they all have to be kept in separate rooms from each other and the puppies, and with the bird . . . well, there aren't enough rooms.'

'Did you say bird?'

'Yes. The cockatoo.' At her blank expression, he says, 'I didn't tell you about the cockatoo?'

'You did not.'

'Ah. There's a cockatoo. Long story. Anyway, that's why I brought the puppies here. But don't worry, we're all clearing out of here.'

'I'm not worried.' In fact, she feels a pang of sadness at the thought of Drew leaving so soon. 'If you can't bring the puppies home, where will you go?'

'To the animal hospital. There's a kennel for them, and I can sleep on the couch in the waiting room.'

'Couch? You mean that hard bench? And they'll hate being in the kennel. Drew, why don't you just stay here? At least for tonight. It's late.'

He checks his watch. 'Not that late.'

'Late enough, and we have a lot of catching up to do. I need to find out what's been going on around here all weekend and . . . well, I didn't even know you were fostering a cockatoo. So there's that.'

'Yes, and I wanted to hear about the wedding, and Chicago, and . . . I'm sure you have a lot to tell me.'

'I do.' *About the wedding, and Chicago, and—*

No. Not that.

As much as she longs to tell someone about seeing Sam at the airport, Drew is probably the last person with whom she should discuss it. As close as they are, and as much as she values his opinion, she never feels comfortable bringing up her late husband.

But that doesn't mean she wants to be alone tonight. Quite the opposite.

'Please stay, Drew. You wouldn't even have to sleep in the parlor.'

He raises an eyebrow.

'No! I don't mean . . . I mean, I have an empty room because of the cancellation, so you can stay there. The, um, the Apple Room, isn't it? Or . . . wait, the Teacup Suite?' she guesses, like a clueless gameshow contestant.

'Tommy and Candace are there, remember?' At her blank look, he says, 'The TV stars?'

'Oh! The Specter Inspectors. I did know that. Which room did you say is vacant now?'

'I didn't, but it's the Jungle Room. And I might just take you up on it, if you're sure you don't mind. Janet thinks she found someone to take the orphaned pair of kittens tomorrow, and then I can go home with this crew.'

'This crew?'

'The dogs.'

'Right! I want to hear all about them, too.'

'Bella? Are you sure you're OK?'

'Yes! Why wouldn't I be OK?'

Max's footsteps bound along the upstairs hall. 'Doctor Drew, I did all the stuff you said! I changed into my pjs and I'm all clean. Can I play with the puppies now?'

Drew looks at Bella. 'Want to see them? They're awfully sweet.'

'Wouldn't miss it.'

They're sequestered in the mudroom off the kitchen, a trio of romping scamps overseen by a large, long-eared brown-and-white hound whose hazel eyes regard the visitors warily as they peek in.

'See, Max? She's a good mama, making sure her babies are safe,' Bella says.

'Actually, that's not the mom,' Drew says. 'It's a male dog.'

'Is he the daddy?' Max asks.

'It's hard to say. They were found under a backyard deck in Forestville yesterday morning. The homeowner had never seen them before, but there's a coyote den in the woods on his property, and . . .' He pauses to clear his throat. 'Anyway, he called me, and I picked them up right away.'

'What about the mommy?'

'She wasn't there,' Drew tells Max, and flicks a somber glance at Bella.

Ah, there's more to the story – and it isn't pleasant. There are so many tragedies in Drew's line of work, she thinks, remembering the orphaned kittens at his place. But there are lots of happily ever afters, too.

'What kind of dogs are they, Dr Drew?' Max asks.

'The big guy is an American foxhound, maybe a purebred hunting dog.'

'How do you know that?'

'His markings, his build . . .'

'What does he hunt?'

Drew, the animal lover, sidesteps the question. 'Maybe bad guys. He can sniff out a bad guy from miles away with that nose.'

'What about the puppies? They don't look like him. They don't even look like each other.'

'I'd say they're a mix of Lab and terrier.'

'Are you sure they're all brothers and sisters?'

Drew laughs. 'I'm sure. Siblings don't always look alike.'

'The St Clair sisters look exactly alike,' Max says, referring to a pair of Valley View regulars who are, indeed, identical, though not twins.

'Are the St Clair sisters puppies?' Drew asks.

Max giggles. 'No! They're old ladies!'

'Well, that explains it. Puppies don't always look like their siblings, even when they're from the same litter.'

'How old are they, Dr Drew?'

'Probably about two months. Their mama must have been caring for them until she – well, until recently, because they're healthy.'

'Maybe you can go back and find her,' Max suggests. 'Maybe she's just hiding. Jiffy's dog Jelly likes to hide.'

'Maybe. Come on, we have a few more minutes before dinner is ready. Do you want to see them up close, Max?'

'Yes!'

As Drew opens the door wider and gestures for them to step into the mudroom, a tiny brown figure darts for the threshold.

'Uh-oh, not again.' Drew scoops him up before he escapes. 'This little guy makes a dash for it every chance he gets.'

He closes the door and redeposits the puppy on the floor, where the others welcome their siblings back with a playful pounce. They're playing with what might be a stuffed animal, or a chew toy, or maybe a wadded-up sock. It's hard to tell in the tumbling, tail-wagging, squealing action.

'They're so cute!' Max crouches on the floor beside them. 'Aren't they so cute, Mom?'

'They are.'

'Can I—'

Drew intercepts the question. 'Hold one? Sure.' He extracts a wriggling ball of white fur from the wrestling match. 'Here you go, Max. She's more fragile than she looks, so I'll show you how.'

He kneels and settles the puppy in Max's arms under the Lab's watchful gaze.

'Like this, Doctor Drew?'

'Exactly like that. Good job.'

'What's her name?'

'I don't know.'

'It should be Krypto. Doesn't she look like Krypto, Mom?' Max asks.

'Krypto?'

'Superman's dog!' Drew and Max say in unison.

Max grins. 'You know Krypto, Dr Drew?'

'Of course. Those were my favorite comics when I was your age.'

'Hey, just like my dad! Right, Mom?'

Bella nods, though it isn't something she'd ever discussed with Sam. This knowledge and this memory belong solely to Max.

'I wish this puppy could be named Krypto even though she's a girl and even though she's not mine,' Max says.

'Then Krypto she shall be.'

'Wow, really? I get to name her?'

'Why not?' Drew asks. 'You can name them all.'

'Even the Daddy?'

'Sure.'

Bella swallows hard and presses her palms over her teary eyes, rubbing them as if she's exhausted – which, of course, she is. That's why she's so emotional.

That, and thinking she'd seen Sam at the airport, and watching Drew with Max, and Max and Drew with the motherless puppies . . .

'Did you hear that, little doggy? Your name is Krypto!' Max gasps, and giggles. 'She's licking my face. That tickles.'

'It means she likes you,' Drew says.

'I wish I could keep her. Hey, Mom, can I please . . . Mom? What are you doing?'

She sighs and looks at him, hoping he can't tell she's on the verge of tears. 'I'm just tired, Max. How about you?'

'No, because it's not my bedtime yet,' he says quickly, and turns back to the puppy.

He knows what she was asking, though. He doesn't want to talk about it, and she's not about to press the matter. Maybe she'll bring it up tomorrow. Or maybe, when she's well-rested and clear-headed in the broad light of a new day, she'll settle on an obvious, scientific explanation for what happened.

But Lily Dale being Lily Dale . . . she wouldn't bet on it.

FOUR

On nights when Luther Ragland doesn't stay over, Odelia Lauder relishes having her full-sized bed to herself. It's nice to indulge in junk food and reality television shows without input from a man who eats health food, has a personal trainer, and pretty much only watches sports on TV.

Really, Luther is her polar opposite in every way.

He's a never-married lifelong ladies' man; she's long divorced and lost her only child, but she's a doting grandma and brand-new great-grandma. She's stout and contentedly sedentary, with gingery hair and freckles; Luther is tall, physically fit, and Black. He's a retired police detective, organized, punctual, and always looks like a million bucks; she thrives in happy chaos – which also applies to her fashion, decorating and culinary style.

They'd met years ago, when Odelia received a message about an unsolved crime from her spirit guides. It wasn't the first time she'd ever walked into the police station with a psychic tip, but Luther was the first law enforcement official to take her seriously – after realizing she wasn't, as he likes to put it, 'a colorful kook'.

Thanks to Odelia and her guides, he'd solved the case, and many others. They'd been unlikely friends ever since. Even unlikelier romantic partners, but . . . here they are, dating since spring and settled into a comfortable routine.

Odelia spends her mornings and afternoons doing readings here in the Dale. Luther lives ten miles away in Dunkirk and works as a private investigator and security consultant. Sometimes they get together during the week, but always have date night on Fridays and Saturdays, and he stays overnight.

They often share a wistful moment when they part ways in the morning, but it passes quickly. Luther has to get back to his dogs and the gym, and she has to get back to . . . well, bed, usually.

They're compatible in every way – as long as they give each other plenty of space to do their own thing.

Tonight, Odelia had attended the Dale's Mainstage event, featuring Candace and Tommy, a pair of married-to-each-other ghost hunters.

Luther wouldn't have appreciated three hours in the auditorium listening to supernatural tales sprinkled with corny banter. Nor would he have appreciated Odelia's bedtime binges back home: the entire first season of *The Specter Inspectors*, and Doritos dipped into Cool Whip.

The paranormal reality show's hosts had always struck her more as entertainers than paranormal investigators. But on the heels of Candace and Tommy's presentation in the auditorium, she'd watched the episodes with renewed interest and far less skepticism. Their Hollywood looks and witty repartee make for good TV, but live and in person, sharing anecdotes to which Odelia can relate, they seem to be the real deal.

Tonight, she has company in bed. Her granddaughter Calla is away on a business trip, and Odelia's been cat-sitting her Russian blue rescue kitten all week. His name is Li'l Chap because he looks like he's formally dressed in a tuxedo, courtesy of the white bowtie-shaped marking on his neck.

Odelia had forgotten how nice it is to have a snuggly pet around the house. Huddled under a down comforter to ward off the nippy night air, she and Li'l Chap had drifted off around midnight, contentedly bathed in flickering television light and nacho dust.

Four hours later, she's jarred awake by Luther talking in his sleep.

She reaches out to poke him, but the bed is empty.

Ah, that's right. Luther isn't here, and Li'l Chap seems to have abandoned her sometime after she'd fallen asleep.

The voice hadn't come from the TV. Luther had programmed it with a sleep timer so that it turns itself off, because 'if I have to wrestle the remote from your death grip one more time when you're asleep, someone's going to get hurt – and I'd bet good money it's not going to be you.'

Well, then, someone must be talking very loudly outside, which would be unusual. Most residents are early risers during the season, and the Dale has zero nightlife. Anyway, she's a sound sleeper.

She gets out of bed and crosses to the two windows overlooking the street. They've been open ever since the Fourth of July and are now so swollen with humidity that she couldn't budge the old wooden sills if she tried. Which she had, just before bed, in an evening chill that now seems to have turned positively arctic.

So much for the heatwave Pandora Feeney had warned her is heading this way. Having grown up in this capricious Lake Effect region, Odelia knows better than to heed weather forecasts – and, for that matter, Pandora's.

And so much for Luther's warning that she needs to be more careful with home security on the heels of a recent break-in and theft at the Slayton house outside Lily Dale's gates.

'Don't tell anyone. It isn't public knowledge yet,' he'd said. 'The police are still investigating.'

She's not concerned. The Slaytons are rich, and they flaunt it. No self-respecting thief would waste time and effort breaking into Odelia's cottage.

Shivering in the wee-hour chill, she leans toward the window and peers into the night, intending to scold whoever's out there raising a ruckus at this hour – probably teenagers hanging out in Melrose Park.

Darkness shrouds every cottage along the lane. She can hear the wind chimes clanking on the porch at Valley View, and the hum of window air conditioners at Misty Starr's place next door on the other side.

Strange on a night like this. Misty isn't the most practical person in the world, but she's far too frugal to run the air conditioners unnecessarily.

The park is deserted, aside from a filmy little girl with long corkscrew curls tied in pink ribbons. She's wearing a midi dress with a sailor collar and bow, and leather ankle boots, and she's swaying on a rope swing dangling from a hickory bough that's suspended in midair.

The original tree had been struck by lightning many times over the years, and finally destroyed in an electrical storm years ago. Odelia doesn't recall whether there had ever been a rope swing when it was still standing, but she thinks not. However, the swing, along with the phantom bough and phantom child, have been hanging around – as it were – ever since the final zap that destroyed the tree.

In Odelia's experience, none of this is unusual. Souls that have passed to the Other Side often manifest by drawing on electromagnetic energy, such as a thunderstorm or even a radio or computer.

Odelia suspects that, like many earthbound spirits she regularly glimpses around the Dale, the girl in the park may not even realize she's dead. She doesn't attempt to communicate, merely lingers in – *haunts* – that spot.

The same is true of Miriam, a spirit who is as much a permanent fixture in Odelia's home as the 1883 cornerstone Miriam's husband had placed on the foundation when he built the place. And Nadine, who's resided next door at Valley View for over a century. Though unlike Miriam, she can be rather mischievous, moving things around the house, knocking objects off shelves, that sort of thing.

Odelia's spirit guides, on the other hand, are highly evolved beings. Some, like the Native American maiden to whom Odelia was wed in a previous lifetime, were once human, but a few – most notably a Great White Hawk – were not, and some never inhabited the earthly plane at all.

Amid the wind chimes and air conditioners, Odelia again picks up the voice – a distant, muffled murmur.

It hadn't come from her guides, or Miriam or the swinging girl. It's most likely a more recently departed soul drawing atmospheric energy to manifest, which would explain the cold that permeates the room on what may indeed have become a warm summer night after all.

'You'd better have a good reason for barging into my good night's sleep,' Odelia informs the newcomer as she shoves a pile of clothes off a chair and sits to meditate.

Bathed in protective white light, she opens herself to Spirit – which is like stepping into a crowded room full of chatty people vying to get your attention.

Odelia focuses, doing her best to zero in on the spirit that had awakened her. And as soon as she deciphers its – *his* – earthly identity, she smiles.

'Why, Sam Jordan. It's about time. Welcome to the Dale.'

FIVE

Y ou don't get a good night's sleep after glimpsing your dead husband, no matter how tired you are or how many glasses of wine you have before bed.

Bella had had two, as she and Drew lingered over lasagna, catching up on everything they'd missed in each other's lives over the last two days. Everything but her Sam sighting, anyway.

She'd found herself yawning deeply as they climbed the stairs to her door. He'd kissed her goodnight – a sweet, gentle kiss, not a passionate heart-thumper. Yet she'd found it impossible to calm her racing pulse, or her thoughts after he'd continued up to the third-floor Jungle Room.

Tucked beneath the covers with Chance curled up at her side, Bella relived the airport experience over and over, while awake, and again when she finally fell into a fitful sleep. Sam was there, as well – not in her dreams, but in a nightmare that involved him, and howling coyotes, and low-flying planes in flames, searing her skin.

At six, the alarm's piercing bleat jerks her back to reality. Sam, the coyotes, and the burning planes are gone, but she's soaked in sweat.

Last night's nippy breeze has given way to humid heat even at this hour. There's no air conditioning here at Valley View, and even if it were a luxury within the renovation budget, there's seldom any need for it.

Bella gets up, goes to the bay windows that overlook the front of the house, and opens the shades. Tree-dappled early morning light floods the room. Beyond the screens, the Dale is hushed, the air heavy with the kind of heat she'd left behind in Chicago.

She quickly makes the bed, noting that Chance is nowhere to be seen. The door to the hallway remains closed but the closet door is ajar. The cat often nudges it open with a paw, and she knows how to release the mechanism low on the back wall, behind the clothes-draped hangers.

Valley View is filled with concealed passageways and hidden rooms and compartments, reportedly once used by bootleggers.

The false wall in Bella's closet leads to a rickety wooden ladder that descends to the basement two floors below. From there, according to local legend, one can access a clandestine network of tunnels built by abolitionists during the Underground Railroad era.

Chance tends to be far less interested in escaping Valley View than she is in mealtime, and has most likely found her way out of the basement to the kitchen.

Sure enough, Bella finds her there along with Spidey. He'd slept in Max's room, where there's apparently a secret exit as well. She's never managed to pinpoint its location and suspects – hopes – that it's just large enough for a small cat, but not a boy.

'Sorry I overslept today,' she tells the cats, who are parked beside the pantry cabinet where their food is kept, waiting for their breakfast.

Ordinarily, she's awake before the alarm goes off. Today, she'd not only slept later than usual, but she'd taken a bit longer with her morning routine, telling herself that it's nice to be presentable for guests when you have a full house.

But who was she kidding? Drew Bailey is under her roof this morning, and, well . . .

There are no coincidences in Lily Dale.

So, after her shower, she'd blown dry her long brown hair and put on a cute blue summer dress instead of her usual shorts and T-shirt. She'd applied lip gloss and mascara, stopping just short of perfume. She'd rummaged in her jewelry box for small hoop earrings and a silver bracelet and had tried several necklaces. The tourmaline was the best match, but it felt wrong, given the circumstances. She'd taken it off at the last minute and put it back in the box, alongside the wedding and engagement rings she no longer wears.

She finds their new bowls, a gift from Drew. They're inscribed with the cats' names – *Chance* in pink lettering, and *Spidey* in Red.

Bella fills them with food and Chance and Spidey dive in, occasionally glancing toward the mudroom, where the puppies are making a squealy, yappy commotion. Drew had mentioned that he'd be checking on them several times overnight. No wonder he's not up yet.

Though the continental breakfast is available starting at seven, her guests usually don't appear until at least eight, and Max sleeps later than that on summer mornings, allowing her to enjoy a peaceful cup of coffee as she makes her daily To-Do list.

After setting the pot to brew, she glances around for her notepad and spots it propped against the toaster. The top page is scrawled in Drew's handwriting: *Call me as soon as you see this.*

That's unusual, given that he's right upstairs. He probably got so little sleep while tending to the puppies that he just wants her to wake him.

But when he answers, he tells her he's been at the animal hospital since he received an emergency call at five thirty a.m.

'Oh, no. What's going on?' she asks, hoping it has nothing to do with coyotes this time.

'Lethargic hamster. The pet owner is seven, and she's here with her mom and grandma.'

'Aww. Is everything going to be OK?'

'I hope so. Bella, I hate to ask, but . . . I need a huge favor.'

'You want me to take care of the dogs?'

'Would you?'

'Of course. You ran this place for me all weekend. Just tell me what I need to do.'

A few minutes later, she's clutching a steaming mug of coffee in one hand and opening the mudroom's exterior door with the other. She pauses to grab some treats from the container on the shelf, per Drew's instructions.

The little brown puppy is the first to scamper out into a small, fully fenced patch of yard. 'His name will be Dash, because he's always dashing toward the door,' Max had decided.

He's closely followed by Krypto and their spotty-coated sibling, whom Max had named Oats, 'because he reminds me of oatmeal with cream and brown sugar.'

The big foxhound hesitates on the doorstep to look up at Bella.

'Aw, it's OK, boy,' she tells him, patting his head. 'It's just a little potty-training break. It's totally safe, and I'll be with you.'

Pandora Feeney, who'd lived at Valley View years ago, when it was a private home, had told Bella that this spot had been intended as a vegetable garden patch, fully enclosed with a tall white lattice fence to keep the critters out. Now, it keeps the canines in, twined with green tendrils loaded with blossoms: deep blue morning glories and bright pink sweet peas.

Both vines, according to avid gardener Pandora, are 'invasive species, Isabella. You really must yank them out. Once they have a foothold, they'll creep in and, before you know it, they'll have taken over.'

'That's fine with me. I love them. They're colorful.'

After rewarding the pups for taking care of business, Bella sits on the low step, sipping her coffee as the dogs play in the sunshine.

She'd been envious of Millicent and George, honeymooning this week on a private yacht in the Caribbean. But in this moment, her own backyard is paradise.

The borders are in full bloom now, bursting with daisies, dahlias, coneflowers, and towering yellow sunflowers. Pollinators and a pair of hummingbirds flit and flutter amid the blossoms.

Beyond the comfortably furnished stone patio and firepit, the wide green lawn extends to the tall grasses and reeds along the lake's pebbly shallows. A pair of red Adirondack chairs face the water, where a lone blue heron perches motionless on the rickety pier. Below, the surface gleams in the bright morning light, reflecting the blue sky and green hills on the opposite shore.

It's all so peaceful, Bella thinks – perhaps deceptively so.

Last June, Valley View's owner, Leona Gatto, was presumed to have tumbled off the pier while trying to secure a kayak in a storm when, in truth, she'd been murdered. Before the year was out, a stranger's corpse had washed up nearby, leading Bella down a treacherous path to catching yet another killer.

Bella's gaze shifts to the massive gingko tree that marks the spot where a bride had been left for dead on her wedding day. And to the tall flat-topped boulder that had concealed a macabre key to a century-old mystery.

But she prefers not to dwell on the dark side of life in the Dale.

The hound sits up and sniffs the air, as if reminding Bella that he can, as Drew had said, sniff out a bad guy from miles away with that nose.

He's looking at the lake, and Bella sees that the surface has begun to ripple around the pier. The heron flutters its wings and takes flight, squawking as it soars into the treetops across the lake.

With a splashing commotion, something emerges from the water. A bad guy? A black-tentacled sea creature?

No, a sea creature wouldn't hoist itself up the wooden ladder. And those aren't tentacles, they're gangly arms and legs, encased in some kind of . . . bathing costume, worn along with a cap, goggles and snorkel.

The dogs are beside themselves, barking so wildly Bella briefly wonders if she's looking at Nadine, a woman who'd lived at Valley View well into the early 1900s and who – according to Odelia, anyway – haunts the place to this day.

Then the figure steadies itself on the pier, removes the snorkel and goggles, spots Bella, and waves.

'Isabella! *There* you are!' Pandora Feeney calls, as if she's been searching land and sea for her.

The dogs, clearly discerning that a visit from Nadine would have been far less intrusive, escalate their barking.

Bella sighs, sets aside her coffee, and gets to her feet. So much for serene solitude. 'Good morning, Pandora. What are you doing?'

'My goodness, what does it look like I'm doing?'

'I'm not quite sure,' Bella returns, as Pandora starts walking, *thunk-flop, thunk-flop*, in rubber flippers that make her feet seem even more enormous than usual.

'I've just finished my morning swim, of course.'

'I didn't know you take a morning swim.'

'I don't.'

'You just said—'

'I take an afternoon swim, Isabella!'

'I guess I didn't know that either.'

'Yes, yes, but today's going to be a scorcher. I don't want to get sunburnt, do I? I'm quite delicate, you know, so I decided to . . .' Tripping over her flippers, she nearly topples off the pier. 'Bloody hell!'

'Careful there, Pandora. Do you need a hand?'

'No, no, I'm quite all right. Splendid, really. But do settle the pups!' she adds above the canine commotion. 'They're creating quite the hullaballoo.'

'I'd say it's a justifiable hullaballoo,' Bella informs the dogs, and doles out a few treats to quiet them.

Pandora plunks down in one of the Adirondack chairs to remove the flippers, then swaddles herself in a familiar large blue towel and heads toward Bella.

'Pandora – is that from Valley View?'

'The swimsuit? No, it's from the Victorian Emporium, an online clothing shop. Smashing, isn't it?'

'I meant the towel.'

'The towel?'

'The towel.' Bella points at the large white VVM monogram.

Pandora looks down, as if she's just noticed it. 'Oh, yes. Yes, it is. I knew you wouldn't mind if I borrowed it. I was so out of sorts, changing my swim time and all, that I forgot my own towel at Cotswold Corner, and I didn't want to trudge all the way back.'

Cotswold Corner is her little pink cottage located just across Melrose Park from Valley View. It's a thirty-second walk, if that.

This isn't the first time Pandora's let herself into the house and helped herself to something without asking. It's been years since her ex-husband sold Valley View out from under her in a nasty divorce.

She's never forgiven 'the wanker' for leaving her homeless and penniless when he ran off with a Hollywood starlet.

Nor has she entirely given up a proprietary attitude toward her former home and everything in it.

For the most part, Bella understands where Pandora is coming from.

Sam hadn't chosen to leave her, but she, too, had found herself penniless and homeless. Young and healthy, he'd allowed their life-insurance policy to lapse and downgraded their medical benefits to add extra money to the nest egg they were saving to buy a house – or so he'd told Bella.

She'd been aware they'd taken some hits in investment accounts, but had no idea how much they'd lost, or that their nest egg was gone, and their credit-card debt was soaring. Only after Sam was gone did she grasp their financial bind, exacerbated by medical bills for doctors and treatments that would have been covered under their old health plan, or at least, worth every penny if they'd given Sam a fighting chance.

Widowed and virtually penniless, she thought she'd hit rock bottom. That things couldn't get any worse.

She was wrong. Within six months of Sam's death, the final blows came: the landlord sold the building and evicted her, and budget cuts eliminated her teaching job.

So, yes. She can relate to Pandora.

But some days – like today – Bella just can't muster the empathy, let alone the energy, to tolerate the woman's lack of boundaries.

Especially now, when Pandora winks as she reaches the fenced yard and says, 'I'd have awakened you to ask about the towel, but I knew you'd had quite the late night with Drew Bailey.'

'Pandora—'

'No worries, Isabella! It will be our little secret.'

'*What* will be our little secret?'

'That I caught Drew sneaking about at half past four.'

'You caught him sneaking about? That's not—'

'Don't worry, love, he was quite discreet as he crept out of the house and drove away. He didn't see me, of course.'

'Where were you? Hiding in the bushes?'

'Of course not! How undignified! I was at Cotswold Corner, peeking through the blinds.'

'How dignified.'

'I heard through the grapevine about a cat burglar at the Slayton manse, and I've been keeping watch for the culprit.'

'I don't know what happened at the Slayton . . . uh, *manse*, but I guarantee you that Drew Bailey wasn't responsible. Cat rescuer, yes. Cat burglar, no.'

'Well, of course not! I must say, I'm chuffed that the two of you finally had yourselves a proper shag.'

Bella feels her cheeks grow hot. 'Pandora! It wasn't . . . it's not . . . like that. He's been staying here all weekend.'

'Yes, yes, while you were on holiday. I'm aware. I came round often to ensure that he was getting on all right. I had rather assumed he'd see fit to vacate the premises upon your return with the lad, but far be it from me to judge, Isabella.' She reaches for the gate latch, clearly planning to join Bella in the fenced area.

The dogs take note, and Dash dashes over, poised to escape.

'Wait, don't open that. The dogs will get out.'

Pandora drops her hand. 'We can't have that. I'm afraid one of them has trampled my petunia patch, and another had a poo in the hosta bed.'

'I don't see how. Drew said they've been sequestered in the mudroom all weekend.'

'Perhaps it wasn't *these* pups, but some frightful mutt has been wreaking havoc about the Dale.'

'Are you sure it wasn't a raccoon? Or a deer?'

'I suppose it might have been. Now then, I'll just go round to the front door and see you inside.'

'Wait, Pandora—'

'I'll get myself sorted in the loo and put the kettle on so that we can have a nice chin-wag over a cuppa.'

She disappears around the side of the house before Bella can tell her . . .

Whatever it is that one should say to Pandora Feeney in this situation.

Like – *Pandora, you need to go back to Cotswold Corner and mind your own business?*

Bella has never been able to come up with anything that wouldn't hurt her feelings. For all her boundary crossing, Pandora herself is a colorful, lovable invasive species – a friend.

Still, Bella is in no rush for a chin-wag over a cuppa.

She finishes her coffee and is playing stick-toss with the puppies when she hears someone calling her name and looks up to see Odelia heading toward her from next door.

Ordinarily, she's the sort of person who ambles, but today, there's an air of urgency about her. She's barefoot, wearing lime green pajamas that clash with her red-rimmed cat-eyed glasses and mop of orange hair that's even more tousled than usual, as though she's just rolled out of bed.

The dogs stop playing and regard her with interest, tails wagging.

'Good morning, Odelia!'

'Bella, I've been trying to call your cell!'

'You have?' Bella pats one pocket, then the other. 'I must have left it in the house. Is everything all right?'

'Yes, but . . . I have a message for you. From Sam.'

SIX

Bella's heart skids into her ribcage and she gapes at Odelia. '*What* did you say?'

'I said, Sam came to me in the middle of the night. Well, that's not what I said, but it's what happened.'

'Sam,' she breathes, closing her eyes briefly and tilting her head back. 'Sam came to you. Then . . . you saw him, too.'

'*Too*? Bella, did you see Sam?'

'Max and I did. Yesterday, at the airport in Chicago. Only I didn't think it could possibly have been real. But if he was here . . .'

Odelia nods. 'He was here. He woke me from a sound sleep, and you know that's not an easy feat for any spirit, especially not a newbie like Sam.'

Bella manages to flash a faint smile. 'I do know that. What happened, exactly? You woke up and he was there, what . . . standing over your bed?'

'This wasn't an apparition. I heard him, and I felt his energy.'

'He gave you a message for me? What was it?'

'I'm still mulling it all over. It wasn't entirely clear. Clairaudience isn't like a telephone call. Well – maybe it's like a long-distance one, back in the day, when connections were static-ridden and kept cutting in and out. Think of it, if you will, as . . .'

She goes on.

And on.

This isn't the first time she's explained mediumship to Bella. She's passionate about spiritualism and considers it her duty to comfort the unenlightened with proof that the soul outlives the body.

As she half-listens to Odelia's familiar spiel, Bella's gaze falls on a tiny hummingbird. It darts toward a sweet pea cluster and hovers, beak dipped into a blossom. Its dark feathers are glossed in iridescent emerald, its whirring wings as invisible as high-speed propellers. Nearby, a monarch butterfly perches on a leaf with a languid flapping, as if summoned to provide visual illustration for Odelia's oft-made point that spirit energy vibrates on a far more elevated frequency than human energy.

Like a professor warming to her subject, Odelia says, 'This is hardly a modern phenomenon. If we go back to the dawn of ancient Greek and Roman civilization, we can—'

'Odelia, I don't mean to interrupt, but . . . you were saying you have a message for me?'

'Oh, Bella! I'm sorry. Here I am going on and on, and of course you want to know about Sam. The very first thing that came through is that he loves you, and Max, and that he's always with you.'

She nods.

'He's happy that you've found your way here. And he knows how much you miss him.'

Bella opens her mouth and then closes it, biting her bottom lip to keep from saying anything.

'Did you have a question?'

'No, I . . . I just . . . I mean, if you were asleep when it happened, how do you know it wasn't just a dream?'

'When you've been doing this as long as I have, you can tell the difference. I can give you more information on that if you're interested.'

'Maybe later?'

Odelia smiles. 'Yes. Back to Sam. He wants you to know that he understands how difficult it was for you to start over and to build a new life without him, and he's proud of you.'

She pauses, as if waiting for a response. Bella bites her lip so hard she tastes blood.

Odelia touches her arm. 'Bella?'

'Sorry. It's just . . . this stuff you're saying is so . . . generic. I feel like it could apply to anyone who's lost a husband, or – anyone who's lost anyone, really. How do I know it's the real thing? Not that I think *you're* not the real thing,' she adds quickly.

'But you're not convinced that I am. And that's OK. I'm not here to convince you of anything. My purpose is to deliver the information exactly as it comes through. And it isn't unusual for a departed soul to express love for those left behind, or to let them know that life continues after they've departed the earthly plane, and that they remain with us always.'

Bella nods, unable to force words past a sudden lump in her throat.

It had been one of the last things he'd ever said to her, when she was at his bedside on that last day in the hospital.

'I'll be with you . . .'

He'd been so weak, his voice a ravaged whisper.

'Promise me you'll . . . stay . . . strong . . .'

She'd promised. In her darkest, most difficult moments since then, she remembers that promise and she manages to keep it.

'Sam kept emphasizing how proud he is of you, Bella,' Odelia says. 'And proud of his boy.'

His boy . . . that does sound like Sam.

'Where's my boy?' he'd call when he came home after a long day.

'That's my boy,' he'd say when Max did something that pleased him.

Maybe a lot of fathers say that about their sons. Of course they do. But Bella wants so badly to believe that Odelia really did hear from Sam . . .

That she and Max really did *see* Sam.

'Oh, and I heard wind chimes,' Odelia adds.

'*My* wind chimes?'

'I suppose it might have come from outside, but now that I think of it, there wasn't any wind.'

'No, there wasn't. I'm sure there wasn't, because . . .'

Because I heard them, too.

She clears her throat. 'Sam gave me the wind chimes on the porch. The ones with the blue glass angels.'

Odelia nods. 'Yes. I know that.'

Of course she does. She knows many things about Sam. About Bella's relationship with him, and their lives together. And she's well aware that it's been frustrating for Bella to live in the town that talks to the dead, among people who believe that everyone can learn to do so – and it seems that everyone but Bella really can.

Odelia is a good friend. She probably wanted to receive a message from Sam for Bella almost as badly as Bella wanted to hear from him.

But sometimes, people hear what they want to hear just as they see what they want to see.

'So, the wind chimes . . . is that why the message was unclear?' she asks Odelia.

'Hmm?'

'You said the message wasn't entirely clear. Because of the wind chimes?'

'No, Spirit sometimes uses sound effects to convey a clairaudient message. I've heard it all – car horns, trumpets, ringing phones. I think the wind chimes were Sam's way of identifying himself to me.'

'So he didn't give you his name.'

'*His* name? No. Again, it's not like a telephone conversation. There's no caller ID. Traditional names can be misleading. Most of us know a number of people who share any given name. In my experience, Spirit prefers to validate earthly identity with details that are more unique to the relationship. That said, I did get *a* name. I'm hoping it means something to you. It meant nothing to me.'

'What is it?' Bella braces herself for it – for the name that will suspend her disbelief, once and for all. It will likely invoke someone from their shared past. Someone who'd been close enough to be meaningful, but not so close that Bella has thought much about the person or shared it with Odelia.

She combs the past for such a person. Maybe their upstairs neighbor, Lena, who'd dropped off that delicious lasagna and a baby gift when Max was born. Or Sam's college roommate, Ahmad, who'd been the best man at their wedding. Or Rebecca, the little girl who'd lived across the street and had an occasional playdate with Max. Or—

'Kevin,' Odelia says.

'*Kevin?*'

'Kevin.'

Bella frowns, unable to place it. 'That's it? Just Kevin?'

'The last name might begin with a B? I heard Kevin Buh . . . something.'

'Kevin Buh . . . Kevin Buh . . . wait, do you mean Kevin Bacon? The actor?'

'Do that mean something to you?'

It does not.

She asks Odelia whether this might be part of her spirit shorthand – a series of symbolic references that mediums use to interpret messages from the Other Side. As Bella understands it, the shorthand is specific to the individual – the same phrase or image might have different meaning from one medium to another.

When Odelia sees rain, it signifies that someone has been shedding tears in grief; when Pandora sees rain, it signifies that a baby is on the way, 'because all seed must be watered in order to grow, Isabella.'

'Doesn't a premonition about rain ever just tell you that there's a storm coming?' Bella had asked, but her friend assured her that the local weather is far too precarious for prediction.

'And life isn't?'

'That isn't the point, Isabella,' Pandora had said in that maddening way she has of brushing past a legitimate question. 'It isn't for us to question why Spirit gives us some information and not other. We must accept what is given.'

Which, in this moment is Kevin Bacon, who is not, according to Odelia, typically included in her personal shorthand.

'So you're saying Sam was sending me a message about the actual actor?'

'Maybe something related to him?' Odelia shrugs. 'My mission is to deliver truth, not to question it.'

'I mean, Sam liked Kevin Bacon's movies – we both did,' Bella muses. 'But I can't think of anything . . . oh! Back when we were dating, we once played that six degrees game at a party.'

'Six degrees?'

'You know the theory that everyone is socially connected by six degrees? It's like that, only you name someone in the entertainment industry, and the others have to name someone connected to them who's connected to someone who's connected to . . . you get the gist. You can pretty much link everyone in Hollywood to Kevin Bacon in six or fewer steps.'

'Including the wanker and the trollop!' a disembodied voice comments.

Bella looks around and spots Pandora, framed in the screened window of the small half-bath.

The wanker, of course, is Pandora's ex-husband, Orville Holmes. The trollop would be Jillian Jessup, the movie star who'd come to town looking for a connection to the spirit world and made an illicit one with Pandora's man instead.

Bella has never met either of them, but she and Sam had seen Jillian's smash romantic comedy film *Wish Come True* on their first date and re-watched it every year on their anniversary.

Odelia scowls up at Pandora. 'What are you doing up there?'

'Tidying up in the loo, of course.'

'Bella hired you as a housemaid?'

'Certainly not. I'm tidying *myself* after my morning swim.'

'*And* you're eavesdropping on a private conversation.'

'That can't be helped when one has a voice like a foghorn, can it?' Pandora shoots back, and adds, 'Not *you*, Isabella.'

Bella sighs, 'Ladies, please. Pandora, was Kevin Bacon in a movie with Jillian Jessup?'

'Of course not! An actor of his stature wouldn't appear in such rubbish. He was in—'

'*Footloose!*' Bella exclaims.

'I don't know about that, but he was in—'

'Pandora! Bella was talking! Stop interrupting!'

'I believe *Isabella* interrupted *me*, as did you.'

'I'm sorry,' Bella says, 'but I think I know why Sam would give me a message about Kevin Bacon. We were dancing to music from *Footloose* at his mother's wedding on Saturday. Maybe Sam is trying to tell me he was there.'

'Kevin Bacon?' Pandora asks.

'Sam!' Bella and Odelia tell Pandora in unison.

'Blimey! You don't have to shout. I'm right here.'

Odelia opens her mouth to retort, but Bella heads her off with a question. 'Odelia, do you think that's what Sam is saying? That he was with us on Saturday?'

Odelia tilts her head, pondering. 'I'm not sure. I'm sorry, Bella. I can only give you the information as Spirit sees fit to give it to me. But I'll tell you what I tell all my clients – that if a message doesn't seem to fit, give it some time. It might become clear when you've had a chance to think about it.'

'But—'

This time, Bella is interrupted by a high-pitched shriek from inside the house. The four dogs launch into a frightened frenzy of barking and howling.

'Ah, the kettle! It's teatime!' Pandora vanishes. A moment later, so does the whistling.

'Oh, for Pete's sake. I'll see you later, Bella. I have to get home to Li'l Chap. Good luck with . . . all this.' Odelia waves at the dogs, and the kitchen, where Pandora can be heard clattering around with the kettle.

As she heads back next door, Bella bends over and scoops up the nearest and most terrified puppy. 'It's all right, Dash,' she tells him, petting him and opening the back door. 'Come on, everyone. Back inside we go.'

In the mudroom, she puts Dash into one of the three miniature puppy beds Drew had set up. There's a larger one for the big guy, but he climbs into the basket filled with the clothing Bella had dumped in from her suitcase last night.

Turning, she spots her phone sitting on the shelf next to the container of dog treats. When she checks it, she finds that there are indeed one, two, *three* missed calls from Odelia.

There's another one as well, from a caller her phone identifies as 'anonymous'. No number.

She checks for a message, but there isn't one. That's not unusual.

But today, for some reason, it makes her uneasy.

For some reason?

For good reason.

Her medium friends are convinced that Spirit sometimes manipulates energy sources like household electronics and appliances.

'If you ever notice the lights flickering, or the television unexpectedly changing channels mid-program, don't worry. It's probably just Nadine,' Odelia told Bella soon after she moved into Valley View – as if *that* was reassuring.

But Bella doesn't really believe that the missed unknown caller was Nadine, does she? Nadine, or . . . or some other Spirit.

'Sam?' she whispers. 'Was that you?'

She waits, clutching the phone, glancing over to see that the dogs are poised and looking at her as if they're expecting something to happen. As if the phone is about to ring, and Bella will hear Sam's voice saying . . .

Kevin Bacon?

Krypto lets out a bark, as if he, too, thinks that's crazy. Looking over, she realizes that the dogs aren't even looking at her. Tails wagging, they're looking past her at the plastic bin of treats on the shelf.

'So much for your psychic powers, guys,' Bella says with a laugh, doling out another round of treats.

Then she opens a search window on her phone, types in *strangers who look alike*, and hits Enter. There's a long list of results.

Clicking the top link, she's taken to a recent article published in a respected scientific journal to which she'd subscribed back in her teaching days.

Researchers have concluded that most people have at least one bona fide lookalike somewhere in the world.

All right, then. If that's the case, then she and Max had simply come face to face with someone who looked just like Sam.

And that, she tells herself firmly, pocketing her phone, is all there is to it. Except . . .

She finds herself reliving the experience again, like she'd missed something.

When it happened, they'd just gotten out of the car. She'd been focused on finding Max's missing backpack. Max had spotted Sam first.

But that wasn't what he'd said. Not at first.

His attention had been drawn to the vehicle, not the driver.

'It's a golden car,' he'd said, as if it were a heaven-sent chariot and not an old Subaru with a dented fender and dingy metallic paint.

No, wait. He'd said *the*, not *a*.

'It's *the* golden car.'

Bella frowns, considering the slight, yet crucial difference.

Calling it the golden car, it almost sounded as though Max had been expecting to see it.

Or as though he'd seen it before.

SEVEN

'No, no, no, of course not!'

That's Pandora, in the kitchen. Bella frowns, heading in that direction, wondering who's there with her.

'What a load of codswallop!'

She can't have Pandora talking to the guests that way – or, for that matter, to Max, who will want to know what *codswallop* means. Bella has never heard the phrase before, but she can guess.

Before she can intervene, uproarious laughter erupts across the threshold.

Pandora, again. Only Pandora.

'Winston, you naughty thing. You *know* I never said that.'

Ah, so she isn't conversing with Max or one of the guests after all. It's merely the late prime minister of England, who drops in frequently, according to Pandora.

Leaving her to her invisible visitor, Bella detours to the breakfast room.

Formerly an enclosed side porch, it's a cheerful nook with white beadboard trim and three walls of windows, all of which are propped open. Still, the room feels like a greenhouse.

Even if she had the time to bake her usual fresh scones or quiche for her guests this morning, the weather is much too warm for Bella to heat up the oven. And she's running low on fresh fruit after her weekend travels, so there will be no melon wedges or fresh berries.

But there's a basket of apples and bananas on the breakfast bar, and the cabinets and mini-fridge beneath are well stocked with alternatives for days like today.

She sets out individually wrapped store-bought pastries, mini cereal boxes, oatmeal packets, and protein bars. Guests can help themselves to milk, juice and yogurt, and can make their own hot beverages using the countertop Keurig machine. She replenishes the pod selection along with coffee condiments, utensils, and napkins, then looks around to make sure she hasn't forgotten anything.

The café tables are covered in blue and white gingham, with fading wildflowers in ball jars as centerpieces. Time to replace them with fresh-cut bouquets from the garden, another task for today's To-Do list, already extended to include puppy training and tea with Pandora Feeney.

She returns to the kitchen. Five minutes. That's it. That's all the time she can afford to waste on sitting around . . . chin-wagging. She'd prefer to avoid it altogether, but she does need to set Pandora straight about what happened – or rather, what *didn't* happen – with Drew last night.

She finds Pandora sipping her tea at the table.

'Isabella, where have you been?'

'I had to get the breakfast room ready for – is that my robe?'

Pandora looks behind her, as if expecting to find a disembodied garment floating in midair – which, Lily Dale being Lily Dale, might not be entirely implausible, but still.

Then she glances down at herself, and back up at Bella. 'Do you mean this dressing gown?'

'Yes.'

'I found it in the laundry room in the basket waiting to be folded, so naturally, I assumed it was meant for guests.'

'*Naturally?* It's mine!'

And it wasn't clean clothing; it was from her suitcase.

Taking some satisfaction in that, she says, 'We don't have guest robes, Pandora.'

'No? They'd be a nice touch, don't you think?'

'This isn't a five-star resort,' Bella says, pouring herself a fresh cup of coffee. 'There's no room in the budget for fancy extras.'

'Ah, yes, your Mr Everard is a regular Ebenezer Scrooge, isn't he.'

Pandora is referring to Grant Everard, Valley View's absentee owner. As a globe-trotting venture capitalist, he'd initially had no interest in even keeping the rundown guesthouse he'd inherited from his Aunt Leona.

Fortunately – for Bella, anyway – selling real estate in Lily Dale isn't a straightforward proposition. All the land here is owned by the Assembly, and only members of the Spiritualist church are permitted to obtain property leaseholds on homes.

So Grant would have had to sell Valley View to a spiritualist who happened to be in the market for an oversized fixer-upper. And of course, the buyer would have to be either a local resident for whom money is no object, or an outsider looking to relocate to Western New York's snowbelt.

Bella had suggested that Grant invest in the guesthouse instead, convinced that it could become profitable in the off-season with some sprucing up and effective marketing.

'Have at it and send me the bills,' he said amiably. 'We'll see how it goes.'

That had been nearly a year ago. She's since become handy with a paintbrush, a caulk gun, and even a wet saw, and is on a first-name basis with the local electrician and plumber. Grant seems content to let her handle pretty much everything, while he oversees it from a distance – often, the opposite side of the world.

Last week, he'd called her from the Tibetan Plateau after she'd sent him the estimates to replace the roof and address the water damage. The entire job is going to be complicated, time-consuming and expensive. Valley View's steep mansard slate roof is intricately patterned and there are dormers, gables and turrets. The third-floor work will involve not just structural and cosmetic repairs, but mold remediation.

Grant had been taken aback by the costs.

'I can try to get more estimates,' Bella had said, 'but not everyone deals with historical homes on this scale.'

'No, it's OK. I'll stop in Lily Dale to discuss it with you next week on my way from here to Newfoundland.'

'Newfoundland, Pennsylvania? Near Scranton?'

'Newfoundland, Canada,' he'd said with a chuckle. 'Near . . . well, not much of anything. Which is why I like it.'

You'd think a guy who enjoys spending so much time in the middle of nowhere might be more interested in visiting the Dale, but he rarely does. When he shows up, it's usually at an inopportune time, like when Bella is dealing with a litter of newborn kittens, or when there's a murderer under this roof, or . . .

A canine quartet in the mudroom?

'When does Mr Everard arrive for his Lily Dale holiday, Isabella?'

'He wasn't sure exactly,' she tells Pandora, sitting in the chair opposite her. 'Any day now, I think, but it isn't a holiday. It's just for one night.'

'Ah, so he's just coming to check up on you, is he?'

'No, we need to discuss some repairs that need to be made.'

'That can't be done over the phone?'

'He's en route to Newfoundland from Tibet, and this is on the way.'

'Is that what he told you? That it's on the way?'

Well, now it sounds lame even to Bella's own ears.

'Grant doesn't come sniffing around here checking up on me, Pandora. He trusts me.'

'But do you trust him?'

'What do you mean?'

'Change is in the air here at Valley View, Isabella.'

Bella sets down her mug and levels a look at Pandora. 'What kind of change?'

'It's hard to say. I'm merely passing the information to you as I receive it.'

'You're receiving it right now? From whom? Winston Churchill? Because I don't think he—'

'Of course not! I received the information from my guides, early this morning – the very moment I set foot in this house.'

Uninvited, nosing around, and borrowing without asking, Bella wants to remind her, but refrains. For all her infuriating meddling, Pandora is the one person in the Dale who has consistently told Bella things she couldn't have uncovered with all the snooping in the world.

She'd somehow picked up on Sam's nickname for her, 'Bella Blue', and had mentioned the phrase 'sushi sky', which had been his unique and poetic description of the sunset one memorable romantic night.

Those details are far more specific than the message Odelia had offered—other than Kevin Bacon, anyway.

It might make sense if Sam was merely confirming that he'd been at his mother's wedding. The connection to *Footloose* could have been his way of validating his presence with a detail Odelia couldn't have otherwise known.

Unless . . .

Well, Bella *had* mentioned it to Roxy yesterday. Not Kevin Bacon himself, but the music from his movie. What if Roxy had mentioned it to Odelia, and Odelia was using it to . . .

To what? Fool you into thinking she was talking to Sam?

No. No way.

Bella might be skeptical about a lot of what goes on around the Dale, but that doesn't mean she suspects that her friend Odelia – or any of the mediums here – are manipulative frauds. They do what they do – what they claim to do, or rather, what they're convinced they're doing – out of a genuine desire to help people.

Pandora included.

Bella asks her exactly what happened this morning when she walked into the guesthouse.

'Spirit touched in to say that change is in the air.'

Touched in. The mediums often phrase it that way, causing Bella to imagine a ghostly figure tapping someone on the shoulder – something Pandora has said Nadine is prone to doing. That has yet to happen to Bella, thank goodness.

'At first,' Pandora goes on, 'I thought it might be because you and Drew Bailey have embarked on a serious relationship that might one day lead you to marry him and leave Valley V—'

'That's crazy! First of all, Drew and I aren't getting married, but even if we *were* getting married – which we are *not!* – I'd never leave Valley View.'

'Not even for love, luv?'

Seeing the gleam in Pandora's eye, she says, 'Not for anything. This is my home.'

'I once felt the same way about it, but things have a way of changing, don't they?'

'What kind of things?'

'Feelings . . . circumstances . . . desires. But I believe when Spirit indicated that change was coming to Valley View, it was in reference to something rather less . . . personal.'

'Like what?'

'I'm not quite sure.' She pushes back her chair. 'I'll go back to Cotswold Corner to meditate and come round for tea later to let you know what I've discovered.'

'Wait, Pandora . . . Spirit didn't give you anything about . . . um . . . Your guides didn't mention Sam?'

'No, luv.' Pandora flashes a rare smile that isn't sly, self-satisfied, or anything other than benevolent.

'But you heard what Odelia said?'

'I did.'

'And you . . .' Bella pauses, about to ask if Pandora believes the message was legitimate.

No. The last thing she wants to do is share even a hint of doubt in Odelia's abilities with her longtime nemesis.

Instead, she asks, 'You don't know what the message means? About Kevin Bacon?'

'I'm afraid I don't . . .' Pandora gets to her feet.

'You're afraid you don't what?'

After the slightest hesitation, Pandora tells her, 'I'm afraid I don't know what it means.'

'That's not what you said, though. That wasn't a complete sentence. You were about to go on, but you changed your mind.'

'You're a mind reader now, are you?'

'Around here, isn't everyone?'

'Very well. I was going to say that I don't get the sense that the message had to do with Kevin Bacon, the actor.'

'There's another Kevin Bacon?'

'Perhaps. Or perhaps our friend Odelia misinterpreted Spirit. It's not for me to say, now, is it?'

'You just did.'

'Did I?'

'You did.'

'Right. Cheers, then,' she adds with a wave, and heads for the door, leaving her teacup on the table.

'Pandora! My robe!'

'I'll bring it round later. We can't parade about the Dale stark naked, can we?'

With that, she's gone.

The next few hours pass in a familiar flurry. Bella gets busy crossing things off her To-Do list, though every time she completes a task, she finds herself adding at least one more that needs to be accomplished today. Between chores, she pops in and out of the breakfast room to greet her guests as they help themselves to food and beverages.

Most are newcomers who checked in during Bella's absence this weekend. Only octogenarian sisters Ruby and Opal St Clair are regulars, having made the trip from Ohio twice this season already.

No one lingers long over breakfast, eager to get on with their morning activities. Some are visiting local landmarks.

Prominent among them are the Fairy Trail, a woodland spot said to be populated by miniature winged creatures, and Inspiration

Stump, the Dale's most hallowed ground. Tucked away in the Leolyn Wood, it is the concrete-encased remains of an ancient tree purportedly charged with potent spirit energy. Daily Stump Readings are held during the summer season, with visitors gathered on benches facing a lineup of mediums who provide messages for a lucky few.

In addition to sightseeing, today's calendar offers a number of scheduled events, including workshops on time travel, poltergeists, numerology, and recurring dreams, about which the St Clair sisters are particularly excited.

'We're hoping to uncover the meaning behind an unusual dream,' Opal says. 'Aren't we, Ruby?'

'Yes, a most unusual dream.'

Hester Garretson, an elderly solo traveler who's become fast friends with the sisters, looks up from her danish. 'What is it about?'

'An enormous white whale swoops out of a beautiful blue sky and swallows us whole.'

'Do you mean the sea?' Bella asks.

Opal tilts her head. 'Do I see what, dear?'

'She really can't,' Ruby tells Bella, opening a packet of salt. 'Not a thing. Blind as a bat, poor dear.' She stirs the salt into her coffee, takes a sip, and makes a face. 'I'm not one to complain, but this new coffee machine really isn't up to par.'

'I'll get you a fresh cup.'

'Thank you, Bella. I take it black, with one sugar.'

'One sugar. No milk. Got it.'

'Milk? Goodness, no. I'm lactose intolerant.'

Ah, yes, Bella is well aware of that fact, which had played an unlikely role in helping her solve a mystery earlier this summer. She tosses the salt-tainted beverage into the garbage and sets the machine to brew another as the sisters chatter on about the recurring dream.

'I'm not quite certain it was a whale,' Ruby says. 'It looked more like a dolphin. Or perhaps a shark.'

'But it wasn't in the ocean?' Bella can't help asking, then wishes she hadn't.

The sisters exchange a glance.

'Did you have a dream about the ocean, dear?' Opal asks. 'That's nice.'

'No, I meant your dream – or was it Ruby's?'

'It was both of us.'

'You had the same exact dream? More than once?'

'They *are* identical twins,' Hester tells Bella, as if that's a logical explanation.

'Oh, we aren't twins,' Ruby says.

'Nor identical,' Opal says.

Hester frowns, looking at Bella and then back at the sisters, mirror images of each other from their snow-white topknots to their black orthopedic sandals.

'But I can't tell you apart,' Hester protests.

'Neither could Papa.'

'Sometimes, neither can we, isn't that right, Opal?'

'Oh, it is,' Opal agrees.

'And you had the same exact recurring dream?' Hester asks. 'That's extraordinary.'

'Is it?' Opal asks, and shrugs. 'Most things are, though, aren't they?'

'Certainly here in the Dale,' Ruby agrees, as Bella sets the new cup of coffee in front of her, along with sugar, rather than salt.

The packets are both white rectangles, but that's where the similarity ends – for Bella, anyway, though she can see why an elderly woman with failing eyesight might mistake one for the other.

As for the sisters, she'd thought they were interchangeable until recently. Now she can discern that Ruby's front tooth is slightly crooked, and that Opal has a faint scar on her right index finger. But if Ruby's mouth is closed, or Opal's hand isn't in view, they're virtually indistinguishable.

Researchers have concluded that most people have at least one bona fide lookalike somewhere in the world.

It makes perfect sense that Opal and Ruby would be each other's. They may not be twins, but plenty of siblings share a striking family resemblance.

As for Sam . . .

Yes, Bella had concluded earlier that she and Max had seen a man who looked like him. *Exactly* like him – cowlick, brown eyes, glasses and all. A stranger.

One who happened to be in Chicago at precisely the right place and time?

A stranger to whom they – Bella and Max – were apparently *not* strangers?

The way he was staring at them, wearing an intense, wistful expression . . .

No matter how Bella tries to reason her way around it, she can't get around one logic-defying detail.

He knew us, just like we knew him.

EIGHT

An hour later, Bella is wiping down the vacated café tables, her hair sweat-plastered to her forehead and the back of her neck, when a pair of impossibly beautiful strangers appear in the doorway.

The man has glossy black hair and blue eyes, and he's wearing black jeans with a black T-shirt that shows off his lean, muscular build. The woman's red hair hangs down her back in tousled waves and she appears impossibly unruffled and unwrinkled in sleeveless white linen and heeled sandals.

'You must be Candace and Tommy.'

'We are,' Candace says with a smile. 'And you must be . . .'

She looks at Tommy. His smile is equally dazzling, his expression equally blank.

'I'm Bella Jordan. I'm the manager here at Valley View.' She transfers the damp rag from her right hand to her left and offers them an even damper handshake.

'Bella – that's right!' says Candace, her grasp cool and dry as a brisk autumn day. 'Your husband said that you'd be back this morning.'

'My . . . husband?' Bella gapes at her, thoughts whirling. 'You saw my husband? Here . . . at Valley View?'

They nod, as if that's unremarkable – but of course it would be, to them. They might be celebrities, but they're in the ghost business, just like everyone else around here.

'He said you were at a wedding in – was it Cheyenne?' Candace asks, helping herself to a couple of bottles of water from the fridge and handing one to Tommy.

'Cheyenne?'

Clairaudience isn't like a telephone call, Odelia's voice reminds Bella, and *I heard Kevin Buh . . . something.*

Maybe Sam had told Candace and Tommy that the wedding was in Shuh-something. Cheyenne . . . Chicago . . .

'Whoa, are you all right?' Tommy asks, peering at her. 'You look a little . . . wobbly.'

She nods, feeling more than a little wobbly. Accustomed as she is to the mediums talking to dead people, this is about Sam. And on the heels of Odelia's message, and Bella herself thinking she'd seen him yesterday . . .

Or had she?

Everyone has a lookalike . . .

But why would Sam's know me?

The baffling facts been rolling around in her head all morning, like pinballs that refuse to drop into place so that she can move on.

'It's just . . . it's . . . *too much*,' she hears herself say.

'It's the heat,' Candace says simultaneously. 'Sit down.'

Tommy pulls out a chair from the nearest table and Bella sinks into it.

'What . . . what else did he say?' Hearing familiar footsteps bounding down the stairs, she adds quickly, 'Was there anything about Max?'

'Max?' Tommy echoes.

'Their son,' Candace reminds him. 'Yes, he was saying that Max would be excited to come home to the puppies. It's so amazing, what he does, isn't it?'

'What Max does? Or what Sam does?'

'What Drew does,' Tommy says. 'Are you sure you're feeling OK?'

'What Drew does?' she murmurs, finding it difficult to keep up with the conversation. Maybe the heat really is getting to her.

'Though I'm sure Max is amazing, too, if he's anything like his dad.'

'He's just like his dad,' Bella assures Candace.

Then it hits her.

'Wait – you're talking about Drew!'

Candace and Tommy look at her, then at each other.

'Sorry,' Bella says, 'but I thought you meant . . . my husband. Drew isn't—'

'Mom!' Max is in the doorway, flushed and sweaty, wearing the waffle knit pajamas he'd dug out of his drawer in last night's chill. 'Mom, why—'

'Max? Let's be polite to our guests. Can you say hello, please?'

'Hello,' he says politely, then, 'Mom, why is it so hot here? It's like Chicago.'

'Ah, *that's* where your dad said you were,' Tommy says. 'Chicago.'

'That wasn't his dad,' Bella says quickly.

But before she can elaborate, Max contradicts her. 'At the airport? Yes, it was my dad. Hey, Mom, can I play with the puppies, and then can I go over to Jiffy's house?'

'Not right now.'

'Which thing can't I do right now?'

'Neither.'

'Why not? I really really *really* miss the puppies. And the Daddy Dog. I still have to name him.'

'Later, Max. They're taking their nap.'

'Then can I go to Jiffy's? He has a puppy. Plus, air conditioning. And a cell phone. Also, Playbox.'

Tommy gets a chuckle out of that. 'Sounds like your friend Jiffy has all the good stuff.'

'He does. His mom likes to give him good stuff,' Max says, shooting a pointed look at Bella.

She can't argue with that.

Misty Starr is one of those overly permissive parents who makes things difficult for parents who try to set reasonable limits. She'd moved to the Dale last year, a few months ahead of Bella's arrival, from a military base in Arizona.

The boys had immediately become inseparable. Bella's relationship with Misty had taken much longer to ignite. Twenty-six, impetuous, and as laid-back in her parenting as she is in everything else, Misty was the last person Bella imagined herself befriending.

But, here they are, irrevocably bonded over the challenges of single-handedly parenting seven-year-old boys. Misty's not widowed or divorced, but she and her husband, Mike, have been going through a rocky patch since she'd failed to consult him about her cross-country move while he's deployed in the Middle East.

He's still there, and swears he'll never live in Lily Dale, but Misty has no intention of leaving when he returns stateside – which will be any day now, according to Jiffy.

'Mom, can I please, please, please go to Jiffy's?' Max asks.

'We don't even know if he's home today.'

'He is. I just talked to him.'

'Where? How?'

Max doesn't have a cell phone. Then again, this *is* Valley View.

If there is a secret passageway in his room, it might not just provide an escape route for a cat, but a means of entry for a small boy.

'He knocked on my window to wake me up because I was sleeping too long and he was having a boring day,' Max explains.

'I think you were dreaming, sweetie. He couldn't have knocked on your window. Your room is on the second floor.'

Then again, this *is* Lily Dale. Max might be under the assumption that Jiffy Arden, a child medium, had somehow teleported himself, or astral-projected, or whatever it is the locals call it.

'I wasn't dreaming, Mom.'

Remembering that Max's windows overlook the flat roof above the side-porch-turned-breakfast room, Bella glances outside just in time to see a small, wiry figure descend the adjacent trellis. His foot gets caught in a sweet pea vine and he drops the last few feet to the ground, landing on his back in the pachysandra bed.

So much for magic.

'Jiffy! Are you all right?'

'Oh, hey, Bella. Yep, I'm fine. By the way, sometimes I jump out of helicopters with my dad, so this is no big deal.'

Jiffy, whose dad is a paratrooper, is the kind of boy who is always having adventures, even if just in his own imagination. And Max is the kind of boy who believes every tall tale his friend shares.

'Jiffy's dad is a real-live hero,' he informs Candace and Tommy. 'And Jiffy's practicing being a hero, too. And so am I. Only my mom doesn't let me do a lot of hero stuff.'

'Most moms don't,' Candace tells him, looking amused as she opens her water bottle and takes a long sip.

Outside, Jiffy gets to his feet. He brushes himself off, plucks a twig from his wiry red hair and wipes his freckled face with grimy hands that leave fresh smudges. 'So, Bella, can Max come over?'

'Why don't you come in and I'll call your mom and tell her where you are?'

'She knows where I am. And it's too hot here. We have an air conditioner.'

'And Playbox,' Max reminds him. 'We can play *Ninja Zombie Battle*.'

'Or some other game.'

'But we like *Ninja Zombie Battle* the best.'

'By the way, I don't know where that game is,' Jiffy says. 'I think I lost it.'

'How did you lose it?'

'I just did,' Jiffy says, avoiding eye contact with Bella in a way that would suggest to any seasoned mother of a seven-year-old that he's lying. 'I'm going back to my house now. I'll wait for you there, Max.'

He takes off, cutting through the shrub border toward home.

Turning away from the window, Bella finds that Candace and Tommy are also beating a hasty retreat.

'It was nice meeting you, Bella,' Candace says over her shoulder as she follows Tommy out the door. 'See you later! We have to get to a Stump reading.'

With any luck, Bella thinks, Spirit will 'touch in' to inform Candace and Tommy that Drew Bailey isn't Bella's husband or Max's dad. And if not, well . . .

At least they hadn't seen Sam hanging around Valley View, any more than Bella and Max had seen him hanging around O'Hare yesterday. Although . . .

'Hey, Max? Yesterday at the airport, when we thought we saw Daddy—'

'We *did* see him.'

'When we saw him,' she amends, 'you said it was "the golden car". Do you remember that?'

'Yep. It was the golden car. Hey!' He grabs a mini box of sugary cereal from the counter. 'I didn't know we have Chocolatey Oaty-Os! You never buy them for me.'

No, but they'd been included in the assorted pack.

'Can I have them, Mom? Please?'

Chocolatey Oaty-Os aren't the healthiest breakfast in the world, but she supposes they're not the unhealthiest, either.

'Sure. Sit down. I'll grab a bowl for you, and the milk, and I'll cut up some bananas, too.'

'Can't I just eat them out of the box?'

That might make them the world's unhealthiest breakfast, but she relents.

'Just this once.' She steers him back to the topic at hand. 'So you said *the* golden car. Not *a* golden car. Right?'

He nods, shoving a handful of cereal into his mouth.

'Why is that? Because it kind of sounded as if you were expecting to see that car, or maybe as if you'd seen it before.'

'Is it OK if I talk with my mouth full?' he asks, doing just that. 'Because you keep asking me stuff.'

'Yes. Just this once.'

'I did,' he says around exaggerated crunching.

'You did . . . what?'

Max, being a seven-year-old boy, shoves more cereal into his mouth before answering, 'I did see the golden car before.'

'You did? Where?'

'It was parked on the street by Grandma's apartment building when George and me were over at the playground. There was a guy sitting in it the whole time, but he was too far away, and I couldn't tell he was Daddy.'

NINE

Bella sits on the mudroom step watching the dogs lap up the cold water from bowls she'd set out for them in the fenced yard after a few minutes of play. Well, the puppies had played. The big guy just lies in a dappled patch of shade watching them. Something tells Bella that he, too, has had his fill of this Monday, though there's no end in sight, with the blazing sun still high overhead.

The midwestern heat and humidity have indeed swept across the Great Lakes and now smother the Dale like a wet towel. Her only reprieve had been a short trip in the air-conditioned car to the air-conditioned supermarket.

At least Max is happy, two doors down at Misty Starr's cottage, keeping cool courtesy of the window air conditioner in Jiffy's room. Predictably, when Bella had called over there to check on him at lunchtime, Max had asked why *he* couldn't have an air conditioner. Oh, and a puppy and a Playbox.

Single parenting is challenging on a good day. This particular day is shaping up to be, well . . .

It isn't a *bad* day, all things considered, but she's had better ones. Every time she believes she's settled on a plausible explanation for the Sam – or *not* Sam – sighting, her logical inner self intervenes, and things go topsy-turvy all over again.

Why would a stranger who happens to look just like her late husband have been hanging around Millicent's building on her wedding day?

There are no coincidences.

All right, then she supposes it makes sense if he was Sam's ghost, haunting his childhood home the way Nadine supposedly hangs around Valley View – not that Bella's ever actually glimpsed the resident spirit.

And not that a ghost makes any sense whatsoever, under ordinary circumstances.

But if Sam was going to visit Chicago from the Great Beyond, his mother's wedding day would be a logical time to do so, wouldn't it?

Even if he was driving an unfamiliar, beat-up Subaru?
How does that make sense, under any circumstances at all?
And . . . Kevin Bacon?

If Sam wanted Bella to know he'd been with them this weekend, why wouldn't the message have been 'golden car', or even 'airport'?

Earlier, she'd tried to call Millicent, intending to ask her . . .

Well, she isn't quite sure what she wanted to ask. She just feels the need to share what's gone on with someone who knew and loved Sam. Maybe Millicent had noticed the golden car parked in front of her building, or maybe she'll be able to solve the Kevin Bacon clue.

Unfortunately, her phone had gone right into voicemail. Bella had left a brief message apologizing for calling her on her honeymoon and asking her to return the call.

She doubts that's going to happen. There's probably no phone service on a yacht in the middle of the Caribbean Sea. Even if there is, who checks voicemail on their honeymoon?

It's probably best to leave Millicent out of this, anyway. She's come a long way from her initial assumption that Lily Dale is run by a cult that's holding Bella and Max against their will, but she might be disturbed by the notion of her son's spirit sending messages through a psychic.

'Kevin Bacon,' Bella mutters yet again, in case saying it aloud will somehow trigger a memory. 'Kevin Bacon?'

It's a question, and she sits, head cocked, listening as if someone – Sam? Spirit? – might answer it.

The only response is a burst of laughter and splashing off to her far right.

Turning, she sees a couple of kids diving into the roped-off area at the small beach. If Max were here, he'd be pestering her to go over for a swim. She recognizes one of the boys as the bully who'd picked on Max and Jiffy when he'd been in their first-grade class.

'Bella?'

It's Drew, calling her from inside the house.

'I'm out here!'

The screen door creaks open and Drew steps outside. He's wearing his scrubs and looks handsome as always, if perhaps as overheated and weary as she is right now.

So much for the care she'd taken in her appearance this morning. She'd long since swapped her summer dress for a tank top and shorts, removed the makeup that had melted off her face, and pulled her sweat-dampened hair off her neck in a plastic clip.

'I'm so sorry,' he says. 'I never expected to be gone this long. First, I had that emergency, and then it was nonstop patients all morning.'

'It's no problem.'

He bends to give the hound a pat as the puppies scamper in to sniff his shoes. 'Looks like I left these guys in good hands.'

'We've all been keeping each other company. How's the hamster?'

'He's going to be fine.'

'Thank goodness. I'm sure his owner is one relieved little girl.'

'And one sleepy little girl right about now,' he says around a deep yawn. 'But who isn't?'

'Why don't you go upstairs and lie down for a while? I'm happy to take care of the pups.'

'That would be nice, but I have to see more patients starting in about . . .' He checks his watch. 'Half an hour. I really just came back to get the dogs out of your way. I'll bring them back to the animal hospital with me.'

'They're not in my way! And why the animal hospital? You can't take them to your place?'

He shakes his head. 'Unfortunately, I've still got a full house. The foster for Sprout and Twixie fell through. Janet's trying to find someone else to take them.'

'Sprout and Twixie? Are they the orphaned kittens?'

'Yes.'

'Those are the cutest names.'

'Well, they're the cutest kittens. Here, I'll show you.' He pulls out his phone and scrolls quickly to a photo, leaning in to show her. 'Can you tell which is which?'

'Twixie has to be the one with the caramel- and chocolate-colored coat and little pink nose,' she guesses, trying not to be aware of how close their faces are. 'And Sprout must be the orange tabby guy with the bright green eyes?'

'You got it.' He scrolls to another photo, and then another. 'Adorable, aren't they?'

'*So* adorable.'

'I don't suppose you'd want to—'

'Hey!' She steps back and looks up at him. 'Are you trying to brainwash me with cute kitten photos, Dr Bailey?'

He grins. 'Absolutely, Ms Jordan. I can just see these two romping around here with Chance and Spidey, can't you?'

'Absolutely *not*. I've got my hands full with two cats, Max, and running this place. But nice try. I'm sorry I can't help you.'

'You've already done more than your share. I'm sure Janet will find someone. Anyway, I really did come back here to take the dogs off your hands, not saddle you with more of my menagerie.'

'Why don't you leave them here for now? It's better than putting them into a cage, isn't it?'

'Kennel. And a lot of dogs feel safer in confined spaces. It's in their canine DNA, going back to ancient times when they were den animals.'

'Does the kennel have bars?'

'Yes, but they won't mind it.'

Yes, they will. The puppies are in their glory, chasing a butterfly that flits around the blooming vines. The big guy is taking a well-deserved rest, lying on his belly in the grass with his long white nose on his paws. He meets Bella's gaze with those soulful hazel eyes, and she leans over to pat his furry brown head.

He's been through so much. They all have. She can't bear to think of them locked up in a cell.

'Please let them stay here, Drew. The mudroom offers plenty of confinement and it's familiar to them now, and they love being outside, and . . . I kind of love having them here. It's a nice distraction from . . . everything.'

'You won't love it in the middle of the night when you have to get up with them every few hours.'

'Oh . . . I . . . I mean . . . I guess I thought . . .'

It's not that she hadn't realized what their care entails. Somehow, she'd just assumed that Drew, too, would be staying over.

Apparently, he isn't interested in doing that again. Why would he be? He has his home, and she has hers, and that brand of change isn't afoot at Valley View, dammit, no matter what Pandora's guides are claiming.

'I'm used to it,' she tells him with a shrug. 'I had a newborn baby, remember? And Chance's kittens. I had to feed them around the clock, too.'

'Well, I can't let you do that. Although . . . I, uh . . . I don't want to presume anything, but . . . if I stayed over again tonight, then I could take care of them?'

'Yes!' she says quickly – too quickly. 'That would be great! *Good*. It would be good,' she amends, and shuts her mouth, feeling her face grow even hotter than it is.

This is about Drew dutifully taking proper care of the animals he rescues, not about his wanting to spend more time with her.

No matter how nice it had been to climb the stairs with him last night instead of watching his taillights disappear into the dark.

He smiles. 'Good. Then I guess I'll get back to work, and see you later?'

'Sounds good. I bought some chicken I can grill for dinner.'

'It's too hot to stand over a grill, Bella. I'll stop and pick up something for all of us on the way back.'

'Sounds good,' she says again.

Actually, it sounds great – all of it. Drew here, morning, noon, and night.

She could get used to this, though she shouldn't.

Darn Pandora and her guides and her assumptions. And Candace and Tommy and theirs, as well. Bella will set everyone straight first chance she gets.

'Is it too hot for this, too?' he asks, leaning in to put his arms around her.

'Not at all.'

His kiss is somewhere between a quick, see-you-later smooch, and something that's . . . well, *hot*. In the best way, and now she can't quite remember the reason why she shouldn't get used to this.

With Drew gone and the dogs back in the mudroom, Bella returns to the day's chores. But after folding a heap of guest towels fresh from the dryer, and unloading the clean dishes from the still-steamy dishwasher, she's drenched in sweat. She pours a big glass of ice water and is guzzling it when she hears the front door open and then close.

Her eyes go to the stove clock, and she sees that it's twenty past two. She wasn't expecting the guests to return until the afternoon sessions are over.

But the footsteps don't continue up the stairs, and someone rings the silver bell on the registration desk. Bella gulps a last sip of water and grabs a couple of paper towels to blot the persistent perspiration from her neck and hairline as she hurries out of the kitchen.

In the entry hall, she finds a young woman peering at the leather-bound guest registration book that lies open on the tall desk. She's wearing khaki capris and a sleeveless pink blouse with a designer logo beneath the left shoulder. Her highlighted blonde mane falls just above her shoulders in one of those cuts that's meant to be styled daily – layers that are shorter in back with angled points at her chin.

Cute, if a bit too high maintenance for Bella's taste – though in this moment, with her own damp hair plastered to her scalp, she's hardly one to judge.

'Can I help you?' she asks.

The woman looks up and gives her a once-over. She seems a bit taken aback.

'Are you . . . you're . . . you're not . . .'

'I'm the manager here.'

'Oh, then you are.' The woman's smile strikes Bella as a little forced. 'I saw your vacancy sign, and I'm looking for a place to stay.'

'For how long?'

'I'm not sure. A night, maybe two? I'm kind of desperate. I really need to get off the road for a bit.'

'We're pretty booked,' Bella hears herself say.

'Tonight? Then the sign is a mistake?'

No, but Drew was planning to stay again, and Bella is selfishly reluctant to give away his room.

But it isn't *his* room, she reminds herself. It's a vacant guest room, and she's responsible for filling them.

'I do have a vacancy tonight,' she admits. 'We had a last-minute cancellation, so if you want it . . .'

'I'll take it for tonight.'

'Great.'

'Great.' The woman opens her tan leather purse.

Bella notes her shellacked fingernails, painted in an intricate glittery pattern, and the gold metal designer logo dangling from the zipper pull.

A lot of people are into luxurious salon treatments and prominently featured brand names. Bella isn't one of them. Though if she were feeling more presentable about her own bedraggled appearance in this moment, she probably wouldn't be feeling so prickly toward her impeccably coiffed visitor's.

She goes around behind the desk and opens a file drawer. There's a row of folders labeled with individual guest room names, sorted alphabetically. Apple Room, Doll Room, Gable Room, Jungle . . .

Wait a minute. The Gable Room is vacant this week for Grant Everard's visit. He prefers it, tucked away in a quiet corner of the third floor, one of the few with a private bath.

'One night, you said?'

'If that's all you have available, that's fine.'

'It is, if you don't mind a room with a damp spot on the ceiling? The roof leaks sometimes.'

'It's not raining, so that's probably fine. I'll take it.' She doesn't ask about the nightly rate, merely pulls out a credit card and hands it over. It's not plastic, but made of sturdy metal, engraved with the name *Polly Green*.

'I'll need to see your ID, too.'

'Oh, sure.'

She flashes a driver's license long enough for Bella to confirm that her name matches the card, and that she lives in Boston.

Bella pulls an envelope from the Gable Room file. Handing it to her visitor, she explains that it contains the code that unlocks the door to Valley View after hours and another for the guestroom, along with a parking tag, and an information packet with breakfast hours, house rules, amenities.

Scanning those, the woman asks about air conditioning.

'We don't have it, unfortunately,' Bella says, wondering if – or perhaps hoping – it's a deal breaker.

It is not.

'It's OK. I'm used to that.'

'In Boston? That's where you're from?'

'It's where I live now. I'm from all over. Army brat, now army wife. Military housing doesn't always have A/C, even in hot climates. Am I all set, then?' She tucks the flap into the envelope and puts it into her purse.

'Yes. And if it does rain, there's a plastic bucket in the cabinet under the bathroom sink to catch the drips.'

'Sounds good.'

Really? She doesn't seem like the kind of woman who'd take something like that in stride. Bella asks where she's parked.

'In the lot by the playground. I wasn't sure where to go. I've never been here before. I'd never even heard of it.'

'How'd you find it?'

'I'm on a road trip – driving cross-country, you know, Boston to

LA. I saw a sign and thought I'd check it out. Just for the day, you know, walk around, and see what's what. But then I spotted your vacancy, and figured I might as well stay. It's a fascinating place.'

'That it is,' Bella agrees as Polly heads out the door. 'Make sure you move your car to one of our reserved spots and leave the pass on the dashboard. And if you need a hand with your bags, I'm happy to help.'

'No, I'm good. Thanks, Bella.'

Only after the door has closed after her does Bella realize that she'd never told Polly her name.

TEN

Ordinarily, Odelia would be irked if a three o'clock client texted a last-minute cancellation at two fifty-five. Today, though, after a string of back-to-back appointments, she welcomes the two-hour break before her next reading.

Given her restless night and busy day, it would have been nice to join Li'l Chap, who's spending the muggy afternoon napping on the couch.

But she's facing a self-imposed deadline for the cookbook she's writing, and she has a few more recipes to perfect before the manuscript will be ready for submission. Unfortunately, she'd saved the dessert chapter for last, and that means baking.

'I probably don't even need to put you in the oven,' she tells her cake batter in progress. 'I can just pour you into a pan and leave you on the counter and you'll be ready in an hour.'

She cracks another egg into the bowl, pauses to press her sweaty forehead against the dish towel draped over her shoulder for that purpose, and consults her notes.

The first time she'd made this cake, she'd used five eggs. That was too many. Last time, she'd tried it with three. That wasn't enough.

Four should do the trick. She adds one more to the bowl. It lands with a fleck of shell. Chasing it around the viscous pool with the spatula, then with her finger, she senses Miriam's disapproval.

'I know, I know, I'm supposed to be cracking each egg into a ramekin before adding it to the batter,' she tells the spirit. 'I decided to take a shortcut today, OK?'

She pins the white shard beneath her fingertip and works it up the side of the bowl, but it takes her several attempts to remove the slippery little bugger. If she didn't know better, she'd think Miriam is interfering, but that's not her style. For the most part, she merely watches Odelia when she's working in the kitchen or garden, where she'd spent most of her time during her own day.

'Gammy? Are you here?' a voice calls from the front of the cottage.

'Oh, hooray! You're back!' Odelia sets aside the spatula and turns to see Calla peek into the room, with a drowsy Li'l Chap in her arms.

'I'm back, and you're . . . *baking*? Gammy! Are you crazy?'

'Yes.' Grinning, Odelia hugs her granddaughter.

'Wow, Gammy, you're soggy!' Calla grabs the dish towel and wipes herself off, then the kitten. 'Either you just took a shower, or it's time to get out of the kitchen.'

'Do I smell like I just took a shower?'

'Time to get out of the kitchen,' Calla says with a laugh. 'Come on, let's go sit on the porch.'

'As soon as I get this cake in the oven.'

Calla puts the cat down and fills his water bowl at the sink. She sets it in front of him and he laps it with his tiny pink tongue.

'Aw, you're thirsty, huh, Li'l Chap?'

'Who isn't?' Odelia whisks oil into her cake batter. 'There's lemonade in the fridge, if you want to pour us a couple of glasses.'

'*Regular* lemonade?'

'Of course.'

'No bizarre additions? Like . . . I don't know . . . fennel? Isn't that what you made last week?'

'That was *fennel-ade*. This is lemonade.'

'Fennel-ade.' She shakes her head, smiling. 'I've missed you, Gammy.'

'I've missed you, too.' Odelia opens a cabinet and roots among the canned goods. 'How was New York?'

'Same as always. Noisy, chaotic, wonderful. How are things in the Dale?'

'Same as always.'

'Noisy, chaotic, wonderful?'

'Among other things, yes.' She plucks a can from the shelf.

'Uh-oh. What's going on?'

'I'll fill you in, but first, I want to hear all about your trip.'

Calla is a novelist. Her first book had been a success a few years back. She's just finished her second, and it's slated for publication next spring. She's been in New York at a writers' conference for the past week.

'It was business. There's not much to tell.'

Odelia fastens the can to the electric can opener. Holding down the button that rotates it around the blade, she watches Calla fill two glasses of lemonade and return the pitcher to the refrigerator. She looks the same as always – lean and tanned in shorts and a T-shirt, her effortlessly pretty face makeup-free, her long brown hair pulled back in a ponytail. But her energy is off, and she appears lost in thought.

'Did you meet with your editor and agent, Cal'? Did they like the finished manuscript?'

'They loved it.'

'Congratulations! Do they want you to do another book?'

'Yes.'

'That's marvelous!' Odelia dumps the can's contents into the mixing bowl and reaches for the spoon.

'Gammy! What's that god-awful smell?'

'Sauerkraut.'

'Please tell me you didn't just put that in the cake.'

'I did. It provides a wonderful texture. Like coconut.'

'Then why not use coconut?'

'Sauerkraut provides a nice acidic touch. Baking is scientific. It's chemistry. Ask Bella. She'll tell you.'

'How *is* Bella?'

'She's well. I saw her this morning.'

'Did she have a nice time at her mother-in-law's wedding?'

'I suppose she did. We didn't really talk about that.'

'What *did* you talk about?'

'About Sam. He paid me a visit last night.'

Calla raises an eyebrow. 'Well, it's about time. I've been hoping to bring him through for her ever since I met her. I still can't believe Pandora beat us both to it.'

'Oh, Pandora.' Odelia waves a dismissive hand. 'I don't believe she channeled him.'

'I think Bella does, but . . . let's not get into a whole big thing about that again, Gammy.'

'Again? When did I—'

'Every single time Pandora's name comes up, there's a whole big thing about something.'

She can't deny that. The woman has tried her patience from the moment Pandora moved in next door at Valley View, years ago. Odelia had pitied her when she'd lost her home in an ugly divorce and been forced to move to a tiny cottage nearby, but she's remained the same old insufferable Pandora.

Unfortunately, there's no avoiding her in a town this size – especially because Pandora is the kind of person who makes it her business to know everyone else's.

'It's not my fault, it's hers,' she tells Calla. 'Do you know what she did the other day? She showed up uninvited to help me weed and prune my garden.'

'She was just trying to be neighborly.'

'But I wasn't weeding and pruning! I just stepped out the door to pick some herbs for the brownies I was making and suddenly, there she was with clippers and a trowel, transplanting things, barking orders and criticisms.' She mimics Pandora's haughty accent. '"*Do* take care as you deadhead the bee balm, Odelia, don't just lop them off willy-nilly – we aren't King Henry the Eighth, are we?" "Blimey, you've let the zinnias go to seed faster than Wallis after the abdication."'

'That's Pandora. She's never been a fan of Wallis Simpson,' Calla says with a shrug.

'That's beside the point. Do you know what she said about—'

'Wait, you were putting herbs in your brownies, Gammy? Were they . . .'

'Lavender-rosemary with just a hint of chive. Here, try one.' She opens the tin on the counter and hands Calla a brownie.

She takes a bite, chews, swallows, and immediately downs a huge swig of lemonade.

'Well? What do you think?'

'You might want to cut back on the chive or eliminate it altogether.'

'But then it would just be a lavender-rosemary brownie. There's nothing special about that. And I have so many chives in the garden this year that I don't know what to do with them all.'

'Why don't you use some in that potato soup recipe, instead of . . . was it cotton candy?'

'For a bit of sweetness and color. But maybe I'll add some chives, too – they'd be so pretty floating in that blue soup, like lily pads on the lake.'

Calla makes a face.

'Anyway, Gammy, we were talking about Sam. What's going on?'

Stirring chopped apples and nuts into her cake batter, she recaps the visit for Calla.

'Kevin Bacon, huh? What's that about?'

'Bella doesn't know. I told her it will probably come to her, but . . . the more I think about it, the more I wonder if I missed something, or . . .' Odelia hesitates, then shakes her head. 'I'm just so exhausted.'

'It's the heat.'

'No, I mean, I'd gone to bed late, and then Spirit woke me up. I never did get back to sleep. I'm just not sure I relayed the right message from the right spirit. And of course Pandora was there, nosing into things as usual.'

'Pandora again? In your bedroom?'

'At Bella's.' She dumps the batter into the greased and floured sheet pan. 'You should have seen her, eavesdropping in the window like a nosy neighbor on an old sitcom.'

Calla rolls her eyes. 'Gammy, you really need to get over this. I thought you two had declared a truce.'

'Yes, but I'm only human. She gets under my skin. I'm not proud of it.'

Calla takes her phone from her pocket, and Odelia sees that there's a message on the screen. Resisting the urge to ask who it's from, she concentrates on smoothing the batter with a rubber spatula.

Calla sends a quick response to the message. Maybe an emoji? Odelia can't quite see it. 'Maybe Sam will be in touch with you again, Gammy.'

'I hope so. I meditated on it, but I haven't been able to get anything more.'

She opens the oven, feeling like she's leaning into a dragon's fiery mouth as she slides in the cake pan. She closes the door, sets the timer, and turns to see Calla leaning against the counter with her phone in her hand, as if she's waiting for the reply to her message.

Odelia flashes back a dozen years or so. Calla, in high school, waiting for the phone to ring. Waiting for Blue Slayton to call.

How many times had he let her down?

What if whoever she's texting now does the same? Why can't it be Jacy? It was supposed to be Jacy. Odelia has always known that. Not because she's always had a soft spot for Jacy Bly, or because she's a psychic medium, but because she's a grandmother.

Calla had come to Lily Dale from Florida after her mom – Odelia's only child, Stephanie – had passed on. Estranged from her own daughter during Stephanie's final years on the earthly plane, Odelia had embraced the opportunity to see her grandchild into adulthood. This time, she was determined to get it right.

Some days, she's convinced that she has. Others, she fears she's let her own staunchly held opinions interfere with the relationship, just as she did with Stephanie. Calla is equally strong-willed, and arguably a more potent medium than anyone in the Dale, Odelia included; though she isn't nearly as experienced – in mediumship, nor in life.

She's made some questionable choices over the years, despite Odelia's attempts to guide her, and to spare her the same mistakes she herself had made.

Now, seeing Calla so fixated on her phone, Odelia experiences a twinge of apprehension – and yes, perhaps a bit of envy – as she wonders who's commanding Calla's full attention on the other end of the text exchange.

She clears her throat loudly. 'So, Bella mentioned that she and Max saw Sam at the airport in Chicago yesterday morning.'

That gets Calla's interest. She looks up from her phone, eyes wide. 'Gammy! Are you serious?'

'I'm always serious.'

'No, you aren't.'

'Well, I am now. She said they both saw him.'

'An apparition.'

'Apparently.'

'So Bella told you this yesterday, and then he came through to you last night?'

'No, he came through to me last night, and then I told Bella about it, and she told me about seeing him. One had nothing to do with the other. Not that I believe it's a coincidence, because there are—'

'—no coincidences.' Calla completes the sentence with her. 'Right. But he's really trying to connect. Maybe you should have Bella sit down and do a reading with you. See if you can bring him through for her.'

'She'd never agree to do that.'

'Are you sure? Did you ever ask her?'

'I don't think so, no. She's determined not to let herself get caught up in spiritualism.'

'If ever there was a time when she might change her mind, this might be it.'

'You might be right.' Odelia picks up the batter-coated mixing bowl and holds it out to her.

'No, thanks, Gammy, I'm good.'

'But you always like to lick the bowl.'

'Not when there's cabbage in it.'

'You really need to get over this,' Odelia says with a grin.

'I'm only human,' Calla returns, and her phone lights up again.

Odelia puts the mixing bowl into the sink with the other dirty dishes and picks up her glass of lemonade. 'Let's go sit on the porch.'

'Mmm, I'll meet you out there in a minute, Gammy.' She types something, sends it with a whoosh, and stands poised, watching the screen.

'Business?'

'Hmm?'

'Is that business?' Odelia asks her.

'What? This? No, it's . . . a friend.'

'Jacy?' She can't help herself.

'Not Jacy.' Calla frowns. 'You know we're broken up, right? And you know he's been dating a doctor who works with him at the hospital?'

Oh, she knows.

Jacy, who'd come to the Dale as a foster child, had been adopted as a teenager by Odelia's friends Walter and Peter, fellow mediums who own the Soul-stice Bistro here in town. He and Calla had endured as a couple for almost a decade – through their college years, her career launch, his med school and residency.

Then, almost a year ago, her old flame Blue Slayton came back into the picture. Calla had assured Odelia that he'd had nothing to do with her breakup with Jacy, but Odelia isn't so sure she believes her.

In any case, her rekindled relationship with Blue hadn't lasted, either. This time, unlike back in high school, Calla had been the one to call it quits, but she refuses to discuss the details. Odelia only knows that they broke up in June, and Blue left the Dale immediately after – hopefully for good.

As far as she's concerned, it's not too late for her granddaughter to find her way back to Jacy.

'Walter mentioned something about his having gone on a date with a doctor,' she tells Calla. 'But—'

'Just a date? Come on, Gammy.'

'Maybe it's been more than one date,' she concedes, 'but it isn't serious.'

'Walter said that?'

Well, no, he hadn't. But unlike many other parents in the Dale, when it comes to their son, Walter and Peter don't overshare – or share much at all. Odelia has to pry Jacy updates from them, and she knows better than to ask them if he's mentioned Calla since the breakup.

Come to think of it, though, she *has* done just that – and Walter and Peter said no, he hasn't.

'Come on, not even once?' Odelia had pressed. 'In passing?'

'It hasn't come up.'

You'd think they might bring it up to him. They're fond of Calla, and she often helps out waiting tables at their bistro.

They should be rooting for Calla and Jacy to end up together as much as Odelia is.

Men.

'Gammy, if Jacy is happy with this woman, then I'm happy for him,' Calla tells her. 'I wish you could feel the same way.'

'Well, I don't.' She mops her sweaty forehead and tosses the dish towel into the sink. 'Let's finish this conversation outside.'

Calla shakes her head and waves her phone. 'I have to make a quick call. But you go cool off and I'll be right out.'

Too wilted to linger another moment, Odelia leaves her in the kitchen and steps out onto the porch with her lemonade.

If anything, it's even steamier outside, and preternaturally still. At this hour on a summer afternoon, visitors should be strolling the streets or relaxing on park benches between workshops and readings. Today, it's deserted, as if everyone is sheltering behind closed windows and doors.

Everyone on the earthly plane, anyway. In the park across the way, the little girl in corkscrew curls is swinging in midair where the hickory tree had once stood. A filmy man in a top hat is lounging on a bench with a newspaper whose enormous headline bears the word *Titanic*. A couple of teenaged boys in knickers and newsboy caps are playing catch.

Settled on the glider, Odelia checks her own phone. There are

no messages from anyone, including Luther. He'd told her she probably won't hear from him until tomorrow morning, as he's working
a private security gig over at Chautauqua Institution.

It's a few miles from Lily Dale, and the two communities have
a lot in common. Both are gated summer colonies founded in the
nineteenth century. Both sit on the grassy shores of picturesque
country lakes and are notable for their charming Victorian architec-
ture. Both have a smattering of year-round residents but come alive
in June, with a vocation-focused seasonal calendar that draw tourists
from all over the globe. Lily Dale's is spiritualism; Chautauqua is
devoted to the arts. The institution has its own world-class symphony
orchestra, ballet, opera and theater company.

Tonight's speaker is an author-historian from a war-torn country.
Having received her share of death threats, she travels with her own
bodyguards. Luther is part of the local security detail.

Odelia sips her lemonade and tries to enjoy the silence, watching
a couple of squirrels nose around the ground beneath the girl and
her swing. They're probably in spirit, she decides, noting that they
seem to be foraging for – and finding – hickory nuts in what has
been a barren patch of dirt ever since the tree fell.

In the distance, a screen door creaks and slams. She looks across
the park to see that Pandora Feeney has stepped onto the porch of
her little pink cottage. She's wearing a broad-brimmed straw hat, a
long-sleeved blouse, overalls tucked into tall rubber boots, and
gardening gloves. Her face is mostly hidden by enormous sunglasses,
but her nose is bright white – likely slathered in zinc oxide, Odelia
suspects: solar protection for that ashen skin of hers.

Pandora grabs a spade and cultivator and descends the steps,
pausing to look up at the sky. Is she cursing the sun, or channeling
Spirit?

Seeing her turn expectantly toward the far end of the lane, Odelia
follows her gaze and sees nothing.

Silly woman.

She swallows some lemonade, scowling, hoping that Pandora
won't notice her sitting here and come over to 'help' again. If she
does, then this time Odelia will give her a piece of her mind. She'll
say . . .

What will she say? It has to be strongly worded if it's going to
put Pandora in her place, once and for all.

She closes her eyes. Maybe something like . . .

Don't . . .

The word comes to mind as Spirit touches in, and she frowns.

Yes, *don't* is a good start, but—

Hearing tires crunch along gravel, she turns to see a white sedan rounding the corner at the end of the lane, as if summoned by Pandora.

Behind her, the door creaks open. 'Gammy? Sorry that took so long. I just had to explain something to someone.'

'It's fine,' she murmurs, watching the vehicle slow as it approaches. The late afternoon glare obscures the driver behind the windshield, and the car, a Chevy, is unfamiliar.

Across the park, Pandora, too, is watching it.

A strange clamminess seeps over Odelia. She sets the glass on the porch floor and sinks back, eyes closed, feeling a bit dizzy.

Calla is saying something, but her voice is faint, and her words are garbled.

Don't—

No, that isn't Calla. It's Spirit, trying to get her attention.

Don't—

'Gammy! Are you OK?' Calla touches her arm.

Odelia's eyes open, and she's back in the moment. 'What . . .'

'I think you passed out. It's got to be heat exhaustion.'

Odelia shakes her head and wipes sweat from her brow.

'Here, drink this.' Calla pushes the cold glass into her hand.

Odelia sips.

'More.'

Odelia gulps the icy, sweet-tart liquid until the glass is empty.

'Better?' Calla asks.

'Much. Thank you.'

'I don't know why you were baking in weather like this. At your age, you should know better.'

'At *my* age?'

'It's dangerous.'

'At *my* age?' Odelia repeats with an indignant glare at her granddaughter. 'It's not as though I'm a doddering little old lady. I'm hardier than a lot of people half my age.'

'That may be, but you don't always know your limits.'

Odelia rolls her eyes and looks away. Pandora is no longer visible in her yard across the park, and the white Chevy has pulled into a guest spot in front of Valley View.

'You're just so stubborn,' Calla is saying. 'I'll go refill your glass. You need to stay hydrated.'

'I'm perfectly hydrated,' she lies.

'You look flushed, and I swear you just about collapsed. You can't . . . Hey!'

Odelia follows Calla's gaze. Over at Valley View, a woman has gotten out of the parked car. She's wearing pink, and her hair is brown with blonde streaks.

'What is it? Do you know her?'

'No, but she was on my plane this morning.'

'From New York?'

'Yes. The airline held the plane for her and a couple of other passengers. They were on a connecting flight from Chicago.'

ELEVEN

When Pandora Feeney had lived at Valley View, and Leona Gatto, too, they'd used the small study off the front parlor for psychic readings. It's suitably private if you close the curtained French doors and draw the window shades.

Bella rarely does either of those things. She'd transformed the space into a bright and cheerful office space, with creamy yellow walls, blue-and-white window-seat cushions, a large desk, and a comfortable leather reading chair.

Guests are welcome to use the desktop computer, print boarding passes, and use the landline to call for appointments with registered mediums. Last week, after the local phone directory had disappeared yet again from her desk, she'd compiled a list of mediums' names and numbers on cardstock and displayed it beside the phone in a large picture frame.

Predictably, that had sparked a squabble among her closest friends. Odelia was miffed to find herself halfway down the directory instead of at the top.

'Why is Andy Brighton at the top of the list? He lives way across the Dale. Don't you think I should be first, Bella? I'm the most conveniently located.'

'Well, I'm only two doors down,' Misty Starr had pointed out. 'And I'm way at the bottom.'

'Neither of you refinished these floors on your hands and knees?' Pandora said. 'It was a dreadful task. My back has never been the same.'

Odelia scowled. 'What does that have to do with anything?'

'I should be at the top of the list. Andy Brighton never contributed a thing to Valley View.'

Bella threw up her hands. 'It's alphabetical, ladies.'

'Then I should be above Odelia and Pandora,' Misty said. 'M comes before O and P.'

'Alphabetical by last name!' Bella said. 'But either way, Andy Brighton would still come first.'

But Misty wasn't letting it go. 'Starr is just my professional name. My legal last name is Arden.'

'I thought it was Grzeszkiewicz,' Odelia said.

'That's my maiden name. But either way, if it's alphabetical by last name, I'd be before you.'

It was one of the more exasperating conversations Bella had ever experienced – which is really saying something, because most are, when those three women are in a room together.

She's spent the last hour catching up on paperwork and preparing for Grant's visit as if she were still a teacher and working on a lesson plan.

She's created a spreadsheet on the desktop computer, referring to the notes she's been scribbling on a legal pad all summer – things like: *Need new fridge – check Labor Day sales for a good deal?* and *Third-floor ceiling leak worse – time to schedule roofers.*

Every so often, she leans in toward the big box fan spinning in the window. It's a futile attempt to cool off. Even on the highest speed, the blades merely move hot air around.

Ordinarily, Valley View's high ceilings and plaster walls tend to keep the rooms comfortable even in warm weather, but not today. The house has grown more oppressive as the afternoon wears on. The sticky heat seems to have smothered the homey scents that had welcomed her last night. Today, the place smells of damp wood and a hint of basement mildew wafting up from below the hardwoods – perhaps down from the water-damaged third floor as well.

Heavy-duty dehumidifiers might be a good idea, she decides, adding that to the spreadsheet.

And maybe it's time to replace some of the overhead lights with ceiling fans. Not on the first floor, where the vintage fixtures enhance the period ambiance. Nor on the third, where the ceilings are too low. But certainly in the second-floor guest rooms.

She wipes a trickle of sweat from her forehead, then saves the spreadsheet file and closes the program. She can continue working on it in another room, or outdoors.

She grabs the legal pad and a pen and opens a drawer to retrieve her laptop.

It sits alongside a stack of bills she'd rubber-banded to her checkbook and flagged with a Post-it note that reads simply: *To Be Paid.*

They're remnants of her old life, with Sam. Mostly astronomical medical bills for doctors and treatments that hadn't saved his life, along with credit card debt they'd accumulated when he'd gotten sick, and collection notices for unpaid utilities back in Bedford.

Every month, she triages the bills and sends what she can manage to spare, but it's going to be years, likely decades, before it's all paid off.

Her eyes go to the envelope Millicent had handed her yesterday morning. It's sitting on the desk beneath a glass paperweight, a reminder that she needs to deposit the check in the bank that holds Max's college fund, though she doesn't even know where the nearest branch is located.

Two hundred thousand dollars would make a huge dent in Bella's debt. But of course, that's not what it's meant to be used for. And Millicent doesn't know about it.

Throughout their marriage, Sam had been steadfast in his refusal to ask his wealthy mother for help. Even after he got sick. Especially after he got sick.

It's so hard to look at that envelope Millicent had given her and not be tempted to use that money – at least some of it – to dig out of this financial hole.

But it isn't Bella's money, and of course she's not going to touch it. She grabs the stack of bills along with the laptop and leaves the room.

She steps over Chance and Spidey, sprawled in the doorway between the parlor and the entry hall. Ordinarily, they prefer to nap on a sunny window seat, and ordinarily, Chance might rouse herself to follow Bella around, keeping her company or perhaps keeping an eye on her.

Today, she opens one eye to glance up as Bella passes, then closes it again.

'Some watchcat you are today. But it's all right, Chance. Everything is fine.'

The house is quiet and feels empty, though earlier, she'd heard someone come in and head up to the third floor. Whoever it was has yet to come back down.

Out on the porch, Bella settles on the cushioned swing and waits for the computer to boot up. It's an ancient model and always takes a few minutes to come to life, but today it, like everything else, seems extra-sluggish.

When it rumbles to life, she goes to the website for the bank that has Max's college savings account. She hasn't checked it in ages, but luckily, she'd auto-saved the username and password, and they still work.

The balance has increased with interest payments, and is about to skyrocket, thanks to Millicent. Bella looks up the nearest bank branch where she can make the deposit and finds that it's in Buffalo. She'll have to find time in the next day or two to make that two-hour round-trip excursion so that this money can start earning interest right away.

The thick air hums with insects, air conditioners, and an invisible jet soaring high overhead, reminding her again of the airport. The golden car. Sam.

She glances up at the motionless wind chimes hanging from the porch eaves. A spider is spinning an intricate web from the lowest glass angel to a hanging basket of purple petunias that look as wilted and straggly as Bella feels.

Jutting her lower lip and exhaling in a futile attempt to stir the damp hair stuck to her forehead, she scrawls on the legal pad, *Get an estimate for central air conditioning?*

Grant might be receptive if the heatwave persists into his visit. The Gable Room is up on the third floor with a sunny southern exposure. Then again, the ceiling there is badly stained from the failing roof, a reminder that replacing it is the top priority.

Maybe that's the big change Pandora says is coming to Valley View. A new roof, or the new furnace that needs to be installed before winter sets in – though in this particular moment, she can't remember what it's like to feel cold.

She crosses out the note about central air and jots instead, *Look into window A/C units for guest rooms.*

Before going back to the spreadsheet file she'd saved to the cloud, she should check prices on window air conditioners. Maybe there's a local appliance store offering late season clearance models.

She opens a search window. Her most recent query is right at the top, synced from her cell phone's history: *Strangers who look alike.*

She enters it again, and rereads the first article, then the next few. They're filled with evidence – scientific, mathematic, statistical, genetic – that most people in the world have at least one lookalike among strangers. This is mainly attributed to a shared variation in a specific DNA sequence.

Having taught genetics – on a middle school level, but still – Bella is familiar with the single nucleotide polymorphism sequence, though primarily as it relates to medical research. Now, it's cited in a number of compelling studies on 'virtual twins' – biologically unrelated people who are physically identical.

It makes sense.

Then she comes across a piece that chills her to the bone.

It isn't about virtual twins, but about evil twins, also called *doppelgängers*. That phrase had originated in German folklore, but the mythology behind it goes back to ancient civilization. It was believed that these were apparitions, or spirit doubles, and thus soulless replications of a living person. Seeing one was considered to be a bad omen, and—

Bella closes the screen.

If she wants to know about bad omens, she can read a horror novel or watch a scary movie.

This is real life.

Her life.

And it's not as though the incident had even occurred here in the Dale, where – depending on what you believe – you might be more open to accepting that something paranormal might have occurred.

Bella prefers the scientific explanations.

Only, those don't account for the fact that a total stranger at the airport wouldn't have been looking at her and Max the way this person had been.

No. It wasn't even that he was looking *at* them.

It almost felt as though he was looking *for* them.

A stranger wouldn't do that.

Nor would a stranger sit parked outside Millicent's apartment building on a scorching afternoon.

She must have imagined it.

All of it. She believes in science, not—

Hearing a familiar tinkling sound, she goes still, breath caught in her throat, afraid to look up.

When she does, she sees that the wind chimes are motionless. The spider's intricate silken web remains intact.

She stares at it for a long time, thinking about Sam – about how she and Max had both seen him.

Something strange is going on. Something . . .
Evil?
She opens a new search window and starts typing D-O-P-P—
'No,' she says. '*No.*'
She quickly deletes it.

TWELVE

Just before five o'clock, Bella hurries toward the post office, located in a little white clapboard cottage near the entrance to the Dale.

'Hi, Bella!' Roxy calls from her post at the gatehouse. 'How are the puppies?'

'They're doing well!'

'I'll come visit them again tomorrow. And Max, too.'

'He'll love that.' She waves and heads inside, fanning herself with the stack of envelopes in her hand.

The gray-haired, bespectacled woman behind the counter greets her with a grin. 'Bella! I hear you've got a litter of puppies at Valley View?'

'We do, Glenda. I don't suppose you're interested in adopting one? Or four?'

'You know I'm a cat person.'

'Drew has a couple of adorable kittens looking for a home.'

'I have seven. Any more, and my husband will divorce me. Now, what can I do for you?'

'I need six, seven, eight stamps,' she says, counting envelopes and handing over a ten-dollar bill. 'I'm hoping it's not too late for these to go out today? Most of them are already overdue.'

'Bills? Welcome to the club. Every time I think I'm caught up, I get hit with something else. Here, I'll put the postage on and get them right out for you.'

Bella thanks her, pockets the change, and heads back out into the late-day sun, deciding to collect Max on her way back.

Like Valley View and Odelia's cottage between them, Misty's home was built in the nineteenth century, though it lacks the gingerbread embellishment and period paint palette of its neighbors. It's white and boxy, fronted by an enclosed porch and sagging steps – far more *old* than old-world charming. The front lawn has more weeds and bare patches than grass, and is often littered with Jiffy's toys, though not today.

A wooden shingle beside the door reads *Misty Starr, Psychic Consultant*. Beneath that, a placard announces: *The Medium Is In.*

After confirming that the *Reading In Progress* sign isn't posted in the window, Bella opens the screen door to the porch that serves as a waiting room and Jiffy's clutter depository. A couple of New Age magazines share table space with a box of sidewalk chalk and a caterpillar chewing a leaf in an empty peanut butter jar covered with netting. One of the plastic guest chairs is heaped with beach towels – damp and probably there for a few days, Bella guesses, based on the mildew aroma. Another chair holds one child-sized sneaker, and the helmet she insists Jiffy wear when he and Max ride their scooters.

'Misty? Hello?'

Beyond the closed door to the rest of the house, Jiffy's dog, Jelly, is barking and the Beach Boys are singing 'Don't Worry, Baby'.

Misty considers herself a musical medium, often channeling messages through melodies, lyrics, and the occasional dead musician. She prefers listening to the radio over electronic playlists and earbuds.

'When you plug in, you tune out,' she'd explained to Bella. 'And you never know when Spirit is going to touch in via the radio airwaves.'

'You mean, spirit voices?'

'Sure, sometimes, if there's static and you listen closely, you can hear them. But it's not just that. You know how you'll be driving along, and a song comes on the car radio, and it freaks you out because you were just thinking about it, or it has special meaning in that moment?'

Oh, yes. Bella knows all about that.

According to Misty, 'It's never random, Bells. It's a message from the Other Side.'

'Misty?' Bella turns the knob and pushes, but the door doesn't budge.

Locked? Really? This is unusual, albeit long overdue for a mother whose child had been kidnapped last winter.

Bella had presumed – wrongfully so – that Misty would have become fanatically cautious after that ordeal, from which her son had emerged unscathed, thank goodness.

Jiffy, being Jiffy, had not only predicted his own abduction months in advance, but had perceived it as an adventure – before, during and after.

Misty, being Misty, prefers not to dwell on difficult times.

'Life should be lived moment by moment. Otherwise, you might miss something great,' she's often told Bella, who supposes there's something to be said for that attitude.

By the same token, though, if you don't take a lesson from the past, you might miss the chance to prevent something . . . not so great. It seems Misty has finally figured that out.

'Misty!' She knocks, then pounds, on the door. 'Misty!'

The music comes down a decibel, then footsteps.

Misty opens the door.

Larger-than-life – physically, and personality-wise – she's barefoot, wearing her usual array of dangly, jangly jewelry with cut-off shorts and a white T-shirt that bears Mick Jagger's face and a large purple stain. Her nose is pierced, a small silver star-shaped stud gleaming among the freckles. Her straw-colored hair, usually a tumble of unkempt waves, is woven into cornrows with colorful beads at the bottoms.

'Bells! What's going on?'

Bells. She'd bestowed the nickname soon after they'd met. It had irked Bella at first, just as Misty had. She'd learned to tolerate both. Now, she embraces both the nickname and Misty herself – the latter quite literally as Misty throws her bare, fleshy, tattooed arms around Bella with a jangling of bracelets.

'I've missed you, Bells!'

'Aw, I've missed you, too.'

'Shh, Jelly, quiet down!' Misty shakes her head, her beads clacking against each other, as the wildly barking puppy bounds around their ankles. 'I hear you have a houseful of dogs.'

'I do! And I see you have a new hairstyle.'

'I do! It's fun, right? Mike hates it,' she adds cheerfully.

That's not surprising. Bella had met her husband only once, when he visited for Christmas. He seemed like a nice enough guy, if a little stiff and controlling. But that was on the heels of Jiffy's abduction, so it wasn't the best timing for his introduction to the Dale, Bella, and the rest of the crowd.

He is an affectionate father to Jiffy, though. That is the most important thing. And he and Misty do seem to love each other, though they have very little in common other than their son.

'Is Mike here?'

'No, I sent him a selfie. Anyway, I had a client on Thursday who couldn't afford to pay me, so we arranged a barter. She's the new stylist at Shear Magique.'

As with many businesses in the Dale, the local beauty parlor has a New Age twist. The front room is used for haircuts and salon treatments, the back for various forms of healing. Last time Bella visited for a simple trim, the stylist suggested that she update her look – 'maybe some nice green streaks?' When Bella declined, she was instead offered 'energy work to pierce your hidden veil wall.'

'Thanks, but no thanks,' she'd said politely. 'I prefer to keep my hidden veil wall intact.' Whatever that means.

'Hey, you should have your hair done like this, too, Bells! It really helps keep you cool in weather like this. Although the braids are a little tight. I've had a splitting headache all weekend,' Misty adds, her voice raised above Jelly's barking and Brian Wilson assuring them that everything will be all right.

'Maybe you should turn that down,' Bella suggests.

'What?'

'The music? It's pretty loud.'

'I know. WDOE is running all-day trivia contests with cash prizes. So far, I've called in a bunch of times, but someone always beats me to it. And it's not fair, because who knows more about music than me, right? Well, Wolfman Jack does, but he's been helping me with the answers.'

'A *wolfman* is helping you?'

'Wolfman Jack, Bells! You've never heard of him?'

'Should I have?'

'Well, he's a famous DJ, but I guess it was before your time.'

And, it would seem, before Misty's, since she's five years younger.

'Anyway, he's been here all day.'

'I didn't realize you had company. I hope Max wasn't a bother.'

'Max is never a bother. He keeps Jiffy occupied. I kind of feel like I should be paying him,' she adds with a chuckle. 'And Wolfman Jack's not company. He's in Spirit.'

Ah. Bella probably should have guessed that.

'Well, thanks for having Max, Misty. If you can just let him know I'm here, we'll be on our way and let you get back to your contest and your, uh . . . Wolfman.'

'No! You can't go yet, Bells! I have to hear all about your trip. How was Chicago?'

'Oh – it was great. Hot.'

'It's pretty hot here, too.'

'Yeah, no kidding.'

'Come on in for a minute and cool off. I've had the air conditioners running all day. We've got one in every room. Hugo Munson' – the local electrician – 'told me not to run them all at once. But it's fine, as long as I remember not to turn on any appliances. I keep forgetting and blowing fuses.'

'That's not good, Misty.'

'No biggie, I just go down and fix the circuit breaker in the basement,' Misty says cheerfully. 'Anyway, come on in.'

Bella hesitates. She really should get back to Valley View. Sweltering, stifling Valley View.

Giving in to temptation, she steps around the still-yapping puppy into the refreshing climate-controlled air. 'OK, but only for a few minutes.'

Misty locks the door behind her. 'You can't be too careful, you know?'

Taken aback, Bella asks, 'Misty, is everything—'

'Jelly, shush! For Pete's sake! It's just Bells, not the burglar!'

The burglar?

As in *the* golden car?

'Misty, why—'

'Come on into the kitchen, Bells, so I can turn the music down, but please don't judge. It's a mess, and so are the boys – Max included. Sorry. We made snow cones.'

'You *made* them?' Bella follows her through the house, which is its usual cluttery disarray.

'In the blender. Jiffy didn't know it had a top, so when he pressed the button . . .'

Bella winces. 'Uh-oh.'

'Yeah. I'm still wiping the splatters off the ceiling. Although that blender blew a fuse, of course, and I saw some paint cans in the basement, so I might just cover the stains with that.'

'Isn't it easier just to clean the splatters?'

'You'd think, but . . . I'll show you. Anyway, I sent the boys upstairs to eat their snow cones. Well, they're not really *cones*. We put them in paper cups.'

'Misty—'

'Did I ever tell you about the first time I met Mike? It was at the snow cone stand at an amusement park in Ohio. We were teenagers – kids, really. At that age, what do you know about anything, right? But I took one look at him and I said, this is the guy for me. I guess I shouldn't have mentioned it to him on our first date, but you know me.'

Bella does know her, and her wistful tone is as out of character as the locked front door.

The messy kitchen is not, though this is above and beyond even for the Arden household. There are purple spatters on every surface, including – *especially* – the ceiling. A stepladder is open in the middle of the room, with a bucket and sponge precariously balanced on the top rung.

'Want a snow cone?' Misty asks, turning down the volume on the ancient radio plugged in on the counter alongside a blender filled with purple slush. 'We used grape juice for the flavoring, but I'm going to make a new batch with Hawaiian Punch.'

'Oh . . . no, thanks.' Bella climbs a couple of steps on the ladder and moves the bucket to a more stable position. 'Misty, why—'

'Are you sure? You look super-hot, Bells.'

'I'm positive. And I feel like you're trying to avoid telling me why you're suddenly locking your front door?'

'Wow, Bells! I know I've asked you this before, but are you sure you're not psychic?'

'Not psychic.' She descends the ladder, careful not to wobble and slosh. 'I just pay attention to the details, and you said, "*the burglar*". What's going on?'

'We had a theft. But I don't want you to worry,' Misty adds quickly.

Yeah, well, neither do the Beach Boys, but it can't be helped.

'Jiffy was afraid that if you knew, you wouldn't let Max come over.'

'Jiffy may have been right about that.'

'But I mean, it's not like we were held up at gunpoint or anything. We didn't even know it happened until we realized some things were missing.' She pours some melted snow cone into a paper cup, takes a sip, and offers it to Bella. 'Here, try it.'

'No, thanks. So someone broke into your house?'

'Well . . . someone *got* in.'

'Through the door? It wasn't locked? Was this when you and Jiffy were home? Asleep?'

'The answer to all of those questions is, I don't know.'

Misty polishes off the melted snow cone, crumples the cup, tosses it toward the garbage can, and misses. She ignores it.

Remembering something, Bella says, 'Pandora mentioned a break-in at the Slayton place.'

'Really? I didn't hear about that. What happened?'

'I'm not sure.' Bella had been much too caught up in debunking Pandora's assumption that she and Drew had had a proper shag to ask questions about the Slayton incident. 'Did you call the police, Misty?'

'Not yet. I guess I should?'

'Of course you should. Why wouldn't you?'

'Because . . . you know how Lieutenant Grange feels about us.'

Bella isn't sure whether she's referring to *us*, as in herself and Jiffy, or herself and Bella, or perhaps the whole of Lily Dale.

Most likely, it's all of the above.

Lieutenant John Grange is always the first police officer on the scene of a crime in the Dale, and somehow, Bella always finds herself involved.

Only as a witness, of course. And she's been far more help than hindrance when it comes to the investigations – which may be why the territorial, egotistical Grange doesn't always come across as an ally. Not because he's suspicious of her, but because he's jealous.

'Do you think this happened today, Misty? Or sometime yesterday, or last night?'

'I'm not sure. We didn't realize anything was even missing until this morning, but it might have been longer. I've been meditating on it, asking Spirit to shed some light, but so far, I've gotten nothing.'

A police investigation would likely shed more light, but before Bella can urge her to call, Misty goes on, 'I think the energy is blocked because I've been so emotional lately, with everything that's going on with Mike. That can happen. I'm—'

Jelly bounds over with a shoe in his mouth.

'Jelly! No!' Misty stoops to wrestle it from his jaws. 'He keeps doing this!'

'Wanting to play?'

'Eating shoes. I did exactly what Drew told me to do – I sprayed an old sneaker with chew deterrent and let him taste it so that he'd be turned off.'

'It didn't work?'

'He *liked* it!' She looks around the cluttered surfaces for a place to put the shoe and shoves it into a cupboard. 'Crazy dog. He gets into everything! Drew says it's normal, but let me tell you, Bells, if shoes were the only things that went missing around here, I wouldn't be thinking we'd been robbed by anyone other than Jelly. Oh! Shh! Listen!'

The Beach Boys song has given way to an announcer.

'. . . and the prize will go to the first caller who can tell me how many number one singles the Beach Boys had, and we'll double your winnings if you can name them all. We'll be back with our winner after this word from our sponsor.'

Misty grabs her phone, hits redial, and addresses the empty air over her shoulder. 'How many, Jack? Four? OK, what are they? Oh, no, it's busy.' She hangs up and hits redial again. 'Yes, Jack, I've got it. "Help Me, Rhonda", "Good Vibrations", "I Get Around", and "Kokomo"! Darn, still busy!'

She hits redial again, and again, until the DJ returns to the air to announce a winner who isn't Misty.

'This stinks.' She tosses her phone aside. 'I really need to win enough to get Jiffy a new scooter.'

'That's why you're doing this?'

'Yes, his was stolen.'

'Are you sure he didn't leave it somewhere again? You know how he's always losing things. Just this morning he was telling Max about a video game he'd misplaced.'

'No, the scooter was definitely stolen, because they took other stuff. You know that pink vase that was on the mantel in the living room? Gone.'

'Was it valuable?'

'Are you kidding? It was from the dollar store. Ugliest thing you ever saw. I hated it. I bought it as a White Elephant gift for a Christmas party, only then Jiffy went missing and I didn't go to the party. Every time I look at it, I think of that.'

'Why did you keep it?'

'I keep everything,' she says with a shrug.

'What else was stolen?'

'That jigsaw puzzle Jiffy's been working on all summer.'

'Wait . . . you mean it wasn't in the box?'

'It was on the table. So was the box. They took that, too.'

'But . . . are you saying they actually picked up all the pieces of a half-finished puzzle and stole them?'

'It wasn't half-finished. It was pretty much done, but you can't solve a puzzle without all the pieces, and Jelly ate a couple that fell on the floor. Just gobbled them up before we could stop him.'

'Wow. I guess you really do keep everything,' Bella says, wheels turning. 'So they stole the scooter, a vase you hated, and a puzzle with missing pieces. Is that all?'

'I think so. I have some cash stashed away from my readings, but they didn't take that. I even counted it, and it's all there.'

'Where do you keep it?'

Misty points to the little shelf built into the corner between the window frame above the sink, and the adjacent cabinet. It holds a couple of knick-knacks, the biggest bottle of ibuprofen Bella has ever seen, and a prominently displayed glass jar full of cash.

'Wow,' Bella says. 'It's kind of hard to miss.'

'Well, so is my wedding ring. It's sitting right out in the open on my bureau, but they didn't take that, either.'

'Then they must have been here during the day, when you had it on,' Bella reasons, glancing at Misty's left hand. The fourth finger is bare.

She makes it into a fist and tucks it under her right arm. 'I haven't been wearing it lately, Bells. Mike and I . . . we aren't going to make it.'

'Oh, Misty. I'm so sorry.'

Bella sees that she's trembling.

Most of the time, Misty reminds her of a high school friend – breezy and exuberant, speaking her mind without a filter.

But in moments like this, Bella grasps that she's an old soul. Certainly her tattoos bear testimony to a whole lot of hard living – and pain – in her twenty-six years.

Her father's initials and birth and death dates are on her right arm. She'd lost him when she was Jiffy's age – her first paranormal experience, she'd told Bella.

'He came to say goodbye in the middle of the night. He told me he could do more good for me on the Other Side than he ever had on the earthly plane. He drank himself to death because he couldn't deal with seeing apparitions and hearing voices,' she'd added in her frank way. 'I was headed down the same path for a while, but Spirit saved me.'

Bella prefers to think that Misty saved herself – and that she'll manage to do the same for her marriage. A recent inked addition to her bare right foot reads 'one step at a time', along with a triangle symbolizing her own hard-won sobriety.

'Mike won't come here,' she tells Bella. 'He wants to live in Pennsylvania, near his family. He says we can make a fresh start on neutral ground, but how is his hometown neutral? It isn't, you know? It's *his* place.'

'That's true. And Lily Dale is yours.'

'*And* Jiffy's. That matters more than what Mike and I want, doesn't it?'

'It does, but kids are pretty adaptable.'

'That's not the point. When we lived on the base in Arizona, nobody understood Jiffy. Teachers, the other kids, their parents . . . everyone thought something was wrong with a boy who sees and hears things they can't see. Not here, though. Here, everyone gets it. Even you.'

'Um . . . thanks?'

'I don't mean it in a bad way, Bells. Just that you don't do what we do – or maybe I should say you *won't* do what we do – but you accept us nonetheless.'

'Of course I do.'

'And that's why I love you.' Misty smiles and heaves a shaky sigh. 'I'm not leaving. I came here because I wanted Jiffy to grow up among people who understand what it's like to see dead people. And for me, too. I'll admit it. This isn't just my home, it's my livelihood. Where else would I be able to provide for my son and practice my mediumship skills for the greater good? That's what I've been doing this summer, and it's been amazing.'

Bella weighs her response before saying, 'Is there a way you and Mike can reach some sort of compromise? Maybe he'd agree to stay here in the summers, and you can spend the rest of the time in Pennsylvania?'

'Summer is only two months long!'

'But it's when you earn the bulk of your income, isn't it?'

'How would *that* be fair? I get two months here, while Mike gets ten months where *he* wants us to be?'

She sounds like a petulant child, but there are tears in her eyes, and Bella can't decide whether to hug her, or try to make her see both sides of the dilemma.

'Plus, Jiffy would have to go to a different school, away from Max, with a bunch of strangers who think he's weird? He'd be ostracized, the way I was? No. No way. He's my kid. I can't do that to him.'

'But Misty, he's Mike's kid, too.'

'Wow. Whose side are you on?'

'I'm on *your* side, Misty. Always. Yours, and Jiffy's. I just hope you haven't given up without doing everything in your power to save your marriage.'

'I'm not the one who's given up. Mike's chosen to be deployed for our entire marriage. It's just me and Jiffy, day in and day out. Do you know how hard it is to . . .' She catches herself. 'I'm sorry. I know you know. You know in the worst way.'

'I do.'

'I'm so sorry. Don't hate me.'

'I could never hate you. Does Jiffy know what's going on? That you and Mike aren't . . .'

'No. We need to sit him down and tell him together.'

Bella nods, refusing to allow herself to dwell on that looming conversation, and the impact it will have on Jiffy.

'Misty . . . getting back to the theft . . . is there any chance it might have been staged?'

'Staged! What do you mean?'

'Did Jiffy know you didn't like that pink vase?'

'Oh, yes. He and I both thought it was hideous.' Her eyes widen. 'You think he did this?'

'Pandora said she heard through the grapevine about the break-in at the Slaytons', so maybe Jiffy did, too. Maybe he thought you'd buy him a new scooter if you thought his had been stolen, and he's smart enough to know it would look suspicious if that was the only thing missing. He knew you wouldn't miss the vase . . .' Bella shrugs.

'That little stinker.' She jerks the radio knob, silencing it. 'Here I am spending my whole afternoon trying to win a stupid trivia contest, when he—'

'We don't know it for sure, Misty. I'm just thinking . . . maybe he left it somewhere again, and he didn't want to get into trouble.'

She steps into the hall and yells, 'Jiffy! Come down here, please! Jiffy! Right this instant!'

Bella follows her to the foot of the stairs, trailed by Jelly.

Overhead, a door creaks open. 'Mom? Did you call me?'

'I did. Come here.'

Jiffy appears at the top of the stairs. He's barefoot and covered in purple stains, including on his upper lip. 'Do you need me to finish up the extra snow cones? Because they were very delicious.'

'No, I need to speak with you.'

'Be right back.' Jiffy disappears, and Bella hears him say in an audible whisper, 'Hey, Max! You need to come with me.'

'How come?'

'Because she won't yell at me in front of company.'

'OK. What'd you do?'

'I'm not sure which thing it is.'

'How many things are there?'

'Two or three. Oh, wait, maybe . . . about seven. Or ten.'

'Jiffy!' Misty shakes her head and thrums her fingertips on the newel post. 'I'm waiting.'

'I'm coming!'

A moment later, he reappears at the top of the stairs with a reluctant-looking Max in tow. He, too, is juice-stained and juice-mustached.

'Hi, Mom!'

'Hi, Bella!'

'Hi, boys.'

'Come on down,' Misty says. 'I need to ask you a question.'

Jiffy descends slowly, jumping down each step with a floppy thump. 'Is the question about making more snow cones? Or about me and Max having a very fun sleepover here tonight?'

'Not tonight,' Bella says. 'The puppies are only at our house until tomorrow, and I know you don't want to miss that, Max.'

'Can me and Jiffy have a sleepover at our house, Mom?' He's imitating Jiffy's stair jumps, more cautiously, holding tightly to the banister and watching his feet.

'That's up to Jiffy and his mom.'

'We'll see,' Misty says.

'By the way, do you have air conditioners yet, Bella?'

'Not yet,' she tells Jiffy, who has arrived at the foot of the stairs.

'We'll talk about that after I talk to you about something else,' Misty says.

'Both of us?'

'Just you. Max has an alibi since he was out of town this weekend.'

'I do?' Max pauses on the step and looks up with interest. 'By the way, what's an alibi?'

'It's when you're in another place so you couldn't have been in the place where something happened,' Bella says quickly.

'Something good, or something bad?'

'Something bad,' Jiffy says. 'Because that's the only reason you want people to know you weren't there. I've got a lot of alibis, too.'

'You don't even know what we're going to discuss,' Misty says, looking amused.

He shrugs. 'Whatever it is, I know I've got one.'

'Except not for the blender mess,' Max says. 'You were there. I saw you turn it on. And it squirted all over everything, and the lights went out!'

'Shh, Max, let's get going home and let Misty and Jiffy talk,' Bella says.

'But what about—'

'Come on, kiddo. Let's go. What do you say to Misty?'

'Thank you for having me,' Max says politely.

'Any time, Max.' She shifts her gaze to Bella. 'Thanks, Bells. I'll text you later with an update.'

'Good luck!'

'Good luck with what?' Max asks as they step out into the steamy sunshine.

'Misty's just wondering what happened to a few things that are missing.'

'You mean Jiffy's scooter and that vase she hates, and the puzzle Jelly thought was treats?'

'Yes. Do you know anything about them, Max?'

'Uh-huh. Some robbers came in and stole them.'

'Who told you that?'

'Jiffy. He said they were really bad guys.'

'What else did he say?'

'He thinks you should let me keep one of the puppies. Then Jelly will have a best friend, too.'

Bella sighs, remembering what lies in store for Jiffy. Even if he remains in the Dale with Misty, he's going to be devastated by his parents' looming separation.

'You and Jiffy are lucky to have each other, Max. I'm glad you're always such a good friend to him. That's important.'

'Yup. Can I keep—'

'What game do you think we should play with the puppies when we get home?' Bella asks.

Max has plenty of ideas, as she expected.

Together, they walk on toward Valley View, unaware that they're being watched from the shadows in the park.

THIRTEEN

D rew brought the perfect supper for a night like this: cold fried chicken, biscuits and side salads. They eat at the picnic table in the backyard, accompanied by mosquitos, yellow jackets, and Jiffy Arden.

They're midway through the meal when he cuts through Odelia's yard with Jelly scampering at his feet.

'Hi, Doctor Drew. Hi, Max. Hi, Bella. Me and Jelly thought we should come over because we smelled something and we didn't know what it was,' he says with an exaggerated sniff.

'It's probably a dead fish,' Max tells him, pointing at the lake.

'No, it's a good kind of stink.'

'Did you eat dinner, Jiffy?' Bella asks.

'Yep, but what are you having? Because I can have two dinners if it's something I love like fried chicken and macaroni salad and biscuits and some ice-cold lemonade.'

'You're in luck,' Drew says with a grin. 'Have a seat, kiddo.'

'I'll go get you a plate. Does your mom know where you are?' Bella asks, standing.

'Yep.'

'Really?'

'Well, she probably does. She's a good guesser.'

'How about if you text her, just to make sure? Tell her that we'll get you home safely in a little while.'

'That's a lot of stuff to write.'

'It's OK. I'll let her know,' Bella says. 'I'll be right back.'

Earlier, she'd left her phone plugged into the charger in the Rose Room. She's been meaning to retrieve it to see whether Millicent had returned her call, and if Misty had learned whether Jiffy had admitted to staging the theft.

The house has yet to cool off, and it feels deserted, probably because the evening message service is under way in the auditorium. She can hear a male medium addressing the audience over a microphone as she makes her way through the first-floor rooms, pausing to draw lace curtains across open windows in the front parlor.

This is her favorite time of day in this room. The mantel clock ticks softly. Stained-glass Tiffany lamps cast a mellow glow over the old woodwork. In the adjacent library nook, three walls of shelves are stocked with books, classic board games and jigsaw puzzles, to keep the guests occupied on rainy days.

Chance and Spidey are dozing on the window seat. Bella pauses to pet them. They purr as she strokes their fur, and she lingers. Through the window, she sees a white Chevy with Massachusetts license plates parked in one of the visitors spots out front.

It must belong to Polly Green from Boston. Polly Green, who'd mentioned that she was passing through on a cross-country road trip, visiting the Dale for the first time.

I've never even heard of this place, she'd said.

And then, *thanks, Bella.*

It's been nagging at Bella ever since – that Polly had known her name.

It's such a small and seemingly insignificant detail.

Or is it?

It's not as if Bella wears an employee badge, and there's no name placard on the registration desk. It isn't even posted on the Valley View website. She supposes it wouldn't be hard to find in an online search. Occasionally, previous guests post comments about her on travel sites, often praising 'Bella's homemade scones'.

But if you'd never heard of Valley View until you wandered by and saw the vacancy sign, would you have stood outside with your phone to comb through online reviews?

Possibly.

Not that Polly looked as though she'd just been lingering in hundred-degree humidity when she walked through the door.

She sighs, staring out into the quiet street.

On a nearby porch, a glider squeaks rhythmically, and she can hear every word of the conversation between the occupants. It isn't particularly intimate, or even interesting, but they're likely unaware that anyone is listening.

Voices carry farther and more clearly at night due to refraction of sound waves. Science again. Physics.

Shortly after Bella's arrival in Lily Dale, she'd mentioned to Luther Ragland that she doesn't believe in the paranormal. She'd fully expected him to agree with her. After all, he's a detective. His livelihood, like hers in teaching, depends on facts and straightforward evidence.

She'd been taken aback when he informed her that what happens here is all about energy – quantum physics. He'd reached into his wallet and pulled out a creased, well-worn slip of paper he'd carried ever since Odelia helped him solve his first case.

Upstairs in the Rose Room, Bella opens her jewelry box and takes out the same slip of paper.

'Keep it,' Luther had said, handing it to her. 'I know it by heart. It might help you while you're here.'

Bella unfolds it now and rereads the handwritten quote that she too now knows by heart.

Everyone who is seriously involved in the pursuit of science becomes convinced that a spirit is manifest in the laws of the Universe. – Albert Einstein

The tourmaline necklace from Sam is also tucked away in the jewelry box.

Rather, the necklace Bella had found in a hidden compartment here at Valley View last July. Precisely the same necklace she and Sam had found in a little shop on a beach vacation a few months before he'd gotten sick. He'd told her that it was going to be her Christmas gift, and they'd laughed about how terrible he'd always been at keeping secrets.

Six months after his death, the necklace had turned up under a stair tread in a house Sam had never visited, in a town she's sure he'd never even heard of. Even if he had, he couldn't have known, when he was alive that summer, that by the following one he'd be gone. He couldn't have known that his wife and son would soon be starting over in Lily Dale, of all places.

'Yes, he did!'

She jumps and whirls around, half-expecting to see someone behind her. Then she hears footsteps on the street below and realizes the voice had floated up through the open window.

'I don't think so,' someone responds. 'He's back in Hollywood, and the son lives in New York City now, and the housekeeper moved out.'

'Mrs Remington? No way. She's been with them for decades.'

Bella instantly recognizes that they're talking about the Slaytons. Like any other small town, Lily Dale has an industrious gossip mill.

As the footsteps and voices fade away, she returns the paper to the jewelry box and unplugs her phone from the charger. There's a message from Misty on the home screen.

Hi Bells. Jiffy swears he didn't fake the robbery. I believe him.

OK, well . . . she's his mother. If she believes him, Bella will certainly give him the benefit of the doubt.

Yes, she will, despite the fact that Jiffy's a creative thinker, and that he'd have known Misty wouldn't miss that vase . . .

And that it's far more reassuring to believe Jiffy had lost his scooter and tried to cover it up than to think an intruder had taken it.

Still, if there had been a break-in at the Slaytons', Misty probably should let the authorities know about this, just in case.

Catching her reflection in the bureau mirror as she returns the Einstein quote to the jewelry box, Bella quickly reaches for a hairbrush, though a hairdryer would be more appropriate. The best she can do is pull her damp hair back from her forehead and off her sweaty neck and hope her haphazard updo passes for presentable.

Then she returns to her phone and starts a text to Misty.

I think you should call . . .

No. She deletes that. Misty isn't big on unsolicited advice.

Are you going to call the police? she asks instead and waits for a reply.

And waits.

She suspects that Misty is there, on the other end of the phone, trying to figure out what to say and do. And Bella doesn't blame her for being reluctant to inform Lieutenant Grange. But if a crime occurred, it should be reported to the authorities.

Then again . . .

An ugly vase, an incomplete jigsaw puzzle, a scooter . . .

There's no way Grange will take this seriously. He's bound to draw the same conclusion Bella had about Jiffy's involvement, regardless of the boy's claims of innocence.

Bella writes, *or maybe you should call Luther?*

A moment later, three dots wobble in the text window, and a reply whooshes in: *Do you have his number?*

It's quickly followed by, *You call him for me, Bells, OK? He likes you better.*

Shaking her head, she types, *That's not true!*

He thinks I'm nuts.

Bella rolls her eyes. It's not entirely untrue.

Please? Call him!

She sighs. *OK.*

Then, remembering, she adds, *Making sure you know Jiffy's here?*

Misty doesn't acknowledge that she's aware, just offers a thumbs-up emoji.

Bella says, *He wants to eat with us. OK w/ you?*

If the situation were reversed, Bella would make sure it's not an imposition, maybe ask what they're having, and what time she should collect her son.

Misty's reply: another thumbs-up.

Bella sighs and calls Luther. It goes directly to voicemail.

'Hey, it's Bella. Can you give me a call when you have a minute? It's not urgent, but . . .'

She reconsiders.

'It's about a robbery. I think. Just . . . call me and I'll explain.'

She hangs up, pockets her phone, and steps out into the hall. About to turn back to lock the door behind her, she catches movement in the hallway out of the corner of her eye and cries out.

'Sorry!' Polly Green says. 'I didn't know anyone was here!'

'Neither did I.' Bella presses a hand against her racing heart. 'Are you on your way out?'

'On my way in. I went out to get a salad.'

'At the Soul-stice Bistro.'

'How'd you know? Oh . . . right. It's Lily Dale.'

'Yes, but I'm not psychic,' Bella says. 'It's the only place in the Dale that would be open right now for anything other than ice cream.'

'I didn't say it was in the Dale, Bella.'

And again, I didn't tell you my name was Bella, either.

Of course she would have introduced herself by name earlier, if the other woman had said, 'Hi, I'm Polly Green, and you are . . .?'

Or if Polly hadn't given her a startled once-over when she walked her perfect self into Valley View, assessing Bella as if she might be the kitchen help, or a vagrant who'd wandered in off the street.

That had put Bella on the defensive, so she'd deliberately identified herself as just, 'the manager'.

She's a hundred percent certain she hadn't mentioned her name in the ensuing conversation, either.

Well, ninety-nine percent certain, given her preoccupation with what had happened yesterday, Odelia's message, having the dogs here, and Drew . . .

OK, maybe there's a larger margin for error.

And maybe Perfect Polly isn't quite so perfect, other than that fussy hairdo of hers. She may not look as though someone just threw a bucket of water over her head, as Bella does, but she's not impervious to the humid heat. Her face is shiny, and her eye makeup is smudged.

'If you're not psychic, Bella, and I didn't tell you I stayed in the Dale for dinner, how did you know? You're not following me, are you?'

Her smile strikes Bella as forced.

'Oh, I'm way too busy to follow my guests around,' Bella returns, suspecting her own breeziness is just as forced. 'I just saw your car parked out front. White Chevy, Massachusetts license plate – that's you, right?'

'Right. That's my car. You sure do pay attention to the little details, don't you?'

Uncertain what to make of that, Bella hears a burst of applause from outside. 'The message service just ended. You're lucky you went to the bistro when you did, because the place will be a madhouse now.'

'That's what the owner said.'

'Walter? Or was it Peter?'

'Tall Black man?'

'Walter.'

Polly nods. 'When I mentioned I was staying at Valley View, he said to tell you hello, and that he's looking forward to hearing about the wedding.'

Bella nods.

'So you got married?' Polly presses.

'Me? No, I . . . no.'

'Who did?'

Bella reminds herself that the woman is merely making small talk. Yet her tone is pointed and there's a shrewd expression in her eyes and . . .

And she just doesn't seem like a Polly, or a New Englander.

Which makes no sense, really.

For Bella, the name evokes warmth and friendliness, but it's silly to assume all Pollys share those traits.

And not all New Englanders call a car a '*cah*' and go around wearing Red Sox caps with . . . with lobsters tucked under their arms.

It's not you. It's me, she silently informs Polly. *This weather is making me irritable. And ridiculous.*

'I'd better get back,' she tells Polly. 'Everyone's going to be wondering what happened to me.'

'In Lily Dale? Seems pretty safe around here.'

You'd be surprised, Bella thinks, but says only 'Good night,' as she turns away and heads downstairs.

FOURTEEN

Before the evening message service, Odelia had polished off three large slices of cake and called it supper. Sauerkraut *is* a vegetable of sorts, and the sugar had helped her bounce back after this afternoon's . . . episode.

Had it really been heat exhaustion?

That's what Calla had called it, and she might have been right.

Immediately afterward, she'd scooped Li'l Chap into her arms and headed for home, telling Odelia to go lie down in front of the fan, be sure to hydrate, and stay out of the kitchen.

Cake had seemed a fine supper at the time, but she'd emerged from the message service far too hungry to go straight home to bed as she'd intended, and has spent nearly an hour waiting to be seated at the Soul-stice Bistro.

Various friends invited her to pull up an extra chair at their tables, although Pandora Feeney, dining alone at a table for two, pretends not to see her. But she's opted to wait, in the mood for solitude. As much solitude as one can find in the midst of a noisy, crowded restaurant, anyway.

Leaning against a brick wall directly beneath the blasting air-conditioning vent, Odelia stares at tonight's specials on the chalk-board, idly listening to snatches of conversation from nearby tables.

'. . . *because it's deep-fried, and it's not good for* . . .'

'. . . *was hoping to hear from Dad, not Uncle Stan* . . .'

'. . . *and now you're eating it all. Why didn't you order it yourself?*'

'*Don't trust her!*'

At that, she looks up abruptly.

She's surrounded by several other people waiting to be seated, but all are silently engrossed in their cell phones. She turns her attention to the tables that are within earshot.

'. . . and you know what the doctor said about saturated fat,' a middle-aged wife is scolding her portly husband as he eats a piece of battered chicken.

'. . . I know, but Dad always deferred to Uncle Stan, even when they were alive,' one young man says to another.

'. . . because I didn't want a whole dessert, just a taste,' a woman informs her scowling husband as she dips a spoon into the chocolate mousse in front of him.

Confirming that none of those people had said 'Don't trust her,' Odelia concludes that it was Spirit.

She closes her eyes, trying to focus, but it's impossible amid the clatter and conversation.

'Excuse me,' a female voice says, and Odelia opens her eyes to see that a woman is trying to move past her toward the exit.

It's Candace, with Tommy behind her.

'Oh, sorry.' Odelia steps aside to let them by.

Candace pauses as a gaggle of women waiting for a table stop Tommy to gush about how much they love *The Specter Inspectors* and how they're looking forward to the paranormal equipment demonstration he's doing tomorrow morning.

'Well, we're both doing it,' he says. 'Me *and* my wife.'

Catching Odelia's eye, Candace offers a smile and little shake of her head. 'Happens all the time.'

'I'm sure it does. To both of you.'

'Sometimes, but he's got more patience than I do. And way more charm – especially with a group like that.'

Odelia has never been one to fawn over celebrities, but she does like to pay compliments where they're due. 'Well, I really enjoyed your presentation last night. It was fascinating.'

Candace smiles. 'Thank you!'

'I'm also a big fan of your television show. Odelia Lauder,' she adds, putting out her hand. 'I live right next door to you.'

'Oh?'

'I mean, right next door to Valley View.'

'Ah. Valley View. So much history there. Tommy and I have fallen in love with the place. It's enchanting, isn't it?'

He rejoins his wife. 'What are we talking about?'

'Valley View. This is Odelia Lauder. She lives next door.'

'Stop by and say hello if you have time while you're here. I'll be happy to share some stories about the house if you're interested.'

'We're *definitely* interested,' Tommy assures her, putting a hand under his wife's elbow.

'I'll make sure I get to your demonstration tomorrow morning,' Odelia says. 'Maybe we can chat afterward.'

'That sounds perfect. Thank you, Odelia. It's always great to meet a fellow redhead.' With a wave, Candace follows her husband out the door.

Odelia watches them disappear into the night.

Don't trust her . . .

The spirit warning couldn't have been about Candace, could it? That doesn't feel right, although it's hard to tell.

Her gaze falls on Pandora Feeney, using a steak knife to saw an enormous hunk of bloody, rare meat on her plate.

A warning about Pandora would hardly be news to Odelia. She's never trusted the woman.

Walter Darwin hurries over to her. 'Odelia, thanks for waiting. I can seat you now.'

'Thanks.' She follows him to the table Candace and Tommy just vacated.

It's adjacent to the one where Pandora Feeney is making short work of her bloody rare steak. Odelia considers telling Walter she'll wait for another spot to open up, but refrains. All the small tables are in this section, so there's no avoiding Pandora in a restaurant this size – nor, for that matter, in a town this size.

She can either sit facing Pandora, or she can take the chair facing in the same direction as Pandora's, so close they might as well be side by side at the same table.

She opts to face in the same direction, avoiding eye contact. With any luck, Pandora will be out of here momentarily . . .

'Oh, Walter?' Pandora says. 'I fancy a triple scoop of vanilla ice cream with chocolate sauce, whipped cream, chopped walnuts – as long as they're English walnuts. If they aren't, do leave them off. Oh, and there should be three cherries, one for each scoop.'

. . . or not.

'I'd better send your server over to take that order,' Walter tells her, and turns back to Odelia, handing her a laminated menu. 'Sorry you had to wait so long.'

'Not a problem.'

'I heard Calla's back from New York?'

'She is. Who told you? Jacy?'

'No, Peter ran into her this afternoon. Too bad about what happened with her editor and agent.'

'What do you mean?'

'Didn't they have a falling out?'

'A falling out? Is that what she said?'

'She didn't tell you?'

'Not in those words, but we only had a brief visit.'

'Oh, well, I'm sure she'll fill you in.'

'I'm sure she will.'

Frowning, she thinks back to their time together this afternoon. Calla hadn't lingered, eager to get Li'l Chap settled back at home.

'What else did she say?' she asks Walter.

'About her meeting? Nothing. We mostly talked about the Slayton house.'

'About the break-in?' she asks, before remembering that Luther had asked her not to say anything to anyone.

'There was a break-in at the Slayton house?'

Oops. 'How would *I* know?' she asks, as if Walter's the one who'd brought it up. 'What did Calla say?'

'David's putting the place on the market.'

'*Calla* told you that?' she asks, perhaps too loudly, though Pandora appears oblivious at the next table, polishing off the last of a baked potato, skin and all.

'Well, she, uh . . . she told Peter,' Walter says, shifting his weight. 'I didn't see her myself.'

'But how would *she* know what the Slaytons are doing with their house?'

'Maybe . . . I don't know.' Walter glances over his shoulder and then around the restaurant, as if longing for an excuse to escape. 'Maybe Peter got it wrong?'

'He must have. Calla's been away for a week. She wouldn't know what's going on back here in the Dale before the rest of us found out.'

'Isn't Blue Slayton living in New York now? Maybe he told her.'

'Is he?'

'I'm not sure. I thought that's what people have been saying, but maybe I got that wrong. Well, I'd better get back to, uh . . .' Walter scuttles away.

Odelia stares into the flickering votive flame on the table.

If it's true that the Slaytons are selling their house, there will be no reason for Blue or his father ever to visit the area again.

Good riddance to them.

But why was Calla the first to know? And why hadn't she mentioned it to Odelia?

Intending to ask her, she reaches into her pocket for her cell phone, then remembers she'd left it at home. For her, the electro-magnetic signal occasionally interferes with spirit energy at the message service.

Oh, well. The call will have to wait until she gets home.

She looks around for the server. Lori, a college student who's been working here all summer, is busy taking an order from the gaggle of women who'd stopped Tommy on his way out the door. They'd all been front and center in the auditorium this evening – and none of them had received a message.

Odelia hadn't been one of the presenting mediums on stage this evening, but she'd sensed the spirit of a shy young man attached to one of the women. She feels him touching in with her again now . . .

No.

She closes herself off to the energy. She has other, more pressing concerns. Like satisfying her ravenous hunger.

She grabs the menu and resumes studying it, as if she hasn't seen it hundreds of times; as if she's not planning to order her usual.

The grilled eggplant and banana on rye toast with mustard isn't on the list of sandwiches, though she's been trying to convince Walter's husband Peter that it should be.

'Listen, nobody wants to walk into a bistro and see the same old fare day after day. You need to liven things up around here.'

'Like you do?'

'Exactly. You can even call it The Odelia. The recipe is featured in my cookbook. Mark my words, it's going to catch on just like wings did in Buffalo. If the Soul-stice Bistro is the first place to serve it, this place will be as legendary as the Anchor Bar.'

'That would be great. Why don't we revisit this when the cook-book is published?'

Ah, but she's been counting on Calla to get the manuscript to her agent. If they've had a falling out, the cookbook won't be anyone's priority, including Odelia's own.

Why would Calla have mentioned that to Peter, and not to her own grandmother?

Again, she flashes back to their time together this afternoon. She recalls scolding her for over-exerting herself amid the heatwave 'at your age', which of course had irritated her at the time.

Really, she should have been more appreciative for her grand-daughter's concern. Calla might even have had a point. Odelia had been feeling a bit faint out there on the porch . . .

Brows furrowed, she remembers that Spirit had been trying to tell her something then, too.

'Don't . . .'

If Calla hadn't interrupted the moment, would she have received the same message she'd gotten this evening?

Don't trust her.

Yes. Yes, that feels right, only . . .

Don't trust whom?

Pandora had been there at the time, out in front of her house, gearing up to do some gardening. She would make the most sense.

Odelia slides a quick sidelong glance at her. She's scraping the last bit of creamed spinach from her plate with a spoon, looking weary, a bit desolate, and not entirely like her usual meddling self.

In rare moments like this, Odelia can't deny that they have more in common than she likes to acknowledge, as mediums, as women of a certain age, and as wives who'd been left destitute by deadbeat husbands.

But Odelia has Luther now, along with her family, and she counts Bella and Max among them.

And Pandora has a large sum of money coming her way, she reminds herself. *She's just fine.*

Anyway, maybe the message wasn't about Pandora. What if it had been about the other person who'd been present when it had attempted to come through this afternoon?

Calla.

FIFTEEN

After dinner, Drew presents the boys with a glow-in-the-dark Frisbee, the perfect alternative to their usual summer night activity: roasting marshmallows around the firepit.

'Cool! Can we play with it right now?' Max asks.

'Yep.'

'But it doesn't turn on!'

'It just needs batteries,' Drew tells Jiffy.

'I hope you've got some, Bella, 'cause my mom never does.'

'I've got them right here, guys.' Drew pats his pocket.

A minute later, the boys are tossing the glowing fluorescent green disk back and forth on the lawn as Bella and Drew settle into the Adirondack chairs.

'Thank you,' Bella says. 'I don't know how you always manage to know exactly what to do when you've never even had kids.'

'I was one, remember? You don't forget what it's like.'

'That's what . . .' She trails off.

'What Sam used to say?'

'How'd you know?'

'Lucky guess?' He reaches over and gives her arm a pat. 'You don't have to erase him when I'm around, Bella.'

She smiles in the dark. 'Thank you.'

'No! Jelly!' Max shouts as the dog intercepts a toss and darts away with the disk in his mouth. 'Get him, Jiffy!'

'No, he's going that way! Grab him.'

'They're going to sleep well tonight,' Drew comments as the boys tackle Jelly.

'Let's hope so.' She yawns.

'You're tired tonight.'

'I'm tired every night.'

'Why don't you go to bed? I'll take care of these two.'

'What? No, I can't let you do that.'

'Why not?'

'Because . . .' She laughs. 'My brain is too tired to think of a good reason.'

'Max! Why didn't you catch it?' Jiffy yells.

'Because you didn't throw it to me!'

Bella spots the luminescent disk floating out in the lake. Uh-oh.

'Now I have to swim way out there and get it!'

'No swimming!' Drew warns Jiffy, on his feet and hurrying over to the boys.

'But what about the Frisbee?' Max wails. 'It's going to float all the way to Chicago!'

'It's OK,' Drew assures him. 'I'll get you another one.'

'By the way, that's not Chicago.' Jiffy points to the hills and homes on the opposite shore. 'It's just Glasgow Road.'

'Uh-uh. My mom and I flew over the lake to Chicago. I saw the water from the airplane window.'

Chicago. Airplane. Sam.

'We did fly over the lake, Max,' Bella says, hoisting herself to her feet, 'but it was Lake Erie.'

Jiffy taps her arm. 'By the way, Bella? Chicago is on Lake *Michigan*.'

'Nope! Chicago is in Illinois, not Michigan. Right, Mom?'

'Right, Max,' she says around a yawn. 'Come on, guys, it's bedtime.'

'Yours?' Jiffy asks.

'Everyone's.'

'Not mine. Good night, Max,' he says. 'I forgive you for throwing the Frisbee into the lake.'

'Come on, Jiffy.' Drew puts a hand on his shoulder. 'I'll walk you and Jelly home.'

'But—'

'Good night, Jiffy!' Max says.

Jiffy waves. 'I'll be back bright and early in the morning.'

'And I'll be back in a few minutes,' Drew tells Bella.

Upstairs, she helps Max get ready for bed, tucks him in beneath just a sheet, with Chance and Spidey curled up at his side, and reads aloud from the quickest book on his shelf.

'Can I have another story, please?'

'Not tonight, sweetie. It's late. Sweet dreams.'

As she walks to the door, he says something around an enormous yawn.

She turns back. 'What was that, Max?'

'I want to dream about Daddy again.'

'What do you mean?'

'I dreamed about him last night.'

'You did? What did you dream?'

'He was here.' He yawns again. 'Not in the golden car. But that wasn't a dream because it was real.'

'Did he say anything about Kevin Bacon?'

'Huh?'

'Never mind.' She slips out the door, shaking her head.

'Mom?'

'Yes?'

'Can I have some bacon for breakfast?'

She smiles. 'We'll see. Goodnight, Max.'

If Drew weren't here, she'd go directly to bed herself. It's been a long day, and there's a lot to think about. Or forget about if she manages to fall asleep. Or even talk about, if by chance Odelia's home and, ideally, Luther is there. He still hasn't returned her call about Misty's robbery, which is unusual.

Back downstairs, she parts the curtains in the front parlor and peers out at the cottage next door, hoping to see his SUV parked out front. It is not.

Odelia had left the window shades open, having departed before dark. When she returns, Bella knows, she'll pull them down, same as always.

In the mudroom, the puppies are demanding to be let out, right on schedule. She heads outside with them and settles on the steps to wait for Drew. She'd turned off the overhead light that attracts insects, the better for her to see the fireflies flitting about the yard and the lake, reflecting a moonlit sky sequined with stars.

The air remains warm and sticky, but it's a little more bearable now that night has fallen. Crickets whir in the tall grasses where the water laps the shore.

The foxhound settles at her feet, dropping something from his paws and then resting his nose on it.

'Hey, fella, what do you have there?'

He lifts his head to look at her, and she sees that it's a T-shirt she'd worn on her trip, straight from the basket of laundry she has yet to get to.

She laughs. 'At least it isn't anything unmentionable.'

She pets his head, and he rests it against her bare leg, almost as if he's protecting Bella as much as he is the puppies.

Struck by the disquieting thought that Drew should have been long back by now, she can't help but worry that something might have happened to him, even along the short distance between Valley View and Misty's cottage.

Like what? This is Lily Dale, not the inner city, where she'd grown up. No speeding traffic or open manholes or street gangs around here.

Still, there have been a couple of murders – and now, perhaps, a break-in and theft.

Right. Misty is probably telling him all about it, or trying to convince him to try a homemade snow cone. Or maybe Jiffy persuaded Drew to tuck him in and read him a bedtime story.

That little boy really misses his dad. For his sake – for everyone's sake – she hopes Misty and Mike can work out their differences and figure out how to become a cohesive family, whether that's here or in Pennsylvania. She hates to think about Max suffering yet another difficult loss if his best friend moves away, and she herself will miss both Jiffy and Misty. But they're truly fortunate because Mike can come back to them, while Sam . . .

'Was that you?' she whispers, closing her eyes and picturing the face behind the windshield at O'Hare.

The only response is a nightbird's call from high in the gingko tree. Earlier, Drew had told her that it's a mockingbird searching for its mate.

I get it, Bella silently tells the bird.

Behind her, the door squeaks open, and she turns to see Drew.

'Oh, good, you're back! I was starting to get worried that . . .' She trails off, suddenly feeling silly for even considering that Drew might not safely return. '. . . that Misty was talking your ear off,' she says, and he chuckles.

'She tried, but I've grown pretty adept at extracting myself.' He sits beside Bella and hands her a white paper bag.

'What's this?'

'I took the long way back, past the ice-cream place. There was a line out the door.'

'I'll bet.' Opening the bag, she finds a pint of bittersweet chocolate gelato and two spoons. 'Oh! My favorite!'

'Yes, and it's already halfway to soup, so we'd better dig in.'

She opens the lid, helps herself to a decadent spoonful, and passes the carton to Drew.

The big dog turns to look up.

'Aw, I think he wants some.'

'He can't have any. Chocolate is toxic for him.'

Bella reaches down to pat the dog's head. 'Well, I think you deserve some other kind of treat, don't you, big guy?'

'I'll take whatever you're offering, little lady,' Drew says in an exaggerated, suggestive drawl.

Bella laughs. 'I hate to break it to you, but *he's* big guy. Until Max gives him a name, anyway.'

'Maybe we should come up with one for him.'

'Maybe we should.' She pauses, leaning in to fill her spoon from the carton Drew holds out to her. 'What's a good dog name?'

'Jack? Buddy? Scout?'

'No, it should be something that captures how sweet he is.'

'Gelato?'

She laughs. 'That would make him Jelly for short, and I don't think there's room in the Dale for two of them.'

'True, but he's not staying in the Dale permanently . . . or is he?'

'He is not,' she says firmly. 'Hey, Drew? When you dropped Jiffy off, did Misty say anything about . . . anything?'

'She said he could go upstairs to his room and play with his Playbox until bedtime.'

'Wow – so he actually has a bedtime?'

'Probably midnight.' He takes another spoonful and hands the gelato back to Bella.

'So she didn't mention the robbery?'

'Robbery! What robbery?'

'She didn't tell you about a robbery?'

'She was up on a ladder painting the kitchen ceiling when I got there.'

'You mean cleaning it?'

'*Painting* it, using a long-handled roller. She's painting it blue – like the sky, she said, and she's going to paint a big yellow sun up there, too. She tried to recruit me to help, but I said I had to get back to you. What's this about a robbery?'

Between spoonsful of gelato, Bella explains what happened at the Ardens', and that there was also a recent break-in at the Slayton house.

'Misty told you about that?'

'Pandora did.' She feels her face grow hot and is glad he can't see her in the dark. Not that she'd ever tell him what Pandora had said about the two of them.

'So you think Jiffy staged the break-in at his house after he heard about the Slaytons?'

'I do. But Misty says he denied it and that she believes him.'

'She must. If she really thinks she was robbed, then she should have called the police, instead of counting on you to tell Luther.'

'But she's Misty. You know how she is.'

'And you're Bella. I know how you are, taking care of everyone's needs before your own. Anyway, Luther's not even available tonight.'

'He's not? I was wondering why he hasn't called me back yet. It's not like him.'

'He's on security detail for that writer who's visiting Chautauqua.'

'The one who gets the death threats? Isn't that dangerous?'

'It is, but all things considered, Luther's been in worse situations over the years. For that matter, so have you.'

Bella puts the now-empty carton back into the bag and leans back with a satiated sigh. 'Thanks for the gelato, Drew.'

'I thought you deserved it, after a day like this.'

Ah, you don't know the half of it.

After a moment of silence, he says, 'Bella? I heard what happened with Sam.'

Her jaw drops.

For one thing, it's as if he just read her mind. For another, she's not accustomed to her late husband's name on Drew's lips.

'What, uh . . . what did you hear?'

'That you and Max think you saw him yesterday at the airport.'

'Max told you?'

'Jiffy did.'

Ah, Jiffy. Of course Max would have shared the experience with him. And of course, Jiffy will now be sharing it with . . . everyone.

Bella reminds herself that it isn't exactly an invasion of privacy, and the boys have done nothing wrong. It's just that in a town this size . . . in a town like this, those who see her as the newcomer who doesn't subscribe to spiritualism might assume she's changed her mind.

Why does that matter?

Unable to answer her own question, she poses one to Drew. 'What did Jiffy tell you?'

'That Sam was following you and Max around Chicago in a golden chariot.'

Bella can't help but laugh. 'More like a beat-up Subaru, and he wasn't following us around.' Her smile fades. 'And, I mean, it wasn't really Sam.'

Drew says nothing to that.

'Drew? You know it wasn't Sam, right?'

'I wasn't there, so . . .' He shrugs. 'All I know is what Jiffy told me. Though I have to admit, I did think the golden chariot was a little far-fetched.'

'But not the rest of it?'

'This is Lily Dale.'

'It happened in Chicago. It happened to *me*.'

'And Max.'

'And Max,' she agrees, 'but we're not part of this Lily Dale stuff, and neither are you.'

Drew is a fellow outsider. Yet he's lived in the area all his life and is long accustomed to people claiming that they've seen Spirit.

Is that what she's doing?

'Why don't you tell me what happened?' Drew asks.

She does, in as matter-of-fact a tone as she can muster, neglecting to mention the profound longing she'd felt for Sam throughout a weekend spent in his hometown, and the tumult of emotions she'd experienced when she'd glimpsed his familiar face.

'Maybe it was just a stranger who looked like Sam,' Drew says.

'I thought that – I want to think that . . .'

'But?'

She voices the detail that's been weighing on her; the fact that won't allow her to believe he'd been a stranger.

'But I didn't just see *him*. He saw *me*. *Us*. He was staring at us. A stranger wouldn't do that, right? A stranger would be oblivious, wouldn't he?'

'Maybe not, if he caught someone gaping at him.'

'True, but . . . it wasn't like that. He didn't just *look* like Sam . . . you know, the way a person can look like someone else at first glance, but then when you look closer, you see the differences?'

Drew nods.

She goes on, 'This was . . . when I got a better look, I saw that he had the same eyes, same hair with the same cowlick, just like Max.'

'That's pretty unique.'

'Exactly. But how could it be Sam? There must be an explanation. Something that doesn't involve the paranormal. Or my imagining him. Right?'

He seems to be weighing his words.

'You'd just spent the weekend in Sam's hometown, with his
mother, at a milestone celebration. I'm sure you were wishing he'd
been there, and you were probably missing him more than usual.'

He pauses, as if to allow her to chime in.

She doesn't. Of course he's correct, but admitting that to him
might be hurtful.

Which is ridiculous, she reminds herself. *Drew knows you loved
your husband and grieves the loss.*

'All I'm saying, Bella, is that . . . well, maybe you saw what you
wanted to see.'

'I'd think that was the case, except Max saw him too. Actually,
so did the security guard. We couldn't have all hallucinated him at
the exact same moment, right?'

He rubs his chin.

'Drew? Do you think . . .' She takes a deep breath. 'You don't
think it might have been Sam's ghost, do you?'

Unlike the mediums, he doesn't correct her phrasing to 'Spirit'.
Nor does he brush off the suggestion of paranormal activity, as she
herself so often has when the mediums chalk something up to Spirit.

But he says, 'I don't know.'

'This wasn't a filmy figure. It was a solid person. Definitely an
alive person. A person who was driving a car! Ghosts can't drive
cars!'

Drew says nothing.

'Wait . . . you think they can? Ghosts can *drive*?'

'It's not that. It's . . . I don't know,' he says again.

'Drew, you don't really believe people can see dead people? You
have a science background, like I do. You don't buy into this stuff.'

'For the most part, I don't.'

'But . . .?'

'But I work with animals, and I've seen them do some extraordinary things. As far as I'm concerned, they have instincts that are
on par with psychic perception.'

She thinks of Chance, rooted in a highway last summer, leading
her and Max to Lily Dale.

And of Chance, perched in the second-floor window last night, looking out over the Dale as the wind chimes stirred without a breeze.

'I can't argue with that,' she says. 'Chance got us here. And whenever I try to convince myself that it was random, I think of my necklace.'

'What necklace?'

She tells him about the tourmaline pendant she'd found at Valley View. 'If Sam didn't leave it here, how did it get here? And there's something else . . .'

Something Max doesn't know, so Jiffy couldn't have told anyone about it. Something she hadn't intended to tell Drew. But, oddly, it feels right to be discussing these things with him. He's the one person in the world – other than Luther, perhaps – whose insight she values, when it comes to this sort of thing.

'Odelia said she had a visit from Sam last night. And she said he had a message for me.'

'What was it?'

She hesitates. It seems too intimate now – that he'd expressed his love for her, and told her that he misses her, that he's proud of her for building a new life without him . . .

If all of that is true, and if she were to believe that Sam really had said those things, then she'd have to accept that he sees her life as it is now. All of it – including the part that involves Drew Bailey.

Suddenly aware of how close they're sitting, her left side up against his right, she fights the urge to move away, to put some distance between them. It's been months since she'd come to terms with her feelings for Drew, finally convinced that she shouldn't carry guilt for moving on.

But right now, here in the moonlight with another man, it strikes her as a betrayal to reveal her husband's words – even if Bella isn't entirely convinced they'd actually come from Sam.

'The message itself really doesn't matter,' she tells Drew. 'Some of it was vague and general, and there were parts that made no sense whatsoever. The main thing is the timing. She's never brought him through before, so why now?'

'Power of suggestion? Unless you didn't tell her you'd seen Sam at the airport?'

'No, and Max couldn't have, either. I didn't even tell *you* about it last night. So there's no way she knew, and . . . you know, dreamed it, or whatever. I keep thinking . . .' She sighs. 'I don't know what to think. What do *you* think?'

'That doesn't matter.'

'But it does.'

'You probably won't like it.'

'Try me.'

'Ever hear of Occam's razor?'

Surprised, she turns to him. 'Of course. The simplest explanation is probably the correct one.'

'Exactly.'

'But . . . there is no simple explanation in this case.'

'There is the way I see it.'

'Which is . . .?'

Drew shrugs. 'You – and Max and Odelia, too – saw Sam's spirit.'

'*That's* simple?'

'All things considered . . . I'd say so.'

She ponders that.

Lily Dale being Lily Dale . . . maybe he's right.

SIXTEEN

Tuesday is just as hot as – if not hotter than – Monday was. Somehow, Bella got a solid night's sleep despite everything. Rising at her usual time, she quickly showers, pulls her damp hair back into a ponytail, and throws on cut-offs, a tank top, and flip-flops. No fussing for Drew's sake now that he's seen her at her worst and is still hanging around.

Downstairs, she finds that he's already made the coffee, and he and Max are out in the yard playing with the puppies. Good. She'd prefer not to start the day rehashing last night's conversation about Sam, and Drew will never bring it up in front of Max.

She steps outside with a mug of coffee. 'Good morning!'

Drew smiles. 'Good morning.'

Crouched on the ground with his arms wrapped around the big dog, Max says, 'Hey, Mom, guess what? This guy has your T-shirt.'

'Again?' She laughs.

Drew shakes his head. 'Sorry, Bella. We couldn't get it away from him.'

'It's fine. I don't know why he's so attached to it.'

'Dr Drew says he's in love with you, Mom.'

For a crazy moment, she misinterprets Max's comment.

Then the light dawns: Drew had said the *dog* is in love with Bella. Not that Drew himself is.

Of course he wouldn't say *that*.

Hoping he can't tell what she's thinking, or that her chuckle is forced, she says, 'Well, I guess it's nice to have a not-so-secret admirer.'

'Maybe that's a good name for him!' Max says.

'Not-So-Secret-Admirer? It does have a nice ring to it,' Drew says, and Max giggles.

'Mom, me and Doctor Drew are thinking up a name for this big guy, and Doctor Drew can only think up silly, crazy names like Spaghetti or Meatball.'

'What's wrong with those names?' Drew asks, with a wink at Bella. 'You said you love spaghetti and meatballs, Max.'

'You asked me what's my favorite thing to eat! And this guy doesn't look like a Spaghetti, or a Meatball! Or a Kitty Cat – that's another crazy name Doctor Drew thought up, Mom.'

'Sounds like Doctor Drew could use some help from you, Max.'

'I'm thinking really hard.' Max pets the dog's head. 'I think Not-So-Secret-Admirer is too much to say. And he needs a super-special name because he's super-special. I love him so much. I wish I could keep him.'

'I know you do.'

'Can I?'

Even the dog seems to be pleading, his big sad eyes fixed on Bella.

She shakes her head. 'Let's just enjoy his visit, Max.'

'But Doctor Drew said all the dogs have to leave now and go back to the Animal Hospital because you're too busy to have them here today.'

She looks at Drew. 'I'm really not. Let them stay. Max and I will take care of them together.'

'And Jiffy, too!' Max adds.

'Bella, you don't have to—'

'But I want to,' she says, and means it. 'It's a welcome distraction, Drew. Trust me.'

He nods. He gets it. Before they'd parted at her bedroom door last night, he'd encouraged her to reach out to Odelia first thing this morning.

'Maybe she can shed more light on what you and Max experienced.'

'She'll just say it had to be Sam's spirit.'

'Occam's razor, Bella.'

Ah, but if there's one place Occam's razor tends not to apply, it's Lily Dale. How many times, since Bella's arrival, has she found herself caught up in the least likely scenario imaginable? She's grappled with murderers, swindlers, grifters, thieves – an inordinate number of criminals for such a small town.

Then again, when you consider the Dale's geographical isolation, and the fact that it's relatively deserted nine months of the year, you can see why it might appeal to anyone who has something to hide. Since it's a tourist destination, nobody gives outsiders a second thought, and since Bella's job entails hosting total strangers here at Valley View, it makes sense that she finds herself involved in criminal cases – to her, anyway. Perhaps not so much to Lieutenant John Grange.

Reminded of Misty's request, she realizes she'd left her phone upstairs on the nightstand without checking to see if Luther had gotten back to her overnight. He wouldn't have called her back in the wee hours, but he might have texted when he got her message about the robbery.

After Drew leaves, Bella heads back inside, telling Max he can stay in the fenced yard and play with the dogs awhile longer. The area is still in the shade, but things are going to heat up quickly out there as the sun climbs higher in the sky.

She keeps an eye on them through the breakfast room windows as she gets everything ready. It's still too hot to bake fresh scones, but she'd bought some from the supermarket bakery yesterday, along with muffins and tarts. She arranges the baked goods in a wicker basket lined with a blue-and-white cloth napkin that matches the gingham tablecloths. She cuts berries, melon and mango into a fruit salad, puts it into a white china serving bowl, and garnishes it with some sprigs of mint from the herb garden.

Once everything is ready for her guests, she wrangles Max and his canine posse back into the house, settling the dogs in the mudroom and Max at the kitchen table as she opens the cabinet to find some cereal.

'Hey! I thought you were going to make bacon for my breakfast today,' he says.

'Oh – I forgot. How about tomorrow?'

Max is agreeable. 'OK. I have to eat speedy-quick anyway because Jiffy said he's coming over bright and early.'

'I'm sure Jiffy's still fast asleep at this hour. He was up late last night.'

'Jiffy's never still fast asleep. He doesn't like to miss stuff.'

Bella smiles. 'How about some Shredded Wheat?'

'Is it the kind with the frosting?'

'No, the plain, healthy kind.'

'I'll just have Chocolatey Oaty-Os. Jiffy said they're super-healthy and I saw a lot more boxes in the breakfast room. I'll go get one.'

'OK, but today you have to have it in a bowl with milk and sliced banana.'

He dashes from the room and returns with five boxes of the cereal before she finishes peeling the banana.

'Max! You can only have one.'

'Well, I want to hide the rest in here so that if the robber comes he won't see them and steal them.'

'Why would a robber steal cereal?' Bella asks, slicing the banana into a bowl.

'Because I think he's the kind of robber who likes Chocolatey Oaty-Os.'

'What makes you think that?'

'I don't know.' He avoids her gaze as she pours cereal into the bowl, topping it with milk.

'OK, kiddo, eat your breakfast and I'll be right back. I have to run upstairs and find my phone.'

'Did you lose it? Maybe the robber stole it.'

'No, I didn't lose it, and nobody stole it, Max, but . . .'

She hesitates, aware that she only has a few minutes to herself before the guests start trickling down for breakfast. Now isn't the time to ask him what he knows about the robbery at the Ardens'.

Still, his mention reminds her to detour to the study to get Millicent's college fund check, just in case. She's relieved to see that the envelope is still right where she'd left it, on her desk under the paperweight, edges fluttering in the breeze from the fan.

That had seemed like a safe enough place before she'd heard about the break-in at the Slaytons' and possibly at Misty's place. Now, Bella decides to tuck it away upstairs in her jewelry box until she can get to the bank.

'Hello?' someone calls in the front of the house. 'Hello? Anyone here?'

She folds the envelope in half, shoves it in her back pocket, and hurries into the parlor.

'Grant!'

'Hi, Bella.'

With flashing black eyes, chiseled features, and broad shoulders, Valley View's owner always looks like a leading man who's just stepped off a film set. Sometimes, he might appear to have been cast as an action hero; others, as a global billionaire or the romantic guy next door. His devil-may-care charisma is palpable, whether he's wearing a khaki utility jacket, bespoke suit, or – today – a chambray button-down with rolled-up sleeves.

He greets her with a quick hug, then gestures at his female

companion. 'This is Eve. Eve, Bella Jordan. She's been managing the place for me.'

'Yep, I have,' Bella agrees in a voice slightly higher – and squeakier – than her own, as she thinks of Polly Green, ensconced in the Gable Room that was supposed to be reserved for Grant.

Bella never expected him to show up at this hour. What if he wants to go right upstairs to rest?

Then he should have told me when to expect him.

Right. That's only reasonable. Grant is a businessman – a rich one who intends to get richer and wants Valley View to make money. He'll understand why Bella decided to allow a paying guest to stay in his empty room last night.

What he might not understand is why she'd given the Jungle Room to Drew Bailey free of charge.

Is that something she needs to share?

It is not. Not yet anyway. She'll just hope that Polly is up and out of here soon, and then she'll prepare the Gable Room for Grant and his . . .

Companion.

His prior visits have always been solo, and it had somehow never occurred to her that he might not be single.

Eve is as striking as Grant is, and well over a decade younger. More likely two, appearing to be in her early twenties. Her raven hair is cropped short in a cut that would probably only look good on a young boy or a supermodel. She might very well be one – tall and thin, wearing platform wedges and a clingy black skirt and top that reveal a flat belly, pierced navel, and long, tanned limbs.

'Nice to meet you, Bella,' she says, with a mouth that appears to have been injected with whatever it is you inject to get lips that appear swollen in a beguiling way.

'You, too.' Bella smiles with a mouth that's still swollen from where her own teeth had drawn blood yesterday in her effort to keep from blurting to the medium next door that her dead husband's message had been generic.

Eve doesn't strike her as a woman who'd bite her own lip to keep from hurting a friend's feelings – perhaps not a fair assessment. But Bella's Mean Girl radar had been honed back in middle school – probably not so long after Eve had been born – and she still knows one when she sees one.

She turns back to Grant. He's looking around the parlor that just yesterday she'd admired for its cozy charm.

Now, seeing it through his critical eye, she notes that one of the three bay windows is propped open with a strip of scrap wood because the sash is broken. Sunlight falls through it in precisely the right spot to highlight the threadbare spots on the vintage rug. The bouquet of pink hollyhocks she'd cut yesterday is already drooping in the heat. The crystal vase, with a crack she hadn't noticed until now, is surrounded by a litter of fallen petals on a mahogany table marred by circular white water stains from coasterless cups.

She pivots to Eve with a belated, 'Welcome to Valley View. Is this your first time in the Dale?'

'In . . .'

'Lily Dale?'

'Oh! Yes. It's my first time in this part of New York. I live in the city.'

'That's where I grew up.'

'No, I mean . . . *New York* City,' she clarifies, as if Bella's a country bumpkin claiming to be the long-lost royal heir.

'Oh, I know,' Bella says. 'New York's the best city in the world, as far as I'm concerned.'

Eve rewards that with a smile and touches Grant's arm. 'See? I told you.'

He just shakes his head, looking annoyed in the most good-natured way imaginable.

'Um . . . you told him I grew up in New York City?' Bella asks.

'No! To be honest, I didn't even know you existed until we got here.'

Ditto.

'What I told him was that you can't compare a city like Toronto to New York, which is what he was doing.'

Grant turns to Bella. 'That's where we flew from Shanghai yesterday. Have you ever been there?'

'Shanghai? No.'

'Toronto.'

'I've never been there, either, but it's only a three-hour drive from here, so maybe I'll get there one of these days. I've heard great things.'

'From Grant?' Eve asks. 'He kept talking about all the cool stuff I'd be able to post about.'

'She's an influencer,' he informs Bella.

'You mean . . . on social media?'

'Um . . . *yee-aaah*,' Eve says, in a tone you'd use on someone very young and naïve. Or, in this case, old and naïve. 'I'm All About Eve.'

'That's your website?'

'My website? No! It's my handle.'

'Oh! Your username!'

There's an awkward pause. Eve shakes her head and turns back to Grant. 'Anyway, I was saying, we should have just come straight here yesterday instead.'

'There's plenty to see and do in Lily Dale,' Bella assures her.

She looks amused. 'I mean, we should have gotten Lily Dale over with so we could have been back in Manhattan for Kylie's event last night.'

'Kylie's event?' Bella asks – not out of naivete, nor even curiosity, but because if she's been cast in the role of bumpkin, she might as well embrace it.

Eve nods. 'She's a good friend of mine. She had a birthday dinner at Clovis.'

'Clovis?'

'Um . . . the *restaurant*?'

Bella shrugs. 'I haven't been to the city in a while.'

'It's been open *for-ev-er*. Well, the one down in Meatpacking has. Since last fall, at least. Maybe even longer.'

Ah, the Meatpacking District. Bella considers telling Eve that her late father had worked in that neighborhood in his youth— 'Before the drug dealers and sex workers took over,' he liked to say, lest anyone mistake the portly, upstanding Frank Angelo for either of those things.

But Eve probably isn't big on familial anecdotes, so Bella offers coffee instead. 'There's a pot in the kitchen, or you can make decaf by the cup in the breakfast room – though I'm guessing you need the *caf*. You two couldn't have gotten much sleep if you spent the night in Toronto and drove all the way here already.'

'Drive! We didn't *drive*. We flew.'

'From Toronto? To Buffalo?'

'Buffalo?' Eve echoes. 'God, no. To . . . what was that place called, Grant? Something about dinky . . .'

'Not dinky,' he says with a chuckle. '*Dunkirk*.'

'There are flights to *Dunkirk* from Toronto?' Bella asks.

'Not *commercial* flights,' is Eve's reply.

To which Bella the Bumpkin says, 'So . . . how about that coffee?'

From Grant: 'Sounds good.'

From Eve: 'You've got to be kidding. It's way too hot for coffee.'

'I know, but unfortunately, there's no air conditioning here at Valley View. That's one of the things I wanted to talk to you about, Grant.'

'Hmm.' Not an intrigued *hmm*, but almost a disinterested *hmm*.

'I can make iced coffee, if you'd rather have that?'

'Actually, that would be perfect.'

'I'll just have water,' Eve tells Bella.

'Got it. One iced coffee and one iced water, coming right up.'

'*Ice?*' Eve echoes. 'No ice. Just tepid is good.'

'You want tepid tap water?'

'*Tap* water?' Eve gapes at Bella. 'Wait . . . don't tell me you don't serve bottled water here?'

'We have plenty, but it's all in the fridge in the breakfast room. You can help yourself, or I can give you a glass to fill from the faucet.'

'No, thanks,' Eve says. 'I'll skip the water. Is there someplace where I can have some privacy to work on some new posts?'

Uh-oh. She turns to Grant.

'Actually, I had the Gable Room all made up for you' – *had* being the operative word – 'but there's only a full-sized bed in there, so it might be a little cramped for two people. I didn't realize you were bringing a . . . date.'

'A date! You are just *too* adorable!' Eve all but ruffles Bella's hair.

And you are just too . . . much.

Bella goes on, 'The Jungle Room is also on the third floor, and it has more space. It was just vacated this morning, so I can get it ready now.'

'Wait – does she think we're *staying* here?' Eve asks Grant, as if Bella isn't right here.

'Well, I usually do.'

'You *do*? *Here?*'

'Here,' Bella confirms. 'After all, he owns the place.'

Eve looks amused. 'Right. About that—'

'Maybe Eve can use the Jungle Room while you and I chat?' Grant cuts in.

'Uh . . . Sure. There's a desk, but the bed isn't made or anything.'

Though maybe it is. Drew is probably the kind of man who makes it every day, as soon as he gets out of bed. Funny that you can know someone as well as she feels she knows him, and yet certain details only come with a different kind of relationship.

'I don't care about the bed,' Eve says. 'How do I get to the third floor?'

'Most people prefer to take the stairs.'

She looks perplexed.

'It was a joke,' Bella explains.

'Oh! Funny.' She doesn't crack a smile. 'What I meant was, I don't know my way around this creepy haunted house, and I don't want to go alone. You'll walk me up, won't you, Grant?'

Of course he will. This woman seems to have Grant wrapped around her finger.

The two of them head upstairs, Eve clinging to Grant's hand as if something is going to leap out from the shadows.

Where's Nadine when you need her?

Grateful for the reprieve, Bella returns to the kitchen.

Max is still at the table with his cereal bowl, but he's no longer alone. Jiffy is sitting across from him, wearing his stained T-shirt from yesterday. His upper lip still bears the traces of grape mustache.

'Good morning, Jiffy.'

'Hi, Bella. I came over to tell Max some stuff. *Private* stuff,' he adds pointedly.

'Don't worry. I'll leave you two alone. Did you eat breakfast?'

'Yep. I had a lot of spoons of peanut butter, but I could eat another breakfast if you want. As long as it's Chocolatey Oaty-Os. Do you have any more?'

'They're in the cupboard,' Max says. 'I hid them in case the guests eat them all up.'

'I thought it was because the robber might steal them because he likes that kind of cereal.'

'Oh, yeah. That, too.'

'What do you think, Jiffy? Do you think the robber likes Chocolatey Oaty-Os, too?'

'Probably, because he's a grown-up and he knows that Chocolatey Oaty-Os are fortified with ten vitamins and minerals.'

'How do *you* know that?' Max asks.

'It says so on the box, see?'

'I don't know those words.'

No, because Max, while intelligent, is reading on an appropriate level for a kid his age, while Jiffy has a genius IQ.

Bella takes out a bowl for him. 'Does your mom know you're here?'

'Yep.'

Bella peers at him. 'Really?'

'Well, she probably does because she's a psychic and she always knows stuff. But she was sleeping when I left, and I didn't want to wake her up because she was up really late painting the ceiling to cover up all the purple from the blender.'

Ah . . . now it makes sense. Sort of.

'Why don't you give your mom a call and tell her where you are?' she suggests.

'Because she doesn't like it when people wake her up.'

Max nods. 'Yeah, and because you don't have your—'

'Max!' Jiffy gives him a warning look.

'Jiffy? What don't you have? Your phone?'

'Why'd you tell her that?' Jiffy asks Max. 'It's private, remember?'

'I *didn't* tell her. She's a good psychic, too.'

'She is not.'

'She is so. Psychics know stuff and she does.'

'But she's not a *psychic*. She's just a mom. She doesn't have a shingle and do readings like my mom. Right, Bella?'

'Right.' Bella pours cereal and milk into the bowl and sets it in front of him.

'Thanks, Bella. I'll have a banana, too, please. And extra milk, because the box says that it magically turns into chocolate milk, and I can drink that when I run out of cereal.'

She obliges. Then she asks, again, 'Where's your phone, Jiffy?'

He glares at Max.

Bella tries a different tactic. 'Did you lose it?'

'Nope.'

'So you know where it is?'

'Yep.'

'Really?'

'I swear, Bella. I'm not lying. I know 'xactly where it is.'

'OK, well . . . that's good. Eat your cereal, boys. I'll be right back.'

She heads for the stairs, intending to text Misty so she won't worry if she wakes up and Jiffy's not there.

Candace and Tommy are on their way down.

'Good morning!' Bella steps back to let them descend. 'You two are up bright and early.'

'We're doing a presentation,' Candace says. 'You should come. We're doing an equipment demo.'

'Equipment?'

Tommy ticks off on his fingers, 'Magnetic field detectors, EVP recorders, EMF readers . . .'

'Ah, ghost-hunting equipment.'

'Exactly. There's a lot of activity in this house.'

'Yes, well, we're at full capacity,' Bella says.

'He means paranormal activity,' Candace tells her.

'Oh, right,' Bella says, as if she didn't already know that.

'Our sensors were going crazy on the third floor last night,' Tommy says. 'Something's definitely going on up there.'

'If you want, we can come back and do a full investigation,' Candace offers. 'Valley View would be a great place to film an episode. We met your friend Odelia last night. She said she has some good stories about this place. I'll bet you do, too.'

'Maybe not as colorful as Odelia's. I've only been living here since last summer.'

'What's it like in the off-season?'

'Quiet and peaceful,' Bella says. 'Well, most of the time.'

When she's not solving murders and chasing down kidnappers.

'Listen, everything's all set up in the breakfast room, so help yourselves, and I'll be back down in a few minutes if you need anything.'

'Take your time,' Tommy calls after her as she hurries up the stairs. 'We don't need a thing.'

In the Rose Room, Bella checks her cell phone. Millicent has yet to return her call, but her home screen shows that she'd missed one from Luther just minutes ago.

She returns it immediately.

He answers on the first ring. 'Bella! Are you OK? You had a robbery at Valley View?'

'No, not here. At Misty's. But maybe not.'

She quickly explains the situation, including her theory that Jiffy staged the robbery to cover up the fact that he'd lost his scooter.

'Misty believed him when he denied it, but I'm not so sure I do. He's here right now with Max, and he seems like he's up to something.'

'He usually is,' Luther remarks.

'I know, and he says he doesn't have his phone. I'm wondering if he lost it, and he's trying to cover it up with this robbery story.'

'Didn't Misty say the scooter and vase were the only things that were missing?'

'And the puzzle. The only things that she knew of so far,' Bella says. 'But you've seen her house.'

'I have. It always looks as if it's just been ransacked. Still, if the phone was missing, either because it had been stolen or because Jiffy lost it, wouldn't he have told Misty that it disappeared during the "robbery"?'

'Probably. And he just looked me in the eye and swore that it isn't lost, and that he knows exactly where it is. I feel like he was telling the truth. But I did hear that there was a break-in at the Slayton house.'

'Odelia told you?'

'Pandora. She said she'd heard it through the grapevine.'

Luther sighs on the other end of the line. 'I guess there are no secrets in Lily Dale.'

'It was a secret?'

'Well, the house has been sitting empty all summer, and it's not a good idea to publicize that.'

'What happened?'

'I don't know all the facts, but the caretaker who keeps an eye on the place found a broken basement window – something like that.'

'Was anything stolen?'

'Not much. Grange and his team are still investigating, and David Slayton doesn't seem to be in any hurry to get here, but it sounds like all that's missing is a diamond necklace.'

'The one with the sapphires?'

'You know about it?'

'Calla mentioned it when she was here one day. She said that Blue's mother took off when he was a baby and was never heard from again. The housekeeper, Mrs Remington, always suspected foul play because she'd left behind that valuable necklace. According to her, it was a red flag.'

'I don't know if that says more about Blue's mother or the housekeeper,' Luther comments. 'You'd think most women would consider a child more valuable than a piece of jewelry.'

'You'd think,' Bella agrees. 'Anyway, Calla said that Blue wanted to give her the necklace when they were dating, but David wouldn't part with it. I guess he thought she might come back some day.'

'Interesting. I wonder how many people knew it was in that house?'

'You'll have to ask Calla. I haven't told anyone.'

She thinks back to that day, wondering whether their conversation might have been overheard. They hadn't even been out in public, though; just chatting on the Adirondack chairs in the yard as Max and Jiffy dug for buried treasure.

'Why don't I stop by the Ardens' and talk to Misty?' Luther suggests.

'Now? Aren't you exhausted? You've been up all night.'

'I'm wide awake. I've had enough coffee to keep me up till next week. I can't stay long – I have to get home to feed my dogs – but I'll see if I can get to the bottom of this.'

'Thanks. Have you spoken to Odelia yet today?'

'Not yet. I'm sure she's still asleep. You know Odelia.'

'I do.'

And Odelia knows me.

She knows, perhaps better than anyone, how badly Bella misses Sam, and that she's been longing for some sign from him on the other side.

She hangs up with Luther and opens the text app to let Misty know that Jiffy's here and Luther's on his way.

There's a new message from *Unknown.*

Bella clicks to open it, and her stomach turns over.

Bella, it's me. Sam.

SEVENTEEN

Odelia has never been one to jump out of bed at sunrise, but she does today.

Well, she doesn't quite *jump*. It's more of an arthritic hoisting, punctuated by a loud sound that's part-groan, part-yawn.

Her sleep hadn't been restful. The bed suddenly seemed big and lonely without Luther and/or Li'l Chap, and Spirit's cryptic message weighed like the humid night air and the sandwich she'd gobbled at Soul-stice.

Don't trust her.

Determined to grasp its meaning, Odelia does her best to meditate on it, as she had last night, but finds that she still can't quite get past her worry over Calla.

There's only one way to find out what's going on.

She throws a bathrobe over her pink chiffon peignoir, and a pair of heeled pink scuffies that can pass for shoes.

You need to stay hydrated, Calla's voice reminds her, and she goes to the fridge to grab a bottle of water to carry along.

Stepping outside, she's greeted by a blazing glare of morning sun.

Goodness, it's hot and bright. Back inside she goes, to shed the robe and retrieve her fuchsia, jewel-encrusted cat-eye sunglasses. Checking the mirror by the front door, she decides that her nightie shows a bit too much cleavage, especially for this hour on a weekday. She fishes through a drawer. A woolen scarf is out of the question on a day like today, but her feathered pink boa is just the thing to drape over her shoulders and across the plunging neckline.

Glancing at Valley View as she descends the front steps to Cottage Row, she's startled to see a big black SUV idling out front. There's a bald man in the driver's seat, wearing a suit and sunglasses.

He looks like the Secret Service type, she thinks, recalling a certain First Lady who'd visited the Dale years ago. Or maybe just some kind of government agent. Or perhaps a security guard? A spy?

Odelia's protective streak kicks in. Why would someone be spying on Valley View? On *her* Bella and Max?

She marches over to the SUV and knocks on the driver's window.

He rolls it down. A blast of air conditioning and country music spill out.

'Can I help you?' she asks.

'Uh . . . excuse me?'

'I'm Odelia Lauder. And you are . . .?'

'Marty.'

'Marty . . .'

'Kowalski.'

'What can I do for you, Marty?' She pastes on a friendly smile to put him at ease.

'Uh . . . I'm not interested in . . . uh . . .'

He's definitely on edge. He must be up to something.

She tries a different tactic.

'Most people who show up here are looking for a session. I'm booked all day today, but I can see if my friend Misty has any availability. She's very good.'

'I'm . . . I'm not . . . I'm just Mr Everard's driver!' he blurts. 'He owns this place.'

'Oh! Grant.'

Odelia's never been a fan. Not since the days when he'd come to visit his aunt Leona here. He'd never had much use for the Dale, or the guesthouse, though she'll admit, he'd been good to his aunt, and she'd adored him in return.

'So you're dropping him off here?' she asks Marty.

'I'm taking him back to the airport as soon as he's finished with his – well, I thought it was some kind of business meeting, but I guess I should have known better, especially the way *she* was dressed.'

'She?'

'His, ah . . . his *friend*.'

'So he's not staying overnight?'

'Guess not.'

Well, that's certainly good news for Bella, who has enough to worry about without Grant underfoot.

'All right, then, Marty. Carry on,' she says, and he quickly raises the window.

About to move on, she notices the white sedan she'd seen yesterday afternoon, driven by the woman Calla had said she'd seen on her flight from New York. There's a Valley View guest parking pass on the dashboard. The car must be a rental, as it has Massachusetts license plates, and Calla had mentioned the woman had been connecting through Chicago.

At the time, Odelia was too busy fainting from heat exhaustion to think much of it, but now . . .

Bella and Max had been in Chicago all weekend.

Sam was from Chicago.

A lot of people are, and a lot of people visit, but . . .

There are no coincidences. Not in Lily Dale.

Frowning at the car, Odelia recalls that she'd seen it right around the time that Spirit had initially attempted to touch in with the message about trust. Is it possible . . .?

Could it have had something to do with the woman in the car, rather than with Calla? Or even Pandora?

'Everything OK there?'

She turns to see Marty, still watching her through his open car window.

'Everything's great,' she lies, taking a sip from her water bottle and moving on.

Calla's East Street cottage is on the opposite side of the Dale – not by design, though Odelia suspects that if she'd had her choice, she'd have put a good amount of distance between the two of them.

If Odelia had had *her* choice, Calla would have moved back into her old room at Odelia's place. It had been Stephanie's girlhood bedroom as well.

I don't like living alone.

The thought catches Odelia off guard. It isn't something she thinks about often, if ever.

She's accustomed to solitude. It's necessary, in her line of work. But sometimes, lately, solitude seems to walk a fine line with loneliness.

Which is silly, because here in the Dale, one is rarely alone.

She passes the phantom girl on the swing, the man in the top hat with the *Titanic* newspaper, and the knickered newsboys playing catch. As she rounds the corner onto East Street, she encounters a filmy white woman.

'Good morning, Odelia,' a familiar voice says beneath layers of sheer scarf that drape her head and cover most of her face, with enormous sunglasses obscuring the rest. 'Fancy meeting *you* about the Dale at this early hour.'

'Pandora? Is that you in there?'

'Of course. I'm taking my daily stroll before it gets too bloody hot. I can't risk becoming sunburnt and freckled like . . . like . . .'

'Like me?'

'Precisely. Ruddiness would be garish on delicate skin such as my own, but on you, it's quite becoming.'

Odelia raises an eyebrow. It isn't like Pandora to offer compliments. Certainly not to Odelia.

'Well, thanks. I like your . . . uh, is that a hijab?'

'A burka. Just the thing for maximum sun protection. And I do say, your gown is quite smashing. Just returning from a night on the town with Luther, are you?'

'No, I'm on my way to visit my granddaughter. I have something to discuss with her.'

'Ah, would that be the falling out with her publishing cohorts? Or her dalliance with Blue Slayton?'

Odelia flinches. 'What are you talking about?'

'I couldn't help but overhear your tête-à-tête with Walter last evening at the bistro, as I happened to be seated at the adjacent table.'

'You *were*?' She feigns surprise.

'I'd have invited you to join me, but I was caught up in a personal dilemma, you see.'

That makes two of us.

'I'm afraid I still haven't gotten myself sorted. Perhaps you can offer some insight, Odelia?'

'Into your . . . personal dilemma?'

'Yes. Ordinarily you're the last person with whom I'd share, but, well, you're the only one afoot at the moment.'

She shifts her weight and looks around the deserted street. 'I'm sure others will be afoot any minute now, Pandora.'

'Perhaps, but as a divorcée of a certain age, I believe you're best suited to provide insight. My dilemma involves finances. I'm about to come into a rather significant amount of money, you might recall.'

She nods. Everyone in town is aware that Pandora had recently inherited a seemingly mundane family heirloom that had turned out to be a priceless treasure.

'My advisors are encouraging me to pay off debts and invest the rest to secure my future.'

'Your advisors? You mean your spirit guides?'

'My financial advisors. My guides haven't quite weighed in on the matter. Unfortunately, I have little experience with stocks and bonds and such. I don't suppose you do?'

'Me? You're kidding, right?'

'Ah, yes, what was I thinking? You're hardly a Wall Street whiz, are you?'

Delivered without a trace of Pandora's usual haughtiness, it isn't an insult.

'I'm not,' Odelia admits. 'But if you're going to invest in stocks and—'

'I'd prefer to use the windfall on something that will make me happy.'

'How about travel? You could take one of those cruises around the world or spend the winter on a tropical island.'

Pandora shakes her head. 'I've no desire to leave the Dale. This is my home.'

'I don't mean forever. Just for a few months.'

'I'd prefer to use the money for something that will make a difference in the long run.'

'Well, you could always donate to charity. There are lots of good causes in need of—'

'That won't make a difference for *me*.' Pandora, being Pandora, doesn't sugarcoat her reply.

Ordinarily, this would be Odelia's cue to make some excuse and extract herself from the conversation. But today, despite being distracted by her own problems, she senses vulnerability in Pandora.

'What would make *you* happy?' she asks.

'A time machine that could transport me to the good old days before Orville abandoned me, but I suppose that's out of the question?'

'No, it isn't,' Odelia tells her, and taps her own temple. 'You have all your memories right here. You can revisit those days anytime you want. But why would you want to?'

'Because I was happy then.'

'With Orville?'

'I was, yes.'

Odelia is tempted to advise her to get over the wanker, just as she herself had gotten over Jack Lauder so long ago. Most days, she doesn't even think of her ex-husband and the pain he'd inflicted, leaving her alone at such a young age with a child to raise. But every once in a while, some detail from that failed marriage comes back to her – not just the worst of it, but the best.

'I understand, Pandora.' She reaches out to find the woman's spindly arm beneath the swathe of fabric and gives it a squeeze. 'But you will be happy again.'

'It's easy for you to say. You've got your family, and of course, Luther. I've got no one.'

'You have all of us here – your friends. And Lady Pippa,' she adds.

Pandora's Scottish fold is arguably the Dale's most pampered pet.

'Yes, yes, but that isn't quite what I meant, is it?'

'I don't know. Is it?'

'It is not.'

Odelia sips her water, eager to move on. She's positive that the warning from Spirit had nothing to do with trusting – or not trusting – Pandora. And yes, her heart goes out to the woman, but her patience is wearing thin.

'Maybe you should let your financial advisors and your spirit guides help you figure things out,' she tells Pandora. 'Or how about talking to a good therapist? I can ask around and see if I can find some recommendations for you.'

'I don't need a therapist! Are you suggesting that I'm—'

'I'm suggesting that everyone goes through a rough patch, Pandora. It sounds like this is yours.'

Though from where she sits, there are worse problems to have than how to spend a fortune.

'Anyway, I really do need to get to Calla's.'

'Of course. Carry on.' Pandora lifts her chin, gives a nod, and walks on.

So does Odelia, not noticing the man who slips into a stand of trees, watching her intently.

EIGHTEEN

B ella stands in the Rose Room, staring at the message on her phone.

Bella, it's Sam.

It had come in the middle of the night from an unknown number.

Who'd play a trick like this on her? Her mind races through possibilities.

Even Jiffy, for all his mischievous pranks, would never be so cruel.

She types, *Who is this?* and hits Send before she can change her mind.

The message whooshes off, far more likely to some human prankster than to the Great Beyond. Whoever it is won't reply, and she can delete the message and move on.

She texts Misty, *FYI, Jiffy's here with Max and Luther's stopping by your house.*

After sending it, she sees that there's a response from Unknown. It's a single word: *Sam.*

She shakes her head. 'No, you're not.'

There's absolutely no way that her dead husband is, what? Sitting on a cloud in a white robe and halo, cell phone in hand?

Then again . . . what about the tourmaline necklace?

What about Einstein?

Everyone who is seriously involved in the pursuit of science becomes convinced that a spirit is manifest in the laws of the Universe.

Science. Physics. Energy.

Sometimes miracles aren't miracles at all.

She considers the vast wealth of commonplace technology that had been unheard of just a few generations ago. Ordinary people had never flipped a light switch, flown in a plane, used a microwave, a telephone, a computer . . .

A hundred years or even decades ago, pressing a button on a handheld device and instantaneously being able to communicate with a loved one on the other side of the world would have been a magical feat.

Now, everyone knows that it's just technologists manipulating energy.

By the same token, what Bella finds utterly inconceivable in this moment might be well within the realm of possibility in the not-so-distant future.

She'd witnessed wind chimes moving without the wind; had seen lights flicker and television stations change seemingly of their own accord.

Why is a text message any more miraculous?

She thinks of Candace and Tommy and their equipment. Maybe spirit energy harnessing electromagnetic communication makes as much sense as the necklace turning up at Valley View and Sam's apparition at the airport.

'Really? Come on. Occam's razor, Bella,' she mutters.

What's the simplest explanation for any of this?

That someone very much alive, hidden behind an unknown number, is playing a prank.

Ellipses wobble in the text window.

A new message pops up. *I can explain.*

'Oh, really?' she murmurs.

She knows better than to engage. Yet, for some reason, she finds it necessary to send a lengthy response, one that takes forever to type on her phone's small keyboard just using her thumb.

What is there to explain? You can't be Sam. Sam is dead.

Send. Done. Now she can walk away, except . . .

The dots are back, and curiosity gets the better of her. She waits for the next message.

When it comes, she rolls her eyes.

I'm not dead.

Ah, Lily Dale semantics. Dead isn't dead.

Who is this? she asks again.

As she hits Send, she hears footsteps in the hall.

Someone knocks on the door.

'Bella?' Grant calls. 'Are you in there?'

'Yes.'

'Is everything OK?'

She clears her throat. 'Everything's fine. I'll, um . . . I'll be right out.'

'Thanks. I've got something to discuss with you, and it, uh . . . it's not going to be easy.'

Five minutes later, seated across from Grant in the parlor, Bella grips the arms of the chair, fighting the urge to double over as though he's just punched her in the gut.

This is too much. First the string of text messages about Sam's faked death, and now Grant announcing that he's going to sell Valley View out from under her?

'I've tried to make it work, but no matter which way I run the numbers, it just doesn't. I'm so sorry,' he adds, like a doctor delivering grim news.

He meets her gaze and then he looks away. She realizes he's checking the mantel clock above her head, and then, almost imperceptibly, his watch.

Her mind flashes back to Dr Stacey Fischer, Sam's oncologist. She'd come so highly recommended, but Bella had disliked her from the start.

'It's twenty minutes slow,' she tells Grant.

'Excuse me?'

She points up at the clock. 'It's an antique. It loses a minute a day. I reset it at the beginning of every month.'

'Terrific. So it's like everything else in this house – broken and useless.'

'Not . . . everything. The . . . the shades are new, and . . . and that lamp,' she adds, looking wildly around the room in an effort to show Grant that he's wrong. 'It was broken, but Hugo fixed it. He's the electrician who rewired the walls and . . . and he helps me. So many people help me. We've done so much work here, and . . . and . . .'

She closes her mouth, unable to push another word past the massive ache in her throat.

Outside, thunder rumbles. Glancing at the window, she sees that the world beyond has gone murky, as if Grant's bombshell snuffed out the sun.

'Bella, you've done an amazing job here,' he's saying. 'Really. You've gone way above and beyond, and I'm not really sure why a young woman like you has been willing to stick it out for this long.'

He doesn't understand. Not at all. But if she tries to explain it now, she's going to cry.

Something tells her that Grant isn't a man who will anticipate a bout of tears in what he views as a business endeavor. Anyway, she'd promised Sam that she'd stay strong, and she's stayed true to her word through enough harrowing situations to last a lifetime. This one isn't life-or-death, and it's not going to be her undoing.

'I mean, it's pretty amazing, what you've done here. It's not even a labor of love for you like it is for me,' he goes on. 'You didn't even know Aunt Leona.'

How can she explain that she had? Maybe they hadn't met when Leona was alive, or since – certainly not in the woo-woo Lily Dale *Dead Isn't Dead* way. But Leona had loved this house and been as much a part of it as Bella is – and Nadine, and Pandora, too. They'd all left a part of themselves here, an imprint as intrinsic as the stone foundation and wrought-iron grillwork that crowns the mansard.

Grant takes a white handkerchief from his pocket and wipes the sheen of sweat from his handsome face.

Bella hears footsteps on the stairs: the St Clair sisters and Hester Garretson, coming down to breakfast.

'No, Opal, that isn't how it happened,' Ruby says. 'Mother and Clark Gable had their torrid affair long before Clark passed on.'

'Are you sure? I've always thought it was afterward.'

'I don't think so, dear. Hester, did we mention that we're from Akron?'

'You did.'

'And Clark's hometown was just a stone's throw away!'

'You mentioned that, too,' Hester tells Opal as the three women enter the parlor.

Grant gets to his feet. 'Good morning, ladies.'

'Why, here's Clark now,' Opal says. 'We'll just have to ask him when it was.'

'Clark? Goodness, no, dear, this isn't Clark. Clark has a mustache.'

Opal scans the room and spots Bella. 'You're right. And that's certainly not Mother.'

'Isn't it?' Ruby lifts the glasses that are on a chain around her neck, peering through them.

'That's not your mother. It's Bella!' Hester informs the sisters.

Bella nods and gives a little wave as they continue on into the breakfast room.

Grant looks at her. 'I can't believe what you have to put up with here.'

Again, he mops his face with the handkerchief.

She wants to tell him that she's charmed by the St Clair sisters
– by all the guests. That they keep things lively; that she enjoys
spending time with even the most eccentric among them.

Again, thunder rumbles in the distance. On its heels, in the back
of the house, a puppy lets out a loud bark.

'Was that a dog?' Grant asks.

Another bark, and Bella realizes that it wasn't a puppy. It was
the big guy.

'Yes,' she says. 'It was a dog.'

'You got a dog?'

'I've got four, at the moment. But it's only temporary.'

'Oh?'

'They're fosters.'

'Oh. Anyway . . . as I was saying, Valley View is my burden,
not yours. It isn't right for me to expect you to keep this crazy place
running and keep your life on hold indefinitely while I'm off living
mine. Especially *here*. Lily Dale is no place for a regular person to
live, and it's certainly no place for a child to grow up.'

'No!' she blurts.

'I know. And I'm sorry your son had to be exposed to—'

'That's not what I meant! Grant, Lily Dale is the perfect place
for a child to grow up. Max loves it, and so do I. It's been our home
for more than a year now.'

'Only by default, though, right? You didn't move here because
you wanted to. You were moving to Chicago when your car broke
down. Isn't that how it happened?'

'It is, technically, but . . .'

Bella had accepted Millicent's invitation to make a fresh start in
Chicago with great reluctance, convinced it was her only option.

Maybe it was, for the person she'd once been.

She's changed, and so has her mother-in-law.

Back then, Millicent was still earning Bella's private nickname
for her, Maleficent, and her Chicago penthouse wouldn't have been
a soft landing spot for a messy kindergartener.

These days, the place has seen its share of Lego blocks and grape
juice stains, and Millicent is positively Mellow-cent.

Maybe that's due to advancing age, or to finding love again.
Or perhaps losing her only child, Sam, had made his mother
reexamine her priorities. Whatever the reason, Bella is grateful for

her mother-in-law's new role in her life, and Max's, though she's no more interested in moving in with Millicent now than she had been last year.

'In any case,' Grant says, 'I'm sure you're eager to get on with your plan for Chicago.'

'Oh, I didn't really want to live there. It was only going to be . . .'

'Temporary?'

'Exactly.'

'I see. But so was this.'

Grant's words land with a thud.

'I was never planning to keep this place forever, Bella. My aunt wouldn't have expected me to. She knew this . . .' He waves a hand around the parlor. 'This isn't me. It isn't you, either. It's a good place for dusty antiques, dotty old ladies, and ghost hunters. But that's about it.'

'Did someone say ghost hunters?' a cheerful female voice says.

Bella turns to see Candace in the doorway.

Her smile fades as she takes in the scene. 'Am I interrupting something? Bella, are you OK?'

She nods, again trying to swallow the ache in her throat.

'You don't seem OK.' Candace turns to Grant. 'Sorry. When I heard you say ghost hunters, I figured you were talking about us.'

'You're a ghost hunter?' he asks.

'Candace. And this is Tommy,' she adds as her husband comes up behind her. 'We're the Specter Inspectors?'

Clearly, that means nothing to Grant, but he offers a handshake and says, 'I'm Grant Everard. I'm the . . . owner.'

'Of Valley View?'

'Yes.'

'I can't tell you how much we've loved being here,' Candace says. 'I was just telling Grant; I wish we could stay for a month.'

'You said you wished you could stay forever.'

'Well, that, too,' she agrees with her husband. 'I'd give anything to find a place like this in Southern California.'

'That's where you're from?' Grant asks.

'Yes.'

'I don't suppose you want to move here?'

'You mean to Lily Dale?' Tommy asks.

'I mean to Valley View. I've got to get rid of it.'

Get rid of it, like it's a soggy wad of chewed bubblegum.

Bella scowls. 'You do know that you can't sell it to just anyone, Grant?'

'I'm aware. It's going to take some time, I know, but—'

'I don't mean to interrupt,' Candace says, 'but – you're selling Valley View?'

Grant raises an eyebrow. 'I am.'

Candace looks at Tommy, who gives a little nod.

'What's your asking price, Mr Everard?'

'I haven't gotten that far. Why? Are you interested?'

'Absolutely. Right, honey?'

'Yes! It's perfect.'

'But there are restrictions!' Bella announces, hearing the panic edging into her voice. 'You have to be a spiritualist to get a leasehold in the Dale.'

'We are spiritualists,' Tommy assures her.

'But are you members of the Lily Dale Assembly?'

'We are,' Candace says. 'We joined a few years ago, when we were filming here.'

Bella's heart sinks. 'Well, you . . . you wouldn't be able to get a mortgage.'

'Not a problem,' Tommy says, mostly to Grant. 'How soon were you looking to sell?'

'As soon as possible.'

'But how can you live here? Don't you need to be in Hollywood, for your show?'

Bella's question comes out in a strangled cry, and they all turn to gape at her.

'*The Specter Inspectors* is shot on location, so we can live anywhere,' Candace tells her. 'This would be perfect, because—'

She breaks off at a loud knock on the front door.

Bella hears it open, and a man's voice calls, 'Mr Everard?'

'In here, Marty.'

A nervous-looking bald man appears in the doorway. He's wearing a suit and tie.

'I'm sorry to disturb you, sir, but if it's going to be awhile, I thought maybe I should leave and come back?'

'Not much longer. Why? Is everything OK out there?'

'Yes, but, uh . . .' Marty glances around uncomfortably. 'I'd rather wait somewhere else, if you don't mind.'

'I thought you'd be better off in the car in the air conditioning.'

'I thought so, too, but I keep getting, uh . . .'

When he doesn't go on, Grant prods him. 'You keep getting . . . what?'

'Propositioned!' Marty blurts. 'I mean, you get used to that kind of thing when you're working a job in the city, but *here*?'

'What do you mean?' Grant asks. 'Propositioned by who?'

'Prostitutes!'

'*Prostitutes!*' Bella gapes at him. 'What are you talking about?'

'Don't play dumb with me. I'm onto you people.'

'But . . . there aren't any prostitutes here.'

'The place is crawling with them,' Marty insists. 'The first one told me that she's booked but she wants to set me up with her friend Misty, and now another one comes along wearing this getup like she's about to do the Dance of the Seven Veils.'

'Maybe it was Salome's spirit?' Candace suggests.

'She was no ghost. She told me she used to be the mistress here, and she offered to, uh . . . "cleanse my chakras".'

'Wait – did she have a British accent?' Bella asks.

'Yes.'

The front door opens again, and as if on cue, a voice calls, 'Isabella?'

'That's her!' Marty looks around as if for a place to hide.

'What's going on?' Grant asks Bella.

'It's just Pandora.'

'Pandora! That's her! Why is she following me?'

'Relax, Marty. She's a medium, not a prostitute, unless . . .' Grant raises an eyebrow at Bella. 'Wait, she's not, is she?'

'Of course not,' Bella assures him, and calls, 'Pandora? We're in here.'

'Just a moment, Isabella. I'm disrobing.'

'Disrobing!' Marty shrinks back against the wall. 'I thought I was clear when I told her I'm a happily married man, but she's obviously got the wrong idea.'

Pandora sails into the room, wearing one of her usual floral print dresses. 'Isabella, I'm wondering if I might ask your advice about—'

She stops short, noticing the others.

'Hi, Pandora,' Grant says.

'Hello, Mr Everard. I do hope you're well.'

'I am, I am. Marty here tells us you offered to cleanse his chakras?'

'Yes, I rather sensed a blockage and had hoped to free his energy.'

Marty turns and makes a beeline for the door, telling Grant, 'I'll be out in the car.'

'If you change your mind, Mr Kowalski, I'm right across the way, as I said, at Cotswold Corner. I take walk-ins, but it's always best to call ahead.' She glances at Candace and Tommy. 'I don't believe we've met. I'm Pandora Feeney.'

'I'm Tommy, she's Candace. Now, Mr Everard, as I was saying, if you're trying to find a a buyer for this place, look no further.'

Pandora gasps. 'A *buyer*? For *Valley View*?'

Bella nods glumly. 'Grant is going to sell it.'

'And we're going to buy it!' Candace announces.

'And do what with it?' Pandora asks.

'Live here. What else?'

'You're going to run a guesthouse? Ah, your television program has hit the skids, has it? I'm afraid every star loses its luster sooner or later,' she adds with a dark gleam in her eye, undoubtedly thinking of her ex-husband Orville.

'We're not going to run a guesthouse,' Tommy says. 'It will be our home.'

'But what about Isabella and the lad?'

Candace and Tommy exchange a glance.

'Well, it's not like we're moving in tomorrow,' Candace tells Bella. 'You and your family will have plenty of time to find a new place to live.'

'This won't do,' Pandora informs them. 'It won't do at all. You can't just barge into Valley View and wrangle it away from us!'

Grant clears his throat. 'With all due respect, Pandora, you don't live here anymore, and I've never lived here and never will, and they' – he indicates Candace and Tommy – 'would love to live here, so—'

'But Isabella *does* live here!' Pandora says. 'This is her home – and her business. She's done a brilliant job of keeping it up. You can't just—'

'Pandora,' Bella cuts in. 'Thank you, but he *can* just . . .' She turns to Grant. 'I'm sorry for all this. I understand. I do. If you hadn't already made this decision, you would have as soon as you saw the spreadsheet. I should have seen it coming, but then, I'm not a medium. I'm just a normal person, like you said.'

'Bella, it didn't even occur to me that you might want to stay on here,' he says. 'Are you interested in buying it?'

She shakes her head.

'I can't. I'm . . . I'm not a spiritualist. But it's OK. Really. Max and I will be fine, wherever we end up.'

'Isabella—'

'Pandora, please don't.' She shakes her head and turns toward the stairs. 'Sorry, if you'll excuse me . . .'

She makes a run for the stairs, determined not to let them see her cry.

NINETEEN

Small and on the dilapidated side, even as Lily Dale cottages go, Calla's home lies on the Dale's wooded perimeter. As far as Odelia's concerned, it's a bit too far off the beaten path, but her granddaughter claims that she enjoys the seclusion.

'I'm a writer, Gammy. Writers need to be alone.'

'You managed to crank out your first novel when you lived with Jacy.'

'Jacy was in med school and then doing his residency. I was even more alone then than I am now.'

'But I didn't worry about you then the way I do now, because I knew someone was there to . . . well, to . . .'

'Don't you dare say to take care of me, Gammy. I don't need a man for that. I'm perfectly capable of taking care of myself.'

That conversation had taken place a few weeks ago. Odelia had interpreted her granddaughter's independent streak as a sign that she wouldn't be jumping back into a relationship any time soon.

Maybe she'd been wrong.

Climbing the porch steps, careful not to catch her foot on a loose tread, she notes that the large potted begonia she'd given Calla earlier in the summer has withered in its plastic garden center pot.

'I'll do my best to keep it alive, Gammy,' she'd said, 'but you know I don't have your green thumb.'

'You don't need a green thumb. All you have to do is water it.'

Odelia dumps her own half-finished bottle into the plant and hesitates with her fist poised over the wooden door, about to knock.

What if Calla is still sleeping? She often wakes up early to write, but just as often seems to write until dawn and then sleep until noon. If this is one of those days, she won't be pleased to find her grandmother on her doorstep. She may not be pleased to see her either way.

Odelia probably should have thought things through before showing up uninvited so early in the morning, but her impulsivity sometimes gets the better of her.

Should she go back home and wait until a more reasonable hour to—

The door opens. 'Gammy?'

Calla's hair is pulled back in a messy ponytail, and she's wearing shorts and a tank top. Odelia can't tell whether she's fully clothed and wide awake, squinting because of the bright morning light, or if she'd slept in that outfit and is blinking the sleep from her eyes.

Odelia greets her with a cheery, 'Good morning.'

'What are you doing here in . . . that?' Calla gestures, and Odelia remembers that she's the one who'd slept in her outfit.

'I thought we could have a nice chat over coffee in our pajamas, just like the old days,' she says, wishing she'd thought to bring along some of that sauerkraut cake, because Calla doesn't look convinced.

'Why are you really here, Gammy?'

'Because you're my granddaughter and I love you.'

'And you're my grandmother and I love you,' Calla says with a sigh, 'but you need to tell me what's going on.'

'What do you mean?'

Calla rolls her eyes. 'Really? Are we going to do this?'

'Do what?'

'Pretend this is just a friendly little visit?'

'What else would it be?'

Calla sighs. 'Come on in, Gammy.'

Odelia steps past Calla into the cottage.

It's small – just one level, with a living area, bedroom, kitchen and bath. She sees an open laptop and cup of coffee on Calla's oversized writing desk, which faces the window.

Li'l Chap trots in from the kitchen, tail crooked high in the air, and nuzzles his face against Odelia's ankles.

She bends to scoop the purring kitten into her arms. 'At least someone's happy to see me,' she says. 'I miss you, too, little fellow. Things aren't the same without you around the house.'

'You need to get a cat, Gammy,' Calla says. 'And I'd be happier to see you if I didn't know exactly why you're here. I've told you a million times, I don't want to talk about this with you.'

'Talk about what?'

'Blue.'

Odelia raises an eyebrow. 'What makes you think I'm here about him?'

'Walter texted me last night.'

Oh. Walter. For a moment there, she'd attributed it to Calla's mediumship or an educated guess.

'What did he say?'

'That he was sorry if he'd caused any trouble between us. He said Peter had told him what I said about the Slaytons selling their house, and that when he mentioned it to you, you got all bent out of shape.'

'Bent out of shape?' Odelia is indignant. 'He told you I was all bent out of shape?'

'Actually, not in those words, but—'

'I barely even batted an eye!'

'Gammy. Come on.'

'All right, maybe I *batted* an *eye*, but only because I was surprised that you'd told Walter and not me.'

'I told Peter.'

'Peter, Walter . . .' Odelia waves a hand in the air. 'Why didn't you mention any of this to *me*?'

'Because it didn't come up.'

'And it came up in your conversation with Peter?'

'Yes. He asked me if I'd seen Blue when I was in New York, because he'd heard that he was staying in their apartment there.'

'And . . . is he?'

'Yes.'

'You knew that when you went there?'

'It was a business trip, Gammy. I registered for this conference a year ago, way before Blue and I ever got back together and broke up. It had nothing to do with him. Anyway, he's been through so much lately, with all the publicity surrounding his father. David really destroyed both their lives.'

'You don't have to tell me. I know.'

'Right. Well, anyway, he's thinking of taking a job in London.'

'London!' Odelia sinks into the nearest chair, imagining Calla living across the ocean, instead of across the Dale. 'But London is so far away.'

'That's the point. Blue wants to get out of the country until everything dies down. Or for good.'

'And you're going with him.'

'What? No!' Calla gapes at her. 'Why would I go with him?'

'You wouldn't?'

'Gammy, didn't I just tell you I need to be on my own for a while?'

'Well, yes, but you and Blue seem to be—'

'*Friends*. We're just friends. Just like me and Jacy.' She gives a little laugh. 'I don't know what's wrong with me, but I can't seem to cut my exes out of my life forever, like you did with my grandfather.'

'There's nothing wrong with you. It's probably healthier to do it your way. I just wish you'd told me.'

'About seeing Blue? Yeah, no. No way. I can't even bring up his name without you freaking out, and – oh, Gammy, he wants you to let him go.'

'Let him go? I'm not the one who's holding on to—'

'I mean Li'l Chap!' Calla says with a laugh, pointing at the wriggly kitty on Odelia's lap. 'His claws are out, and I don't want you to get hurt.'

'Ah. That's exactly it, Calla. I don't want you to get hurt, either.'

'Clever. I see what you did there, Gammy.'

Odelia sets Li'l Chap on the floor, where he chases something only he can see, as felines tend to do. She smiles fondly, remembering her own late great cat, Gert.

'Why can't you just trust me to make good decisions, Gammy?' Calla asks.

'Trust you . . .' Odelia tilts her head, pondering the phrase. 'No, that's not it.'

'I feel like that's exactly it. You think I'm still the same person I was when I was seventeen, and that I'm going to—'

'No, Calla, what I mean is, I came over here to talk to you because I believed Spirit was warning me that you had betrayed my trust, but—'

'What do you mean?'

'Do you remember how you thought I'd fainted yesterday?'

'When we were on the porch together? You did.'

'I don't know if I actually fainted, but I do know that that was when Spirit first reached out to me with that message.'

Calla's eyes widen. 'You're kidding. That's exactly when . . . wait a second, Gammy, why would you even think that warning was about *me*?'

'Heat exhaustion?'

Calla narrows her eyes.

She tries again. 'Because you were there?'

'Those aren't good reasons. I can't believe you think I'd betray you.'

'Not *just* you. And it's the truth. You were there. So was Pandora – I saw her out in front of her house. I also considered that it might be about her. She and I have our issues, but I don't think Spirit was referring to her, either.'

'What was the message, exactly?'

'"Don't trust her."'

'OK, this is going to sound crazy, Gammy, but I got a similar message from my guides around the same time.'

'When we were on the porch?'

'Yes. It was a warning about an untrustworthy woman.'

'Why didn't you mention it?'

'Because I thought . . . well, I thought . . .'

'You thought it was about me?'

'Yes.'

'Calla! How could you—'

'Um, you were there? Heat exhaustion?' Calla shrugs.

'Touché.'

Thunder rumbles outside.

'It's going to rain,' Calla says. 'You should get home.'

'In a minute. First, tell me if you were having a text exchange with Blue Slayton yesterday when you were at my house?'

'What? No! Why would you—'

'You seemed so captivated by it. I just assumed . . .'

'Gammy, it was an agent I met at the conference. I had told him about this idea I have, and . . .' She shrugs. 'He wanted to hear more.'

'An idea for a new novel?'

'For a new book, but I really don't want to get into that right now.'

'This isn't your love life, it's your career. You can share. Maybe I can offer some sage advice from an old lady.'

'You're not an old lady.'

'That's not what you said yesterday. At my age—'

'Sorry, Gammy. I just worry about you.'

'And I worry about you. Let me help.'

'I don't think you can. I just need to figure out what I want.'

'You want to be a writer. It's the only thing you ever wanted.'

'No, I know, and I still do want to write. Just not the book everyone seems to want from me. My agent said my readers are expecting another novel like the first one and the one I just finished. And my editor said it has to be different enough to be different' – she wags finger quotes in the air – 'but similar enough to be exactly the same. Does that make any sense to you, Gammy?'

'Of course. It's all anyone ever wants, isn't it?'

'In a book?'

'In a book, in a relationship, in a day . . . if it was a good one, we want the next one to be the same as the last, but just different enough to keep things interesting.'

Calla digests that. 'Sometimes, you really are wise.'

'I am, aren't I.' Odelia smiles.

'Anyway, my agent and editor and I agreed to disagree and part ways. And I've been going back and forth with this other agent who likes my idea, and he might want to represent me. We have a call scheduled for nine. I've been up since four, trying to pull together notes for the book idea.'

'What's it about?'

Calla winces. 'I knew you were going to ask that. I'm not sure you'll approve.'

'Is it about the Slaytons?'

'What? No! It's about Lily Dale.'

'So it's . . . New Age? Historical?'

'I'm not sure yet what it *is*, but I know what it *isn't*. I have to trust my instincts. And speaking of trust – I think I know who Spirit was warning us about,' Calla says. 'She was right there when we were on the porch.'

'Pandora?'

'No! The woman on my flight. The one from Chicago.'

Yes. The one who'd checked into Valley View.

TWENTY

Safely behind closed doors in the Rose Room, Bella grabs the tissue box from the nightstand and plunks herself down on the window seat, ready to let the tears flow.

Beyond the screens, rain is falling softly, pattering through the trees. But somehow, the deluge that had swamped Bella's eyes just moments ago seems to have evaporated.

It's just as well. A good cry might be cathartic for a few minutes, but it won't change her predicament. She can't prevent Grant from selling Valley View any more than she was able to prevent their landlord from selling the building back in Bedford after Sam died.

She's going to be homeless again, and jobless.

'Really?' She shakes her head. *'Really?'*

How is this even possible? How is it fair?

Fair? You know better than that, Bella Blue. Life isn't fair. If it were, we'd still be together, raising our boy.

It's exactly what Sam would say if he were here. That, and *stay strong*.

'I will,' she whispers. 'Just like I promised.'

A strong person doesn't allow things to happen to her. She makes things happen.

She puts aside the tissue box, stands, and starts pacing. There must be some way to preserve her home, and her livelihood. It can't be impossible.

All right, then, what are your options?

First, and most obvious: persuade Grant not to sell.

But why wouldn't he? He's got qualified buyers ready to make an offer.

Forget option number one.

Option number two: convince Candace and Tommy to buy Valley View as a guesthouse instead of a private residence, to pay Bella to keep managing it, and allow her to keep living here free of charge.

Scratch option number two. This is their dream house. Why would they share it with Bella, Max, a couple of cats and a horde of strangers?

What she needs is an idea that doesn't hinge on other people's actions. She has to take charge of the situation and do whatever it would take to keep Valley View as her home *and* as an income-generator.

Whatever it would take?

It would take buying the place herself.

OK, so that's option number three – and the only one that's viable.

But is it?

She'd have to find a way around the Dale's real-estate requirements. She might even have to become a spiritualist.

And she'd have to come up with a large sum of money, very quickly. But how?

Her debt load and credit score ensure that no bank would ever give her a loan.

She'd need to win the lottery, or Max needs to find that pirate treasure he's always hunting in the backyard, or . . .

She remembers the hefty check Millicent had given her.

What if . . .?

'No!'

It's out of the question. That money is for Max. For his college education.

Still . . .

If Millicent knew what was going on, she'd probably tell Bella to use the money to secure their future at Valley View, and then, when the guesthouse is consistently turning a profit, pay it back into the college fund.

When *it's turning a profit? Don't you mean* if*?*

It's a mighty big *if*, at that.

But the longer she lives here, the more she believes in its potential. This is the largest and most alluring guesthouse in the area, always fully booked in the summer. The key is to lure guests in the off-season; to make Valley View a destination in and of itself.

That means funneling more time and money into advertising and marketing and into the four R's: restoration, renovation, repairs and replacements. Bella's never been able to get Grant fully on board, but if *she* had the freedom to make the big decisions, without interference from an unenthusiastic absentee owner . . .

I can do it. I know I can make this into a successful business.

If only Millicent would return her call. This can't wait until after she's back from her honeymoon. Candace and Tommy are willing to make a deal with Grant *now*.

Bella goes over to her jewelry box to find the check. Lifting the lid, she expects to see the envelope right on top where she'd left it.

It isn't here.

How can that be? She clearly remembers taking it from the study, worried it might blow off the desk in the breeze from the fan, or that someone would steal it. Thinking it would be safer in her jewelry box, she'd brought it right upst—

No, that's not right.

She'd been *about* to do that when Grant showed up.

Reaching into her back pocket, she finds the envelope and heaves a sigh of relief.

She quickly takes out the check and unfolds it.

It's made out to *Isabella Jordan* in her mother-in-law's perfect penmanship.

Does it make sense to save the money for something her son can't even use for another decade when he's about to lose the roof over his head today? Isn't it up to Bella to ensure that he has the bare necessities?

Millicent would be none the wiser if she borrowed it, just temporarily.

Neither would Max.

Anyway, it's *his* money, and Bella is certain that he'd want her to do anything in her power to keep them here.

Really? A seven-year-old is capable of rationalizing that decision?

Of course not.

She pictures Max, at eighteen, storming out of her life upon discovering that his education has come to a screeching halt because Bella had absconded with the tuition money Sam's mother had so generously provided.

This should be enough for Max to go wherever he chooses.

'It will be,' she promises Millicent.

She folds the check, puts it into the jewelry box, and closes the lid with a thud.

Using it for anything but Max's college fund is out of the question.

'It'll be OK. Just keep thinking,' she tells the woman in the bureau mirror, who gazes back so bleakly that Bella turns away.

Her gaze falls on her phone, still on the bed where she'd tossed it when Grant knocked.

She walks over, picks it up, and finds that there's a new message from Unknown.

It's Sam.

It's a response to the question she'd asked right before she'd gone downstairs: *Who is this?*

'You aren't Sam,' she mutters, and starts typing again.

Leave me alone.

As soon as she hits Send, she regrets it. She knows better than to engage.

Oh, well. Maybe Unknown gave up on her and won't even see it.

But three pulsating dots appear instantaneously, confirming that her anonymous texter is still lurking like a bully in an alley.

'Never let him know he's getting to you,' she'd counseled Max and Jiffy when that boy at school was picking on them. 'That's what he wants. Just ignore him. Turn your back and walk away. He'll get bored and move on.'

Jiffy had shaken his head. 'Kevin Beamer never gets bored and moves on. He always thinks up more mean stuff to do.'

Wait a minute. Kevin . . . Beamer?

Before she can focus on that, a follow-up message comes in: *Bella, it's Sam. I swear.*

'No,' she mutters. 'No way. You're not Sam. Sam is dead.'

Another message whooshes in, as if this person can see and hear her, alone in this empty room.

Please believe me.

She shakes her head, typing *No*, and sending it.

It's just kids, goofing around – the modern equivalent of a crank phone call. Thanks to modern technology, there's a sure way to put an end to this. All she has to do is block incoming texts from this person.

'Then why don't you?' she asks herself aloud, though she knows the answer.

A part of her – a lonely, foolish, wistful part of her; a remnant of the old, fragile Bella – wants to believe that it really is Sam.

Not just here, now, on the other end of the phone, but Sunday morning at the airport, too.

Sam's apparition. Sam's spirit.

A year of living in Lily Dale will do that to a person, she supposes. It will allow you to entertain the idea that the soul outlasts the body and that anyone – any old person, even Bella Jordan – really can communicate with a lost loved one.

It would be so comforting to think that she really has finally figured out how to breach the gap between this world and the next.

Comforting?

It would be sheer lunacy.

About to block the message-sender, she sees that there's another new text from him.

How can I convince you?

Ah, that's easy.

You can't.

A moment passes.

Another.

She exhales.

Then he's typing again, this depraved stranger who wants to hurt her; this creep who's trying to undercut every hard-won shred of healing in her soul.

She writes, *Stop*.

She hits Send. Her message crisscrosses with an incoming one. Her breath catches in her throat.

I was at the airport on Sunday.

'What?' she whispers, shaking her head. 'How do you know that?'

Another message has already rocketed in.

You saw me. You both did. You and Max.

She'd told no one other than Drew and Odelia. Neither of them would dream of doing something like this to her. Not in a trillion years. And there's no way anyone else can possibly—

'Jiffy.'

Of course.

Jiffy, who'd told Drew.

Jiffy, who'd insisted he doesn't have his phone.

Jiffy, who's downstairs with her son at this very moment.

It doesn't feel like something a seven-year-old would do.

But this is Jiffy. He has a genius IQ, has her phone number, and is undoubtedly tech-savvy enough to conceal his.

She hurries from the room, remembering to lock the door behind her this time.

When she reaches the first floor, the parlor is empty. Good. The last thing she wants is to be dragged back into Grant's conversation with Candace and Tommy about their impending purchase of Valley View.

They can't have come to terms so quickly. They must have moved the discussion elsewhere – probably the study, as the French doors are closed, but now isn't the time to investigate. Now is the time to catch Jiffy Arden red-handed.

A new message has come in, beneath the one about Sam at the airport.

You can't deny it. You know you saw me, Bella.

She pauses to ask: *Your ghost?*

Jiffy, like anyone here in the Dale, will bristle at the wording. How many times has he said, 'By the way, Bella, it's not *ghost*. It's *Spirit*.'

As the dots again begin to pulsate in the message window, she scurries on toward the back of the house. Past the breakfast room where the guests are chattering; past the dining room, where Chance and Spidey are sitting on the window seat, watching the rain; past the mudroom, where the pups are quiet.

Another message: *Not my ghost.*

Ah, he's still typing, undoubtedly, about to reprimand her phrasing. It's *Spirit*.

Approaching the kitchen, she hears Jiffy, sotto voce: 'Because you can't tell your mom, Max! It's a private secret!'

Bella's stomach flip-flops. It's one thing for Jiffy to send those texts, thinking it's a harmless practical joke, but her own son? Max should know better.

She glances down at her phone to ensure that Jiffy's still in the midst of typing. Yes. The dots are there.

Stepping over the threshold into the kitchen, she finds the boys sitting at the table, right where she left them. Their cereal bowls are now empty.

So are Jiffy's hands.

She exhales. He doesn't have his phone. He's not texting her. But someone is.

She looks down just as a new message pops up from Unknown. *I'm not dead. I'm alive.*

TWENTY-ONE

Odelia rounds the corner onto South Street, walking toward home as quickly as she can in her heeled slippers. It hadn't been raining quite this hard when she'd left Calla's.

'Gammy, let me drive you,' Calla had said. 'It'll take two minutes.'

Odelia wouldn't hear of it. She'd told Calla to go back to preparing for her call with the prospective new agent.

'What about Bella? We have to tell her—'

'I'll handle it. You just focus on what you have to do to land a new agent. And find out if he represents cookbooks,' she'd added.

She really doesn't mind walking in the rain – not at this time of year, anyway. It's a bit of a drag on a bone-chilling March day, but today she hopes it might cool things off. So far, it seems to be ramping up the humidity and turning to steam on what little pavement the Dale has to offer. At least her garden will get a nice soaking.

Up ahead, she sees Roxy in the little gatehouse. Things are quiet this morning, though visitor traffic will likely pick up when the rain subsides.

Roxy has her nose in a book and doesn't see Odelia until she knocks on the window.

She lets out a startled gasp, revealing a wad of pink bubblegum. 'Odelia! What are you doing?'

'Walking home from Calla's.'

'In the rain? And geez, what is up with people today? First Pandora comes along looking like a mummy, then some guy wants to play twenty questions with me, and now you show up looking like Alabama Beggs.' She snaps her gum.

'Wow, Roxy, that's—'

'No! Don't say it.'

'Don't say what?'

'Pandora told me that "chewing gum is a revolting habit for a dignified young lady",' she says in a near-perfect imitation of the woman.

'Oh, well, you know . . . *Pandora*.' Odelia rolls her eyes. 'I figured you're just making up for lost time now that you finally got your braces off.'

Roxy flashes a straight white grin. 'Exactly.'

'What I was going to say was, if you know Alabama Beggs, you must be reading *Save Me the Waltz*.'

Roxy holds up the Zelda Fitzgerald novel, using her finger as a bookmark. 'How'd you know?'

'Calla must have read it a dozen times when she was your age.'

'This is her copy. She loaned it to me. Did you ever read it?'

'No, but Zelda and F. Scott touch in at the Stump from time to time.'

'I wish I could see them.'

'How are your mediumship lessons going?'

'Not great. My mom says that at my age, I've probably got too many other things on my mind to be able to focus on Spirit. But the next time Zelda touches in, tell her I'm a fan, will you?' Roxy blows a bubble and snaps it between her teeth. 'Oh! Speaking of fans, guess who showed up here this morning? All About Eve!'

'Bette Davis?'

'Huh?'

'You said *"All About Eve"*,' Odelia reminds her. 'I assumed that was a clue, so I guessed Bette Davis. She played Margot Channing.'

'She's an actress?'

'Was. She touches in at the Stump, too. But you weren't talking about her, were you?'

'No, it was Eve.'

'Of Adam and Eve?' No wonder. Biblical spirits aren't her thing.

'Of All About Eve! She's an Influencer. Wait, I'll show you.' Roxy pulls out her phone, opens an app, and gasps. 'Ooh! She's posting from the Dale!'

Roxy holds up the phone, careful to keep it dry beneath the gatehouse overhang. Odelia leans in to see a silent video of a bored-looking young woman against a backdrop of familiar green frond-patterned wallpaper.

'That's the Jungle Room at Valley View! Roxy, was this Eve person driving a white Chevy with Massachusetts license plates?'

'No, she was in a black SUV with a chauffeur.'

'Ah – she was with Grant Everard?'

'Yes, but I know the woman in the white Chevy. The one with the gold glitter manicure, right?'

'I don't know about that, but she got here yesterday?'

'That's her. Her nails were awesome. I asked her if she'd gotten them done around here, and she said no, and then we got to talking about her trip, and I said I've always wanted to do that.'

'Do what?'

'Drive across the whole country.'

Odelia frowns. 'Is that what she told you she was doing?'

'Uh-huh. She started in Boston and she's on her way to LA.'

That woman isn't on a cross-country road trip if she'd connected from Chicago to Calla's flight from New York. Odelia has no idea why anyone would lie about something like that, but she's now certain that Spirit's warning had been about her.

'What else did she say?' she asks Roxy.

'Nothing, really. She just asked me for directions to Valley View and that was it. Why?'

'Just wondering.'

'It's so funny. You're the second person to ask about her this morning,' she adds, setting her book aside as a car turns from Dale Drive into the entrance.

'Who was the other person?'

'Twenty Questions guy.'

'Is he an influencer?'

'No, just some random guy who wanted to know a lot of stuff.'

'Like what?' Odelia asks, well aware that she's blocking the car's path to Roxy's window and holding up a finger to indicate that she won't be long.

'Like Valley View, mostly. He asked me if I know Bella and Max, and when I said I know them and I babysit Max, he asked what that's like – if he's a good kid, and if Bella's nice . . . that kind of thing.'

The waiting driver, one in a carload of women, sticks her head out the window. 'We're trying to get to the Specter Inspectors' paranormal equipment presentation!'

Odelia considers waiting so that she can ask Roxy to elaborate, but it's raining harder now and she's getting drenched. She can dry off and come back.

She hurries toward home, doing her best to camouflage her cleavage in bedraggled pink boa and hoping her nightie isn't transparent when wet.

She's on Cottage Row when a car splashes up behind her. She

steps off to the side of the road so that she won't be splashed when it passes, but it slows, and she hears a wolf whistle. Whirling, she sees a familiar SUV with Luther behind the wheel.

'Hop in!' he calls and leans over to open the passenger's side door for her. 'Where are you coming from?'

'Calla's,' she says as she closes the umbrella and climbs in beside him. 'What are you doing here?'

'Bella called me.'

'What happened? Is she OK?'

'She is, but she wanted me to look into something for her.'

'The woman from Chicago?'

'No, the robbery at Misty's. What woman from Chicago?'

'What robbery at Misty's?' she asks, simultaneously.

'She told Bella a couple of things were stolen.'

'Last night?'

'No, sometime over the weekend, apparently. Why are you out and about so early? And why are you wearing a skimpy nightie?'

'Because it's too hot for flannel, of course. Why are *you* wearing a suit at this hour?'

'I just came from an all-night security gig, remember? Tell me what's going on.'

She gives him a capsulized version as they bump and splash along Cottage Row.

'Maybe Calla got it wrong,' he suggests. 'Maybe this woman's connecting flight was from Boston and not Chicago.'

'Even if that was the case, she told Roxy she was driving cross-country, not flying. And who is this Twenty Questions guy, asking about her and Bella and Max?'

'Maybe Roxy got it wrong.'

'Luther! Why are you being so difficult?'

'I'm just trying to be reasonable.'

'Well, you're being *un*reasonable, because nobody got anything wrong. Roxy and Calla and I – and Spirit – got it right. I'm going to give Bella a heads-up that that woman's up to something, and I think you'd better figure out what it is. And if you don't, I think I see someone who will,' she says, spotting Lieutenant John Grange's car parked in front of Misty's.

'That's strange. Bella said she wasn't going to report the robbery.'

'Maybe she got it wrong.'

'Why are you being so difficult?' Grinning, he pulls up in front of Odelia's cottage. 'Want to come over to Misty's with me?'

'Dressed like this?'

'You're right. We don't need Grange to see you in your sexy nightie and get any ideas.'

'As *if.*' She opens her door and steps out into the rain.

Luther also gets out, pulling on a belted raincoat and grabbing a big wooden-handled umbrella from the back seat.

Of course he'd been prepared for the weather; of course she hadn't. On days like this, she wonders how they've made the relationship work for this long.

As he holds the open umbrella over her head and walks her up to the porch, she notices that the SUV that had been parked in front of Valley View is still there with the driver, Marty, inside. So is the white Chevy, which she points out to Luther. 'That's her car. You've got connections in law enforcement. Can you run the plate or something?'

'I'll see what I can find out after I go to Misty's. Hey, don't you think you should keep that locked, under the circumstances?' he asks as Odelia opens the front door.

'I should probably do a lot of things that I don't do.' She steps into the house. 'For now, I think I'll just make some coffee and get dressed.'

'Oh, don't do that.' He flashes a sly grin.

'No coffee? That's right, you said you've had enough,' she says, just as slyly, before closing the door.

She doesn't lock it – mostly out of sheer obstinance, but also because the Dale is a safe place, all things considered.

Catching a glimpse of herself in the full-length hall mirror, she decides that she doesn't look half bad – for her age, as her grand-daughter might say.

Sensing disapproval from Miriam, whose spirit is hovering by the stairs, Odelia says, 'Oh, don't worry. I'm not going to make a habit of parading around town in my nightie. But it's fun to keep Luther on his toes, isn't it?'

In the kitchen, she measures coffee grounds into a filter and adds a shake of cinnamon and a smidge of cayenne pepper. Not as much as usual, because Luther doesn't appreciate the spicy kick in his caffeine fix as much as she does.

She stands at the sink filling the carafe with water, gazing out the window at the rain. Thunder grumbles as the wet wind stirs tree branches in her yard. Beyond, the gray sky hangs low over the choppy gray lake. Rarely does one need a watering cans or garden hose here in Lily Dale. Mother Nature usually keeps the grass and flowers sufficiently watered.

'Always a silver lining,' Odelia tells Miriam, though she seems to have faded away.

Too bad Li'l Chap isn't still here. He'd perched on the windowsill whenever it stormed, as mesmerized by the raindrops as he is by birds and butterflies on nice days.

You need to get a new cat.

When Calla had made the comment, it had been lost on her. Now, she considers the idea. By the time she's poured the water into the coffee maker and pressed Start, she's decided it's a good one. It would be nice to have someone other than Spirit hanging around the house on a daily basis.

Turning her attention to her cell phone, she googles 'All About Eve Influencer' and is instantly rewarded. The young woman seems to be very famous indeed, though Odelia has to install an app and create an account in order to see her posts.

She's in the midst of doing just that when the front door opens, and Luther calls, 'I'm back!'

'That was fast.' She meets him in the hall. 'What's going on over there?'

'As far as I could tell before Grange kicked me out, she called him this morning when she realized that Jiffy's video game console is missing.'

'How did she not know that sooner? He plays with it constantly.'

'It disappeared overnight, apparently. She seemed pretty agitated. Meanwhile, that white Chevy turns out to be a rental.'

'You already ran the plates?'

'I've got connections, but they're not *that* efficient. I just walked over and checked it out.'

'You can identify a rental car at a glance?'

'You can if you're in my line of work and know what to look for. While I was at it, I talked to a guy parked out in front of Valley View.'

'Marty?'

'You know him?'

'He's Grant's driver.'

'That's what he said, but . . .'

'You don't believe him?'

'He was pretty jumpy. When I asked him to roll down the window and tried to find out what he was doing there, he got all skittish.'

'Well, some people get nervous around cops.'

'I'm not a cop.'

She raises an eyebrow. 'You *were* a cop, and you look like a cop, and you act like a cop.'

'What do you mean?'

'You're wearing a suit and a trench coat and you're asking a lot of questions.'

'Huh. Maybe that's why Marty kept insisting that he hadn't done anything wrong. Anyway, I have to get back to the dogs, but I'll feel better if we go over to Valley View first and and . . . what was that?' he asks, as Odelia's phone chimes in her hand.

'I was waiting for this app to load so that I can watch a video.'

'What—?'

'Shh!'

The video launches. Now she can hear what the bored-looking young woman is saying.

Luther leans in over her shoulder. 'What is—?'

'Shhh!'

'. . . and, yeah, this place is the worst dump ever,' Eve is saying, 'and the town is super-creepy and it's full of looney losers who think they can talk to ghosts, and . . .'

'*Spirit*, not ghost,' Odelia mutters, glaring at her, 'and don't look now, but there's one right behind you.'

Luther glances over his shoulder.

'Not you. Eve.' She skips the video back a few seconds and replays it for Luther, pointing at the screen. 'See that, behind her?'

'The wallpaper?'

'The orb!'

'Where?'

'It's right there!'

'I don't see it.'

'Well, it's Nadine. She hangs around the Jungle Room. And she won't take kindly to this influencer calling her home a dump.'

'I'm sure she won't. Come on. Let's go talk to Bella about this woman from Boston.'

'Chicago.'

'Chicago.'

'All right. Just let me run upstairs and get dressed in something decent.'

'On one condition – I want to be around the next time you decide to put on something indecent. Deal?'

'Deal.'

She smiles. That man is most definitely on his toes.

Upstairs, she strips off the wet clothing. Wondering what to wear, she glances out of the window to see if it's still raining.

It is, though over in the park, the spirit world carries on as if it's a beautiful day. The phantom child swings from the invisible branch, the gentleman in the top hat reads about the *Titanic*, and the newsboys play catch.

Spotting another familiar figure, Odelia leans closer to the window, squinting, wishing she hadn't left her glasses downstairs.

Ah, yes. That does appear to be Sam Jordan, walking along with an open umbrella in one hand and a cell phone in the other.

TWENTY-TWO

'm not dead. I'm alive.

Bella stares at her phone, as furious at the person behind the texts as she is at herself.

There's a part of her that wants to believe that Sam isn't really dead. There are moments when her brain refuses to grasp that it had actually happened. When she wonders whether it had all been a terrible misunderstanding, a delusion, nightmare, because any of those possibilities seem more plausible than the shocking reality.

How could her strong, capable husband have gotten so terribly sick, without warning? How could he have vanished from her life in a matter of weeks?

Three months from diagnosis to death, spanning a season. Autumn.

It had always been her favorite time of year, especially when she was married and living cozily in Bedford with Sam and Max. Pumpkins on porches; vibrant mums in borders and baskets; a glorious foliage canopy overhead; the air thick with the scent of ripe fruit and fallen leaves and woodsmoke.

She'd seen it so differently when Sam was dying. *Everything* was dying. Overnight, vibrant leaves were withered brown, strewn across the landscape amid rotting apples; flowerbeds frost-blackened; mornings cold and dark; days ever shorter, days running out.

'Mom?'

Max's voice crashes into her memory, and she looks up from her phone to see him beside her.

'*Can* we?' he asks. 'Please?'

'Can you what?'

'Can me and Jiffy play with the dogs outside?'

'No, it's raining.'

'Jiffy says dogs love rainy days, right, Jiffy?'

'Yep, they do, Bella. Jelly's most favorite thing to do is roll around in mud puddles. And Max and me love to jump in them and pretend we're army guys landing in the ocean.'

'Yeah, it's so fun. Can we, Mom?'

Her phone vibrates with a new text from Unknown.

I needed you to think I was dead.

Her jaw drops.

'Can we, Bella?'

She stares at the phone.

I needed you to think I was dead.

'Mom, we want—'

'Bella, can we—'

'No!'

It comes out far more sharply than she ever speaks to them, and she glances up to find them gaping at her.

'Sorry, guys, I just . . . I, um . . . Why don't you go watch *Ninja Zombie Battle* on TV for a while? I . . . I have to do a few things.'

'*Yes!*' The boys fist-bump and race into the back parlor before she can remind them to clear their cereal bowls from the table. Ordinarily, she'd call them back to do it, or she'd do it herself before leaving the kitchen to hurry upstairs. And ordinarily, she'd check on the guests in the breakfast room to make sure everyone has what they need.

But ordinarily, she isn't in the midst of a text exchange with someone purporting to be her dead husband.

Rather, her husband who needed her to *think* he was dead?

At the top of the stairs, she sees that she'd left the door to the Rose Room ajar when she rushed out to confront Jiffy.

Chance is perched on the threshold, as if she'd been guarding it in Bella's absence. She greets Bella with an unblinking stare, or maybe a reproachful one.

'It's OK, sweetie,' Bella tells her softly. 'Everything's OK.'

The cat follows her into the room.

She closes the door behind her and sits on the bed. Chance hops up beside her. Not settling in for a nap, not nudging and purring, not wanting to play. Just there, warm, solid, protective, watchful, perhaps wary. As if she knows about the texts from Unknown that are wreaking havoc on Bella's emotions.

She rereads the latest message yet again.

Of course this isn't from Sam, because Sam isn't alive, although . . .

His being alive *would* provide a non-supernatural explanation for the airport, and the necklace.

A non-supernatural explanation that makes no sense whatsoever.

Still, Bella painstakingly types out a question with a trembly thumb: *Why would you do that?* She hits Send before she can change her mind.

The answer is prompt.

I got into trouble.

Another message pops up before she can respond – not that she knows what to say.

I borrowed money from the wrong people.

'What are you talking about?' she mutters. 'And how are you writing these so quickly on your phone?'

A lot of money.

Messages stack the window, one on top of another, so rapid-fire that he's either typing on a laptop, or dictating them.

I couldn't pay it back.

They were going to kill me.

It was the only way out.

'*What?*' she whispers. 'What are you saying?'

She waits for more. It doesn't come.

After a long pause, she clicks on the window. Her cursor blinks there, ready for her to start typing, as if this were an ordinary exchange.

As if she believes that the man she'd loved – the man who had been terrible at keeping secrets – had kept one so monumental, faking his death like a character in a movie.

Had Kevin Bacon ever portrayed someone who'd done that? Maybe that's—

Wait, that doesn't make sense. Not if that message had come from Sam's Spirit, as Odelia had said, and not Sam, still alive.

Does any of this make sense?

You can't solve a puzzle without all the pieces.

Bella has to keep him talking, whoever he is. She replaces the flashing cursor with a question.

What do you mean?

The response comes quickly.

We faked my death.

She flashes back to the events that have haunted her for nearly two years now.

The sudden onset of his symptoms – could he have faked them?

The diagnosis – had Dr Stacey Fischer been in on it? Was she even an oncologist?

The tests and hospitalizations – had they been elaborately staged?

Sam's transformation into a gaunt, ravaged shadow of himself – had it been an act?

That awful last day at his deathbed . . .

'I'll be with you . . . Promise me you'll . . . stay . . . strong . . .'

'I promise.'

Those were the last two words she'd ever said to him.

Until now, if she were to believe that he's alive and texting.

We faked my death.

'No. No, no, *no*!'

The man she'd loved would never have allowed her – allowed their child – to endure the worst pain imaginable.

Jaw set, she asks, *Who is we?*

She waits for a response.

I can't share that.

Stoic, Bella repeats the question.

I can't tell you. They saved my life.

You can't tell me? I'm your wife! she responds, as if it really is Sam sending these messages.

It can't be. It isn't.

I'm so sorry. I'll explain in person.

Really? In person? OK, now this is getting ridiculous.

When? she asks. *Where? How?*

First promise me you won't tell anyone.

Why?

For your own safety. And Max's.

She shakes her head. It's one thing for this person to toy with her. But to hint at danger, and invoke her son's name?

'No,' she mutters. 'No way.'

Bella is no longer interested in disengaging and walking away. Now she wants – needs – to know who's behind this.

They're watching. They're dangerous.

Who?

'Wait, I know . . . you can't tell me,' she says.

I can't tell you.

'Right. Of course you can't.'

They found out I'm alive.

He's still typing. She waits.

They want their money, Bella.

More typing.

If this is going where she suspects it is . . .

Can you help me?

Ah. So she'd been right.

Help you how?

No hesitation in the reply: *I need to give them the money.*

'Of course you do,' she mutters, and asks, *how much?*

Waiting for the response, she starts taking screenshots, capturing the messages all the way back to the beginning and saving them to her photos file. She has a feeling Luther is going to want to see them when she tells him about this.

A text pops up in response to her last question.

200.

Seeing the figure, she's taken aback.

Two hundred dollars?

She spells it out, just to be absolutely clear, though she already knows what's coming.

200K.

There it is. Two hundred *thousand* dollars. Precisely the amount of the check Millicent had given her.

Lily Dale. No coincidences. Right.

This isn't just kids – not even that bully, Kevin Beamer – playing a harmless prank. A kid wouldn't ask for *200K.*

Someone has been snooping around Valley View and knows about the check.

It's her own fault, she supposes, for leaving it right out in the open, under the paperweight in the study. At least now it's safely put away in her private quarters – which doesn't do her much good if she doesn't close and lock the door to the Rose Room.

But there's not much worth stealing in here. Her wallet, which she keeps in the top drawer of her bureau, holds her ID, her maxed-out credit cards, and very little cash.

The only thing of value in this room would be her gold and diamond wedding and engagement rings. A year into widowhood, she'd taken them off and put them away, thinking that she might one day give them to a daughter-in-law or granddaughter.

She hurries over to the bureau and opens the lid of her jewelry box. The envelope is right on top where she'd left it. There's the ring box, and yes, the rings are inside. Relieved, she puts it back . . .

Only to realize that something just as precious is missing: her tourmaline necklace.

TWENTY-THREE

'**B**etter lock the door,' Luther tells Odelia as they step out onto the porch.

She obliges without protest and quickly turns to scan the park across the way, looking for Sam Jordan's spirit.

When she'd glanced out the upstairs window, she'd been surprised to see him among the others. Then again, she supposed it would be a logical spot for his energy to linger, right there in Valley View's shadow. It's just that she doesn't often see apparitions of the recently departed.

Under ideal circumstances, she'd have attempted to channel his energy and see if she could get him to expand on his message for Bella, but that would have to wait. Her priority is to let Bella know that there's something duplicitous about the woman staying under her roof.

Odelia had been in such a hurry to get dressed that she'd failed to note that unlike the other regulars who haunt the park, Sam hadn't been oblivious to the downpour. No, he'd been walking under an umbrella, and wearing a raincoat and looking at a cell phone. When she looked out the window again to confirm it, he'd vanished.

There's no sign of him now, either, as she and Luther hurry next door to Valley View beneath Luther's umbrella. Nor is there any sign of Marty in the black SUV.

'If he was Grant's driver, then Grant must have left,' she tells Luther, relieved.

But when they walk into the guesthouse, Grant is in the entrance hall, talking on his cell phone.

Pandora Feeney is there, too, pawing through the garments hanging on the coat tree by the door.

'Luther! Splendid! I'm in need of a brolly, and here you are with your massive one.'

He blinks and looks at Odelia.

She shrugs and echoes, '*Brolly?*'

'Yes, you see, this simply won't do.' She waves a bright yellow, child-sized umbrella imprinted with ninja zombies. 'I'll just borrow yours, Luther, if it isn't a bother.'

'Of course it's a bother!' Odelia snaps. 'It's pouring out.'

'Well, yes, that's rather the very point, isn't it?' Pandora returns with a beatific smile.

'Yes, I will,' Grant is saying into his phone. 'I'll have it sent to you right away but start drawing up the contract.'

Pandora plucks the wet umbrella from Luther's hands. 'I promise I shall return it posthaste. I'm going across to Cotswold Corner to make a few calls.'

Grant hangs up the phone. 'Hi, Odelia, Luther. Sorry about that. It was my attorney.'

'Yes it was! Cheers, then! Ta!' Pandora sails out the door.

Odelia turns to Luther, frowning. 'Well, that was bizarre.'

'Hey, what can I say? I'm a sucker for any woman who notices my massive brolly.'

Grant snickers.

Even Odelia can't help but grin. 'What I mean is, when I ran into Pandora on my way to Calla's this morning, she was a hot mess. I wonder why her mood turned around so quickly.'

'Maybe it's the weather. She probably prefers the rain because it reminds her of London.'

'I don't think—'

Odelia pauses, hearing a door bang open upstairs. Bella appears, looking utterly distraught.

'Bella! What's wrong?'

She looks around and then down the stairs, spotting Odelia and the others. 'My necklace! It's gone!'

'Necklace?' Grant frowns. 'What necklace?'

'Your tourmaline?' asks Luther who, like Odelia, is well aware that Bella Jordan wouldn't react this way over any old necklace.

'Yes.' She hurries down the stairs. 'I opened my jewelry box, and it was gone.'

'Maybe you just misplaced it,' Odelia suggests.

'No, that's the only place it would be, if I'm not wearing it.'

'When was the last time you had it on?'

'At Millicent's wedding.'

'Ah, then it's probably tucked away in your bag, or maybe you left it in Chicago.'

'No, Luther. I unpacked and put it away. I saw it in my jewelry box yest . . . wait.' She frowns. 'I did put it on with my blue dress yesterday morning. But only for a minute, because I realized . . . I realized, uh . . .'

Odelia to the rescue: 'You realized it was much too hot for jewelry.'

Bella flashes her a grateful smile. 'Exactly.'

Odelia had seen Bella in that blue dress, wearing makeup, with her hair styled, and suspected it was because Drew Bailey was still hanging around.

'Well, you must have put it down somewhere when you took it off,' Grant says.

'I didn't. I just turned the Rose Room upside down. It isn't there.' She turns to Luther, holding up her phone. 'And there's something else—'

A shrill scream erupts somewhere upstairs, and a woman's voice yells, '*Heeelp!*'

'Eve!' Grant rushes up the steps, taking them three at a time, with Luther right on his heels.

Bella looks at Odelia. 'That's his girlfriend. She's . . . a lot. I'm sure it's nothing major.'

'How about you, Bella? Are you all right?'

'I'm . . .' Her voice breaks, and she shakes her head.

'Your necklace. I know.'

'Not just that. It's everything. Sam—'

'Sam! Yes. I just saw him.'

'When?'

'About ten minutes ago. I was in my room.'

'And he came to you again? Did he have a message?'

'No, not like before. This was different. I saw him outside, in the rain.' She turns and points out the window at the park across the way. 'He was over there. But I turned away, and when I looked again, he was gone.'

'That's it? He was just . . . there?'

'Yes. Walking. He had an umbrella and a cell phone.'

Bella gasps. 'He . . . he had a *cell phone*?'

'And an umbrella, which I thought was unusual because—'

'Bella?' Luther calls down the stairs. 'Can you come up here, please?'

'What's going on?'

'Rainstorm, old house, leaky roof. Does that answer your question?'

'Oh, no!'

'Things could be worse,' Odelia reminds Bella.

'You're right. A lot worse, considering what goes on around here. Odelia, the boys are watching TV. Can you—'

'I'll make sure they're OK. In fact, why don't I take them back to my house for a while and give you a break? You have a lot to do here.'

'That would be . . . I don't even know how to thank you.'

'No need.' She lowers her voice. 'Luther and I have some concerns about one of your guests. Make sure he tells you.'

As Bella hurries up the stairs, Odelia heads for the back parlor.

Candace sticks her head out of the breakfast room. 'Odelia? What's going on? We heard—'

'Everything's fine,' Odelia assures her, along with Tommy and the other guests who are there, looking concerned.

'No, dear, we're not talking about our *dream* now,' one of the St Clair sisters tells the other. 'Hester was saying that somebody *screamed.*'

'My goodness, what happened to Hester?'

'Nothing happened to *me*, Ruby. I'm right here. You see? I'm perfectly fine.'

'Then why are you screaming and carrying on?'

Odelia heaves an inward sigh.

'Who *did* scream?' Tommy asks her.

'It's probably just the television. No worries. I'll go turn it down. Go on back to your breakfast.'

'Thanks, but we were just getting ready to go.'

'We'll see you there, right?' Candace asks.

'Where?'

'At our ghost-hunting equipment presentation.'

She'd all but forgotten. Their conversation last night seems so long ago.

'I'm not sure I'm going to make it. Bella asked me to keep an eye on the boys – her son and his friend.'

'Bring them! It's totally G-rated,' Candace says. 'Kids are always fascinated with the equipment. We can even have them come up on stage and help with the demonstration. Just make sure you come early to get a seat down in the front. It's going to be crowded.'

'Yes, we're all going,' Ruby says with a smile.

'Where are we going, dear?' her sister asks.

'We're going . . . where are we going again, Hester?'

Odelia continues onto the back parlor, where she finds Max and Jiffy curled up on the couch with Spidey between them. They're so engrossed in their favorite ninja zombie program that they don't seem to notice Odelia until she picks up the remote and pauses the TV.

'Hey!'

'No!'

'It's just me, boys.'

'Oh, hi, Odelia,' Max says.

'Hi, Odelia,' Jiffy parrots. 'By the way, we were watching ninja zombies, and you froze them.'

'I thought you two might want to join me for something fun?'

'I would!' Max shouts.

'Me, too, I guess.'

'Everything OK with you today, Jiffy?'

He replies with a lackluster, 'Yep.'

'Except for your phone and your play . . .' Max winces as Jiffy elbows him. 'Sorry. Everything's OK with Jiffy today, Odelia.'

Hmm. Thoughtful, she asks, 'You haven't seen your mom's tourmaline necklace, have you, Max?'

'Her what necklace?'

'That special blue necklace she likes to wear.'

'Oh! She wore it at my grandma's wedding.'

'Right. I thought maybe you'd seen it around the house.'

'Nope.'

'Jiffy? Have you seen it?'

'Nope, it's not around my house, either.'

'Well, she can't find it, so let's keep an eye out for it, shall we?'

'We shall, but that's not the fun thing, is it?' Max asks.

'It is not. We have a few minutes before we have to go, so I'll let you two finish your program.' She presses Play, and the show resumes.

As she leaves the room, she hears Max whisper, 'What if Kevin Beamer stole my mom's necklace, too?'

That stops Odelia in her tracks.

Kevin . . . Beamer.

'Why would he steal that?' Jiffy asks.

'Because Odelia said it's blue, so maybe it's worth a lot of money like that other one.'

'I told you, he's not the one who stole that.'

Wide-eyed, Odelia sneaks back toward the doorway, eavesdropping.

'Anyway, he doesn't steal stuff,' Jiffy goes on. 'He just makes people give him their stuff.'

'Oh, right.'

Odelia shakes her head. Kevin Buh . . . something.

Buh . . . *Beamer*. Not *Bacon*.

It happens all the time—with many spirits eager to get the medium's attention, one message can easily get muddled with another. When someone as seasoned as Odelia is focused – say, doing a reading for a client – she's adept at sorting things out. But Sam had woken her from a sound sleep, and, well, *he's* certainly not a pro at this.

'But isn't that the same thing as stealing?' Max is asking Jiffy. 'I mean, you didn't *want* to give him your Playbox and all that other stuff.'

Jiffy's response makes Odelia's blood run cold.

'I had to, because if I didn't, he was going to tell the police I stole the fancy necklace from the Slaytons.'

'Yeah, but that was *his* idea.'

'Yeah, but I did it.'

'Because you had to because he made you!'

A pause.

'Not really,' Jiffy admits in a voice Odelia has seldom heard him use. 'I had to because . . . I just had to, that's all.'

'Because Kevin Beamer's got video and he's going to give it to the police if you don't do what he says, right?'

'Well, yeah.'

'This stinks,' Max says, and then, 'Wait, I know! You need to get a lullaby!'

'You mean an alibi. I don't have one.'

'You can say you were with me.'

'It was the middle of the night, Max. Everyone would know I wasn't with you.' Jiffy sounds glum. 'I don't want to talk about this anymore. Let's just watch *Ninja Zombie Battle* until we go do Odelia's fun thing.'

Needing a cup of coffee and a place to sit and ponder everything, Odelia is glad to find the breakfast room deserted. The others must already be on their way to the auditorium. That's fine. She can be a few minutes late with the boys, she decides, as she waits for her coffee to drip from the Keurig.

She has to figure out what to do about Jiffy and—

'Bells?' Misty's voice calls. 'Bells! Where are you?'

Odelia leaves the coffee and hurries to the front hall.

Misty is there, her braided, beaded head soaked from the short walk over.

Lieutenant Grange is also there, wearing a trench coat and propping an umbrella against the wall. Odelia wonders whether he'd offered it to Misty. Then she wonders whether he's here to handcuff Jiffy and take him away.

Which is illogical, of course. You don't arrest a seven-year-old boy. You . . .

Well, whatever you do, she's certain it's pretty horrible.

'Oh, hi, Odelia. What are you doing here?' Misty asks.

'I was just heading out to the auditorium with the boys,' she says quickly, and shouts, 'Boys! Let's go!'

'Where are you going?'

Why, she wonders, does Grange always sound as if he's interrogating a criminal when he asks a question?

'To the auditorium, if that's OK with you?'

'Fine with me,' he says.

'I meant, if it's OK with you, Misty. I know you' – she indicates Grange – 'don't need to talk to him, or anything.'

Misty shrugs. 'It's fine with me.'

'Good, and we're late, so . . . Boys!'

Grange winces. 'I'm here to talk to Bella Jordan. Where is she?'

'Upstairs. I'm sure she'll be right down. Why don't you wait in the breakfast room? There's coffee and breakfast and . . . Boys!' she calls again, eager to get them out of here before they – or she – slips up in front of Grange about Jiffy's role in the robbery at the Slayton house.

TWENTY-FOUR

Hurrying along the third-floor hallway toward the supply closet, Bella spots Polly Green in the doorway of the Gable Room.

'What happened?' she asks Bella.

'It's just the weather – there's a leak in the room down the hall.'

'Really? I heard someone scream. I still do,' she adds, as Eve wails in the Jungle Room.

'Oh, well . . . the guest was . . . startled.'

The guest should have been an actress instead of an influencer. The way Eve is carrying on, you'd think the entire ceiling crashed down, instead of a small chunk of it. Unfortunately, it had been right above the desk where she'd been sitting.

'Is everything OK in your room?' Bella asks Polly. 'The leaks are worse in there than anywhere else up here.'

'It's fine.'

Is it Bella's imagination, or does she say it too quickly? 'Really? Mind if I take a look? Just to be sure, you know, it's not . . . damp.'

'You've got your hands full. Don't worry about me. Really, it's all good.'

'Well in that case . . . I'm just going to grab the spare bucket from under the sink in your bathroom.'

'Oh. I, uh . . . sure. OK.'

She doesn't have much choice. Bella is already stepping around her into the Gable Room. She scans the space for anything unusual, not sure what she's expecting to find.

Certainly not the bucket from the bathroom, positioned beneath the drippiest spot in the gabled ceiling. Bella looks from it to Polly.

Her perfect hair is . . . crooked.

It's a wig, Bella realizes. She must have thrown it on quickly when she heard Eve screaming down the hall.

Standing by the desk, she's casually closing her open laptop as if it's the most natural thing in the world.

A *laptop*.

Bella thinks of the extensive but quickly typed messages from 'Sam', and her heart pounds.

She clears her throat. 'I thought you said the ceiling was dry?'

Polly meets Bella's gaze without flinching. 'I said it was *fine*.'

Had she? Bella isn't sure.

'*And* I said you have your hands full, which you seem to,' Polly adds, 'so I didn't want you to worry about anything in here.'

'Oh, well . . . thank you. I guess I'll leave the bucket then.'

'Thanks. I'll be out of here soon.'

'Out of here?'

'You said the room was only available for one night, didn't you?'

'Oh . . . I did. Yes. Thank you.'

'Thank you,' Polly returns.

There's nothing for Bella to do but walk out of the room, closing the door behind her. As she moves on down the hall, she hears Polly turn the lock inside.

She's probably just skittish about all the wailing down the hall, Bella tells herself as she opens the door to the supply closet and finds a couple of buckets.

Of course Polly isn't hiding anything. A lot of women wear wigs. Maybe she's prematurely gray, or maybe she's sick. And maybe didn't close the laptop because there was something incriminating on it . . .

Say, fake texts from Bella's dead husband, demanding two hundred thousand dollars?

She weighs that prospect against her own paranoia and Odelia's warning about one of the guests.

Luther. She has to talk to Luther. Now.

Returning to the Jungle Room, she finds him standing on his tiptoes on a chair, straining to get a closer look at the hole in the ceiling above the desk. Grant is examining Eve's right thumb, using his phone like a surgeon lighting an operating theater. Eve is crying, though more softly now. One can't keep up hysterics indefinitely, thank goodness.

'Does it hurt when I do this?' Grant asks.

'Ouch! Yes!'

'I didn't even bend it yet.'

'Don't bend it! It hurts!'

'What happened again, exactly?' Bella asks Eve.

'I was sitting at the desk, you know, working, and the roof caved in, and that boulder fell on me.'

Bella eyes the chunk of drywall on the floor. Hardly a boulder; it's the same shape and size as a small banana and would fit the ceiling hole like a puzzle piece.

'I'm so sorry,' she tells Eve. 'You must have been so startled.'

'Startled? It was sheer terror! That rock crushed my hand and my phone and it's broken!'

'I don't think it's broken,' Grant says, gently moving her thumb.

'I mean my phone!' She grabs it with her left hand and shows him, then Bella and Luther. The screen is shattered. 'Now I can't film this!'

'Film what?' Bella asks.

At least that's what she thought she'd asked, but Eve looks at her as if she's speaking in tongues.

'Um . . . my life?'

'No, I get that's what you do, but when you said film *this*, I thought you meant . . . *this*.' Bella waves a hand to indicate the ceiling, the floor, and Eve's wounded thumb. Seeing her expression, she mumbles, 'And you did. Sorry.'

'Well, she *is* All About Eve,' Luther says.

Eve's face lights up and she turns to him as if she hadn't noticed his presence until right now. 'You're a fan.'

It's an assumption, not a question.

His answer is matter-of-fact. 'Of course.'

He's a *fan*? Bella gapes at Luther, who hardly seems like the type of man who'd be interested in influencers. He gives her a wink.

Eve is howling again.

'Stay still,' Grant says. 'I need to blot the cut.'

'Cut? I'm bleeding? *Noooo!* I'm bleeding!'

'Why don't you go into the bathroom down the hall and clean that for her?' Bella suggests to Grant. 'There should be first-aid stuff in the medicine cabinet – bandages, peroxide.'

'Peroxide!' Eve screams. 'Are you insane? That will hurt!'

Grant escorts her from the room.

Bella looks up at Luther. 'What do you think?'

'I think you're perfectly sane, Bella Jordan,' he says dryly, 'and that she clearly mistook *peroxide* for *battlefield amputation*.'

'I agree on both counts, but I mean about the ceiling?'

'The joists and insulation are pretty dry here, so it's strange that this is the part that gave way, unless . . .'

'Unless?'

'Nadine?'

'Nadine . . .'

'Your household spirit.'

'No, I know who Nadine is.'

She remembers what Tommy had said earlier. *Our sensors were going crazy on the third floor . . .*

'Odelia says she's the orb in the video Eve posted. If you pull it up on your phone, I can show—'

'My phone!' She pulls it out and opens the text messages. 'Luther, come look at this.'

'The video of Eve?'

'No, something way more important,' she says quietly, closing the door to the hallway while he climbs off the chair. 'Just read these texts from the beginning.'

She hands him the phone and watches him scrolling through the messages.

'What in the . . .?' He looks up at her, wide-eyed. 'Who's sending them?'

'Not Sam.'

'Of course not Sam,' he agrees, so quickly that she feels a twinge of . . .

Disappointment? Really?

Is it because she so highly value's Luther's opinion, as a detective and fellow Lily Dale outsider, and she believed that he might consider, even for a moment, that it's in the realm of possibility that the messages actually *are* from Sam?

Especially now that Odelia mentioned seeing him outside in the rain with an umbrella and a cell phone.

'I took screen shots of the texts for you,' she tells Luther as he hands back her phone.

'Good. Send them to me right away. I'll look into this.'

As she quickly scrolls through and highlights the photos, she says, 'Odelia told me you have some concerns about a guest who's staying here. Is it Polly Green?'

'Is Polly the woman who's claiming to be on a cross-country road trip from Boston?'

'She isn't?'

'It's a rental car. She probably picked it up at the airport, saw the license plate, and came up with that story.'

'Airport? So she flew here.'

'From Chicago.'

'Chicago!'

Before she can tell Luther about the wig and the laptop, the door jerks open without a knock. Grant is there, unaccompanied.

'Our driver abandoned us,' he announces. 'I don't know what's up with him, but he's not parked out front and he's not picking up the phone and I need to get Eve to urgent care. She's feeling faint, and I think we'd better have her hand x-rayed. She's in excruciating pain, poor thing.'

Oh, Grant, Bella thinks. *How can such a smart, worldly, successful man be so very stupid?*

Reminding herself that he's selling Valley View, she decides that he and Eve deserve each other.

'Maybe you should call an ambulance,' Luther suggests.

'Oh, I don't think *that's* necessary. Can one of you drive us? It's in Dunkirk – only fifteen minutes away.'

'I live there,' Luther says. 'I was just on my way home to take care of a few things. I'll take you, but I can't hang around at the urgent care.'

'That's OK. I'll find a driver to take us right to the airport from there.' Grant turns to Bella. 'I'll call you later. I wanted to make sure you're OK with everything.'

'Am I *OK* with your selling Valley View?' She shrugs. 'It is what it is, Grant.'

'You're *selling* Valley View?' Luther looks at Grant. 'Why?'

'It's OK, Luther. Candace and Tommy will take good care of it, and they'll fit right in here, and they'll be good neighbors to Odelia, so—'

'I'm not selling it to Candace and Tommy, Bella.'

'Who the heck *are* Candace and Tommy?' Luther asks, looking from Grant to Bella.

She's focused on Grant. 'What do you mean?'

'Pandora made it very clear that it wouldn't be fair to rob this town of its most brilliant guesthouse,' he says, rolling his r's like she does. 'And it wouldn't be fair to expect you and Max to move out. It's your home.'

'It is.' She swallows hard. 'So . . . you're keeping it?'

'Oh, no, I'm selling it. To Pandora Feeney.'

'*What?*' Bella and Luther ask in unison, gaping at each other, and then at him.

'Grant!' Eve yells, down the hall.

'We're coming!' He hurries out the door. 'Luther!'

'Right behind you.'

'Go,' Bella says.

'I'm going. But he just said he's selling it to—'

'Yes. He did.'

'What do you think she's—'

'I have no idea, but if I think about it now, my head is going to explode.'

'Just take it one minute at a time. And if you get another text, let me know, and don't engage.' He gives her hand a quick squeeze and is gone.

Left alone in the room, she sinks onto the bed. For the first time, she realizes that it's neatly made.

Drew.

Swept by a fierce need to connect with him, she dials his number. It rings into voicemail.

'Hey, it's Bella. There's . . . I have . . . Can you . . .' Choked up, she swallows hard before saying quickly, 'Just call me, OK? Thanks.'

She exhales and closes her eyes.

In a perfect world, she'd be buying Valley View.

This world is tilting farther from perfect with every passing moment.

'Pandora?' she whispers, shaking her head.

She checks her texts. There's not another message from Sam.

She thinks of Polly, who'd lied about where she's from. Polly, under Valley View's roof, where she might have seen the check. Polly, closing her laptop so quickly, and wearing a wig.

Bella steps out into the hall. The house is quiet.

Odelia had taken the boys, and the guests were heading to the auditorium. All but one.

Bella walks to the closed door to the Jungle Room and knocks.

'Polly?'

Is that even her real name?

'Polly?'

She knocks again. Waits. Tries the door, expecting to find it locked.

It opens.

She looks in. The room is empty.

Right, because Polly is checking out this morning. Bella hurries over to the window and scans the street below.

The rain has stopped, and the white Chevy is no longer parked at the curb. Across the park, stragglers are heading toward the auditorium.

Her eye falls on Pandora Feeney's pink cottage.

She's always longed to come home to Valley View. Fate seems to have set her up to do just that. But what . . .

Bella gasps. He's there, standing in the park, gazing up at Valley View, holding a cell phone.

Sam.

TWENTY-FIVE

Leading the boys into the auditorium, Odelia finds that it is indeed packed.

Not only are there no seats down front, but she doesn't see three together. Spotting two, she points them out to Max and Jiffy.

'Go sit over there,' she says, 'and don't move. I'll watch from back here.'

'That's OK, Odelia. You can sit with Max,' Jiffy tells her.

'How come you don't want to sit with me?' Max asks.

'I'm being a gentleman.'

'You're hardly ever a gentleman.'

'I know, but right now, I'm being one.' Jiffy looks up at Odelia and gives a courtly gesture at the aisle.

Odelia narrows her eyes at him.

'I'll stand back here with Jiffy and be a gentleman, too,' Max decides, and imitates the courtly gesture. 'You can go sit, Odelia.'

'No, thank you. Is there any reason you'd prefer to be back here, Jiffy?'

'I told, you, I'm being—'

'Other than being a gentleman?'

'Nope.'

But he flashes a glance at the exit, right behind her.

'All right, then go sit.'

'Hey,' Max says, grabbing Jiffy's arm and pointing. 'Look who's there! Isn't that—'

'Shh!' Jiffy elbows him, and Max clamps his mouth shut.

Following his gaze, Odelia sees a couple of boys their age seated in the row behind the two empty seats.

'Why, is that Kevin Beamer?' she asks, putting two and two together.

Max turns to her, wide-eyed. 'You know him?'

'Of course. I'll walk you to your seats and say hello. Come on.'

She puts a firm hand on each boy's shoulder and steers them down the aisle.

'Sit down,' she tells them, and turns to the boy in the row behind.

He's noticed Max and Jiffy and is snickering to his friend behind a cupped hand.

'Kevin?' she calls sweetly, and he turns, startled. She waves as if they're old pals. 'Hello, there!'

'Uh, hi.' He turns back to his friend.

Max and Jiffy slink down in their seats as if hoping to make themselves invisible.

'Kevin!' Odelia calls again. 'Come here! I have to tell you something!'

He looks at her, suspicious. 'About what?'

'About . . .' She points at the stage, where Tommy and Candace are setting up equipment. 'It's about the Specter Inspectors. Come here.'

'What about them?'

'Kevin, if you're going to lallygag, I'll just tell Candace and Tommy to choose some other kid to help them with the demonstration.'

'I'll do it!' Jiffy says, sitting up straight.

Max does, too, saying, 'I'll do it, too!'

'They only need one kid,' Jiffy tells him. 'And I said it first.'

'Maybe they need two.'

'They need one,' Odelia says. 'Sorry, boys, but they've asked for Kevin.'

He stands, gloating, steps out into the aisle, and starts for the stage.

Odelia stops him with a firm hand on his arm. 'Not that way. I have to take you backstage.'

'Oh! Right.'

'Max, Jiffy, stay right where you are. I'll be back in a few minutes.'

She leads Kevin up the aisle to the exit.

'Wait, isn't this the wrong way?' he asks, hanging back, and she experiences a flash of guilt. Then she thinks of Jiffy, and she says, 'No, we have to use the VIP entrance. Come on.'

Spotting Peter and Walter sitting in the last row, she asks them to keep an eye on Max and Jiffy.

Then she steps outside with Kevin.

The rain has stopped. The Dale has been washed clean, and everything is dripping.

'First, things first. I need to get a picture of you for the newspaper article,' she says, pulling out her cell phone.

'What newspaper article?'

'The one about the Specter Inspectors.'

'Oh. Right.'

She opens the camera on her phone. 'Stand right here and smile nice and big. Say Cheese.'

'Cheese!' he says around a toothy grin, and she hates herself for doing this.

He's a kid.

But a kid who has some tough lessons to learn, and she's determined to set him straight.

'Nice,' she says, pressing a button on her phone and then lowering it, holding it at her side as she leads him around the side of the auditorium. Glancing across the park, she sees that Lieutenant Grange's car is still parked in front of Misty's house, and that the white Chevy no longer occupies a guest spot at Valley View.

'OK, Kevin, let's stop and go over a few things before we go backstage, OK?'

'I guess.'

'First things first. It's never, ever a good idea to let a stranger talk you into going somewhere with them. You do know that, don't you?'

'Yep.'

'But you just left the auditorium with me.'

'You're not a stranger.'

'Do you know who I am?'

'You're Odelia Lauder.'

'That's right. I live right over there.' She points.

He glances over, nods, shifting his weight from one foot to the other. 'Are we going backstage?'

'In a minute. We're talking.'

'I'm not really talking. You are.'

'Let me talk, Kevin. Listen up. You may know who I am, but that doesn't mean you should have left the auditorium with me. Got it?'

'Huh?'

'I'm trying to help you. Be smart. Be careful. The world is full of bad guys, you know?'

'Uh, I guess.' He takes a wary step back from her.

'Not *me*,' she says quickly. 'I'm just the friendly medium who lives next door to Jiffy Arden. You know him, right?'

'Yeah.'

'I hear you're the one who talked him into breaking into the Slayton house.'

Wide-eyed, he just looks at her.

She goes on, 'You got him to steal the necklace, and then—'

'I didn't even know about the necklace until he told me about it! And all I did was dare him to take it, because he was going on and on about finding some stupid pirate treasure so that he can be rich. I didn't make him steal it.'

'Oh. Glad we straightened that out.'

'Yeah.'

'But you were with him? When he broke into the Slayton house?'

'Yeah, but it's not like we smashed in the door or something. The basement window was already broken. Everyone in the Dale knows about that.'

'I didn't know about that.'

'I mean all the *kids*. Can we go backstage?'

'We're almost through. I'm just wondering what you stole that night?'

'Nothing!'

'So he stole the necklace, and that's it? Why would he do that?'

'He thinks he's going to sell it somewhere and get all this money for it.' He grins. 'Dumb kid.'

'Detective Grange is trying to pin this thing on him. He's over at Jiffy's house right now, investigating.'

Kevin follows her gaze and lifts an eyebrow when he sees Grange's car parked in front of the Ardens'.

'He said there's a huge reward for anyone who comes forward with any kind of evidence that Jiffy is behind it. Pictures, or a video.'

'Wait, I've got evidence! I got the whole thing on my phone.'

That makes two of us, Odelia thinks, looking down to make sure hers is still recording.

'Wow, that's genius,' she tells Kevin. 'Can I see?'

'Sure.' He takes out his phone, scrolls through the files, and opens a video. He tilts the screen, and she sees a dark blur.

'What am I looking at?'

'I took this when he was crawling through the window. It's kind of dark, so you can't really see him, but you can hear him. Shh, listen.'

She hears a voice that doesn't sound like Jiffy's at all. It sounds small and scared, saying, 'Are you sure? What if we get caught?'

'We won't. And you said you need the money bad, don't you?'

'I need it really bad. It's kind of an emergency, by the way.'

'Then get in there. I'm right behind you.'

Odelia carefully slides her own phone into her pocket and reaches for Kevin's. 'Can I take a closer look? I couldn't tell that was him.'

'It is.'

'Are you sure?'

'Yeah, see?' He presses Play and hands her the phone.

'I need more light,' she says, and steps into a patch of sun just starting to peek through the clouds. 'That's better.'

Holding the phone close to her face as if she's watching it intently, she swiftly highlights the video and deletes it.

'Wow,' she says, as if marveling at Kevin's prowess. 'You must be really smart to set a clever trap like this.'

'I guess.' He can't hide his smug smile. 'Everyone's always saying Jiffy's the smartest kid in the class, but I'm way smarter.'

'Are you guys enemies, then?'

'Not really.' He holds out his hand. 'Can I have my phone back?'

She hands it to him, and he shoves it back into his pocket without looking at it.

'I'm sure you were trying to do the right thing, Kevin. Theft is a serious crime, you know?'

'Yeah.'

'*You* would never steal, right?'

'Me? No.'

'So you didn't steal Jiffy's Playbox, and his cell phone, and his other things?'

'Huh?' He blinks. 'He gave me all that stuff.'

'Why?'

'I guess he didn't want it anymore.'

Applause fills the auditorium on the other side of the wall, and a voice booms over the speakers, 'Ladies and gentlemen . . .'

'I'd better get back to *my* gentlemen,' Odelia says. 'The show is starting.'

'But . . . what about backstage? I'm the demonstrator.'

Odelia presses a button on her phone to stop the recording and waves it as if she'd just gotten a text. 'Oh, they're saying that they no longer require your services.'

'Huh?'

'Sorry, Kev. Go back to your seat, now. You and I can talk more about this later. Should I let Detective Grange know you might have some evidence to show him? For the reward?'

He grins. 'Yep. Thanks, Odelia.'

'No problem.'

TWENTY-SIX

Bella races from the room and flies down two flights of stairs, ready to bolt out the door and hurl herself into her husband's arms.

Someone steps into her path, and she skids to a breathless halt.

'Mrs Jordan.' Detective John Grange looks her up and down with flinty gray eyes. 'Where are you going in such a hurry?'

'Bells!' Misty is there, too. 'Are you OK? You look upset.'

'I'm not upset . . . I was just going to catch one of my guests who just left. I think she, uh, forgot something in her room.'

'Too late. She drove away,' Grange says.

'In a white Chevy?' Bella asks, peering through the window in the door as if looking for Polly's car.

'She was in almost as much of a hurry as you seem to be.'

The spot where Sam had just been standing is vacant.

Where is he? Where did he go? Had she imagined him?

I think you're perfectly sane, Bella Jordan.

'Mrs Jordan?'

'*What?*' She whirls on Detective Grange. '*What?*'

'I have a couple of questions for you.'

'About what?'

'I'm conducting an investigation.'

'*Now?* Can it wait? I have to—'

'Now. According to Mrs Arden, you have some information about the case.'

Bella looks at Misty, who mouths, *Sorry.*

Think, Bella! Think! You aren't insane, and you didn't imagine Sam, and you have to get out of here and find him.

She clears her throat and asks Grange, 'Which case is that?'

'The break-in over at the Slayton place.'

'Oh, that's right. Of course. Let's go into the parlor. Do you want some coffee?'

'No coffee,' Grange says.

Misty shakes her head. 'No, I'm good.'

'Do you mind if I go grab mine, Lieutenant Grange? It's already been such an exhausting morning.'

'Exhausting how?'

'Oh, you know . . . the usual . . .'

'Bells, are you sure you're OK?' Misty asks. 'You really seem—'

'Totally fine. I just need my coffee.' She hurries toward the back of the house, calling, 'Have a seat, detective. You, too, Misty. I'll be back in two seconds.'

In the kitchen, she pulls her phone out of her pocket and quickly opens the string of texts from . . .

Polly?

Or Sam.

Sam, whom she'd seen outside just moments ago, with her own eyes, holding a phone.

Yes, there's a slight chance that she's delusional, because the delusional probably don't know they're delusional.

But if there's also a chance that he really is alive, and needs her help . . .

She starts typing in the message window, ignoring her own inner voice, and Luther's warning not to engage.

'I have to do this,' she whispers, breathing hard. 'I have to. Right now.'

Yes, I'll help you. Meet me at the Stump in fifteen minutes.

She hits Send.

'Mrs Jordan?' Detective Grange calls.

'Be right there!' She opens a cabinet door and slams it. 'Just grabbing my coffee!'

Wobbling dots appear in the message window.

She sucks in a breath of air and holds it until a message appears.

With the money?

'Yes!' Bella whispers.

Yes, she replies.

She leaves the kitchen quickly. Not with coffee, and she isn't returning to the parlor.

Slipping into the mudroom, she finds the puppies sound asleep. The hound, curled up in her basket of dirty clothes, looks up at her.

About to rush past him, she pauses to give his brown head a quick pat. 'Shhh, it's OK. Don't tell them I left, OK? I'll be back. I promise.'

Then she's out the door, across the fenced area, and through the gate.

Praying that Grange hasn't already come looking for her in the kitchen, she darts across the yard in full view of anyone who happens to look out of a back window.

Ducking into the trees, she begins the long, circuitous route across the Dale toward Inspiration Stump.

She'd chosen it because it's far enough off the beaten path that no one will see her, and because it will be deserted at this hour, with no Stump reading until later in the day.

As she reaches the trail into Leolyn Wood, her phone vibrates with an incoming call.

It's from an Unknown number.

She holds her breath and answers. Her instinct is to say, *Sam?* But is she really convinced it's him?

Not one hundred percent.

'Hello?' she croaks into the phone.

'Bella! It's Millicent. I'm so sorry I didn't call back sooner. I just got your message this morning. Can you hear me?'

'Millicent! Yes, I . . . I hear you.'

'Good. I had to borrow a phone. Mine keeps dropping service out here. What's wrong, Bella?'

'Oh . . . nothing's wrong, I just . . .' She chokes back a sob.

'Bella! Is Max OK?'

'Yes! He's fine, it's nothing like that. It's just . . . I know this is going to sound crazy, but I saw Sam, in Chicago and now here in the Dale.'

Whatever response she was expecting, it isn't, 'You saw him in Lily Dale?'

'Yes. And in Chicago. He was driving a gold car, and Max saw him in front of your building, and then we both saw him at the airport.'

Millicent says nothing.

'Millicent? Are you there?'

There's crackling on the other end of the line, but the call hasn't dropped. Bella can hear George's voice, rumbling in the background.

'Now? Like this?' Millicent says, but not to Bella.

George says something else. Bella strains to hear but can't make it out.

'Yes,' her mother-in-law is saying, 'I know I should have told her, but it wasn't the right time.'

'Millicent!' Bella calls. 'What are you talking about? Tell me what?'

'I'm sorry, Bella. It's a long story, and it's about my first husband, Thierry.'

'Sam's father?'

'Yes. It turns out he'd had—'

The line crackles again and goes dead.

Bella looks at the phone. There's a notification: Call Failed.

There's a new message, too, from Unknown.

Not Millicent, on her borrowed phone.

I'm here at the Stump. Where are you?

'Sam!'

She shoves her phone into her pocket, hurries up the trail, and bursts into the clearing.

She scans the rows of benches, and the Stump.

'Wow. You really came.'

Hearing the voice behind her, Bella whirls to see a figure stepping out from a clump of trees.

She gasps. 'Sam!'

TWENTY-SEVEN

Standing in the back of the darkened auditorium, Odelia sees Jiffy get to his feet and hurry up the aisle.

She intercepts him before he can walk out.

'Where are you going?' she whispers.

'I have to do something.'

'Jiffy? Come back here.'

'I can't, Odelia. I have to go.'

Ah, a bathroom break? All right, but she's not letting him go unescorted. She sticks her head between Walter's and Peter's in the back row and whispers, 'Watch Max for me. I'll be right back.'

Then she follows Jiffy out into the daylight.

'Jiffy, stop!'

He keeps walking, and he isn't heading toward the restrooms, but toward the park.

'Michael Arden! You stop right this instant!'

He stops. When he turns back to her, she sees tears on his face.

'Oh, my goodness. Jiffy, what's wrong?'

'Did you know that my dad's name is Michael Arden, too?'

'I did, yes.'

He nods, looking down at his shoes.

'You must miss him.'

'Yeah. He's supposed to be coming home soon, but . . .' He shakes his head. 'He said the Dale isn't home for him, so he doesn't want to live here with us.'

'How do you know that?'

'He told my mom, on the phone.'

'And you heard?'

'Yeah. They always talk really loud. They kind of yell at each other. Well, not kind of.'

'That must be hard for you to hear.'

'No, it's easy for me to hear because they're really loud, like I said.'

'Ah.' She tries a different tack. 'It probably makes you sad when two people you love are so upset with each other.'

'It makes me sad, and mad. They're always talking about the stupidest stuff.'

'Like what?'

'Money.'

'Money?'

'Yeah, they need a lot of it. And if someone could just give it to them, they wouldn't yell anymore.'

Odelia digests this. 'Sometimes, Jiffy, the thing people are fighting about isn't the thing they're really fighting about. Do you know what I mean?'

'Nope.'

'No, I don't suppose you do. Well, sometimes people who love each other very much just can't get along no matter what happens. Even if the thing they yell about all the time goes away. And sometimes, the person who loves those two people more than anything in the world – the person those two people love more than anything in the world – well, that guy can't do a darned thing to fix what's wrong between them.'

Jiffy says nothing.

She rests a hand on his shoulder and finds him trembling. 'And sometimes,' she says, gently, 'that guy does a bad thing in order to do a good thing.'

He turns to look up at her, as if he isn't sure she's talking about what he thinks she's talking about.

'Where's the necklace, Jiffy?'

'How do you know about the necklace?'

'This is Lily Dale.' She shrugs. 'Where is it?'

'It's in a secret hiding place.'

'Jiffy—'

'I can't tell you where it is, Odelia! But I'm going there right now, so please don't follow me.'

'It doesn't belong to you! You can't just—'

'I know!' He swipes a hand across his eyes. 'That's why I'm going to get it! I'm going to give it back to the Slaytons right now and I'm going to tell them I'm sorry. I just thought . . . I thought . . .'

'I know,' Odelia says, and pulls him into her arms as he cries. 'I know what you thought. Everything's going to be OK now, Jiffy.'

'Are you going to tell anyone what I did?'

'Anyone . . . like who?'

'Like my mom? And Lieutenant Grange? My mom called him up when she found out my Playbox wasn't in my room anymore.'

'And that's why you went over to Max's?'

'Kind of. Are you going to tell them?'

'No. You are.'

For a moment, she expects him to protest. But he considers it, nods, and lifts his chin. 'OK. But will you be with me?'

'Every step of the way,' she assures him.

TWENTY-EIGHT

'Sam!' Bella breathes. 'I can't believe you're really here. *Are you here? Are you alive?*'

'Oh, I'm alive.' He laughs.

She rushes toward him, then stops short.

It isn't Sam's laugh.

And that isn't Sam's face, though it looks like him, so much like him that Bella can't seem to breathe.

Or maybe that's because he's holding a gun, aiming it at her.

'S . . .' His name strangles in her throat. No. He isn't Sam.

And she'd known, of course she'd known, that it couldn't be real; that he couldn't be alive. But her life is disintegrating around her, and she'd needed him so badly; needed to let herself believe in magic, just this once; needed . . .

But Sam had been so long ago. Sam is gone.

And Drew's words, not Sam's, come back to her now.

'*If ever there was a woman who didn't need rescuing, it's you.*'

She takes a deep breath and forces herself to look him in the eye, this stranger who somehow looks so very much, and yet so very little, like the man she'd loved.

'Who are you?'

'You haven't figured it out yet, have you? I can't say I'm surprised she didn't tell you.'

She?

Her thoughts race.

She . . .

In Bella's back pocket, her phone vibrates with a call, and a puzzle piece drops into place.

'Millicent?'

Something flickers in his gaze, and she knows she'd guessed correctly.

'Of course she told me.'

She'd been about to, anyway.

'What did she tell you?'

Right before the call dropped, Millicent had mentioned . . .

'She told me about Thierry.' Not allowing herself to look at that gun, Bella keeps her voice steady, and her eyes focused on his.

Again, she sees a gleam of acknowledgement.

'What about him?'

'He's Sam's father and . . .'

Of course. That has to be it.

'. . . yours.'

Yes. That's it.

Now it makes sense.

Sam hadn't been an only child after all.

This man is his brother.

His half-brother.

Sam couldn't have known he existed; if he had, he'd have told Bella. Sam, who was terrible at keeping secrets, would never have kept that from her.

Millicent had. She'd admitted she'd kept it from Bella, but . . .

Would she really have kept it from her son?

The man with the gun takes a step closer. 'If you knew about me, why did you call me Sam? Why did you tell your boyfriend that you and your kid had seen him at O'Hare?'

So she *had* been overheard last night.

O'Hare.

Polly had flown here from Chicago. She does have something to do with this.

'Why do you think?' Bella asks. 'I was baiting her.'

'What are you talking about?'

'Your friend Polly. I knew she was snooping around, eavesdropping.'

He says nothing to that, just takes another step toward Bella.

It takes every ounce of strength in her body to stand her ground.

'I knew what she was after,' she goes on. 'What you were both after.'

'Did you bring it?'

'The money? You do know that it's not in cash, don't you?'

'Of course it's not in cash. And it would have been so much easier if you'd just left it where it was on your desk.'

So that he could steal it.

'But what are you going to do with a check made out to me?'

'You're going to deposit it.'

'What makes you think I'm going to do that?'

He merely smiles, and it's an ugly, cruel smile.

'I don't understand.'

'You're going to take the check to the bank. You're going to show them your ID, and you're going to give them a deposit slip for that account. And when the check clears, you're going to transfer the money to your other account.'

'What other account?'

'The one that's linked to this one.'

'There is no account linked to this one.'

'Are you sure about that?'

Bella thinks of her laptop with the saved username and password for the bank that holds Max's college fund.

Stupid. She'd been so, so stupid. Anyone with those credentials could have logged in and linked an account. Just as anyone could have seen her stack of unpaid bills and noted, based on the balances, that she's long been mired in debt. Anyone could have grabbed a deposit slip – and her ID, she realizes, heart sinking as she remembers her wallet and tourmaline necklace sitting there in the Rose Room before she'd been cautious enough to lock the door.

How carefully would a busy downtown Buffalo bank branch check the ID of a woman depositing – not withdrawing – a huge check? Anyone with that ID and a passable disguise – perhaps just a wig – could probably pass herself off as Bella.

'Now, if you'll just hand over that check,' says the man with the gun, 'we can get on with things.'

'You and Polly.'

'Right. Me and *Polly.*'

Which, by his tone, isn't her real name. Of course it isn't. Not her name, not her credit card or her ID.

'And that's a rental car she's driving. But how did she know in advance she'd get one with Massachusetts plates so that she'd have the right fake identity?'

He raises an eyebrow. 'You really do notice the little details, don't you, Bella *Jordan*?'

Yes. She does. Like the mocking emphasis on her last name.

'I'm sure you can answer your own question,' he says. 'Think about it.'

'You come prepared,' she guesses. 'Because you don't just use one fake ID. You have a whole bunch to choose from, don't you? Doesn't she? And now mine is going to be part of that.'

'You're smart,' he says. 'But of course you are. My dear brother wouldn't have married just anyone. He thought he deserved to get everything he ever wanted, didn't he?'

Yes, Bella is smart. Smart enough to read between the lines and grasp where this stranger is coming from.

'And you got nothing, right?' she asks. 'Not your father's money, or his name, or even his love.'

'Nothing but his DNA,' he agrees.

'He didn't know you even existed.' It's another educated guess, and a correct one, apparently.

'Nope,' he says. 'But them's the breaks for guys like me. By the time I found the match in the database, my father was long dead, and so was . . . well, you know. Although I'm kind of surprised someone as smart as you believed some dead guy might be alive.'

Some dead guy . . .

Sam.

He'd put his DNA into a database after he got sick, looking for not a long-lost sibling, but a hereditary marker for his disease.

'We need to know,' he'd told Bella. 'For Max's sake.'

The test came back after he was gone. Bella had logged into the database only to confirm that Sam carried no telltale marker that would explain his terminal illness, not bothering to scan the other information, like genetic matches to distant relatives.

It hadn't mattered. Nothing mattered, but that Sam had died.

'Now, let's take care of business. I'd like the check, please. *Polly* is waiting. And she doesn't like to wait.'

He's going to take it, and then he's going to kill her, and dump her body where no one will find her until long after that money has been deposited into, and transferred from, her bank account. Probably to an offshore one that will be difficult, if not impossible, to trace.

It's her own fault. She's the one who'd suggested meeting in this remote spot. She's the one who'd snuck out without telling anyone where she was going.

Grange and Misty might actually be looking for her by now, but how likely is it that they'd think to search here?

Certainly not in time to save her life.

Oh, Drew was so wrong. She does need rescuing. But he's not going to be the one to do it. Nor is Luther. Nor Sam.

Stay strong.

I'm trying, Sam. I'm trying.

But all the strength she can muster would be no match for a loaded gun. There's no way out of this without a rescuer.

Or a miracle. And there are no miracles.

Dead is dead, even here in Lily Dale.

'I need the check,' he says again, gesturing with the gun like a pointer finger. 'Right now.'

'Well, I need my necklace right now.'

'What makes you think I have it?'

'Either you do, or Polly does. I want it.'

'Because your dead husband left it for you? A gift from beyond the grave?'

Her heart lurches. She isn't just terrified. She's furious. How dare he talk about Sam in that mocking tone?

She lifts her chin and holds his gaze. 'I'm not giving you the check until you give me the necklace.'

'Oh? You want to trade?'

'Yes.'

Sure. They'll swap, and then he'll let her go home to her son and her life.

But Valley View can't be home, not anymore. Nothing is going to be the same. This whole new life she's built for herself, and Max – it's being taken away.

She feels her rage mount. White-hot rage. Dangerous, reckless rage.

'If you don't have the necklace, then you'd better get Polly to bring it to me,' she hears herself say.

'Oh, I've got it. It's right here in my pocket.'

The hand that's not holding the gun disappears into his pocket and pulls out her tourmaline necklace.

With a gasp, Bella reaches for it.

He laughs, dangling it beyond her grasp.

'Come and get it,' he taunts her.

She takes a step closer to him. Closer to the gun.

It's the last thing she should do; the only thing she can do.

'What's the matter? Are you scared?'

'Of *you*?' It's her turn to laugh, a shrill, hollow burst of hysteria that almost, almost drowns out a rustling, thrashing sound.

It's coming from behind her, back on the trail, as if someone, some hero, is rushing in to rescue her.

But that doesn't happen in real life.

No, in real life, you have to save your own.

Bella hurls herself at the man with the gun – the man with the necklace, *her* necklace.

She catches him off guard, knocking him off balance.

He's falling backward.

Bella, too, is falling. Falling forward, falling on top of him.

She reaches for the gun, but it's gone, and the necklace is gone, and his hands are empty now. They clamp her arms, twisting her, shoving her.

Now she's on her back, and his full weight is on top of her.

She manages a scream before his hands are around her throat, cutting off her voice . . . her air . . .

You don't need rescuing, Bella . . .

You have to save yourself.

Save your life.

Don't let him take it away.

Fight! Fight!

She tries, but she can't fight; can't breathe.

This is how she's going to die.

She thinks of Max, and of Drew, Millicent, Luther, Odelia, Misty . . .

Please be there for him, she begs them all, as darkness begins to block out the milky sun overhead, and it's because her eyes are closing, and because she can't breathe . . .

Please never let him forget how much his mom loved him. And his dad . . .

Oh, Sam.

Is she going to see him again? Is he waiting for her?

She listens for his voice, or even for the wind chimes, but she hears only a roaring in her ears.

And then somehow the hands are gone, and his crushing weight is off her.

She's gasping.

Choking.

Gulping air.

Breathing.

Thrusting herself up on her elbows, she spots the gun, lying on the ground in arm's reach. Spots her would-be killer, pinned beneath her ferocious rescuer.

It isn't Drew, or Luther, or Sam.

No, it's a foxhound with pleading eyes and a nose that can sniff out a bad guy – or Bella – from miles away. A hero who's spent the last few days in a basket filled with Bella's clothing; her scent.

She grabs the gun. It's heavy, and shaky in her grasp. She steadies it with one hand, grabbing her phone from her pocket with the other, and dialing just three digits.

The call connects immediately.

'9-1-1. What is your emergency?'

'I need—'

Her voice cracks in her throat, which aches from those fierce hands doing their best to choke the life out of her.

But he hadn't. Bella Jordan had saved herself . . . with a little help from a hero, she thinks, as her gaze falls on the enormous dog pinning her attacker to the ground.

Nearby, something glints in a sudden burst of sunshine.

It's her tourmaline necklace.

'Are you there?' the operator is asking. 'Hello? What is your emergency, ma'am?'

She clears her throat and finds her voice, now clear as the patch of sky that's emerged from behind the clouds. 'My name is Bella Jordan, and I'm at the Stump and I need help.'

EPILOGUE

'Time to get up, sleepyhead.'

A groggy grumble from Max as he burrows under the covers: 'I'm cold.'

'You'll be warm once you're up and dressed. Come on. I'll go get your breakfast ready.'

'Chocolatey Oaty-Os?'

'Only if you can get yourself downstairs in five minutes, washed and brushed and dressed for school. And the countdown starts . . . now! Go!'

Max bolts from the bed.

Smiling, Bella heads back down the hall, past the vacant second-floor guest rooms. Things are quiet now that the season is over, and it's nice having the place to themselves again.

Wearing a warm sweatshirt over her pajamas in lieu of the bathrobe Pandora has yet to return, Bella can't deny the nip in the air.

An unusually hot August had quickly given way to an unseasonably chilly September.

Well, not unseasonable for Lily Dale, according to Odelia, who is predicting snow before the month is out.

'Mark my words,' she'd said at last night's book club meeting. 'We're in for an early winter this year. Mother Nature isn't going to be kind to this little corner of the universe.'

Yeah, well, Bella will take whatever Mother Nature dishes out, as long as she and Max can continue to call this little corner of the universe *home*.

It might be slightly more challenging to take whatever Pandora Feeney dishes out when she takes over as mistress of Valley View next month. She claims that she isn't planning to actually move in – not yet, anyway.

'Maybe one day,' she'd said. 'But for the time being, just think of me as your silent partner, Isabella.'

'You? Silent? I'll believe that when I see it,' Odelia had muttered.

'Gammy!' Calla had said in a warning tone.

'What? I'm just observing a fact.'

'The fact is, Pandora is doing Bells a huge favor by buying Valley View,' Misty said. 'Actually, Pandora, you're doing all of us a huge favor. Especially Jiffy. I don't know how he'd get through any of this without his best friend Max.'

By *any of this*, she means her separation from Mike, and the ongoing fallout from Jiffy's role in the theft at the Slayton house, and the subsequent one he'd staged at Misty's to cover up the loss of his own belongings.

He'd intended to confess the truth to both Misty and Lieutenant Grange, but when Odelia had escorted him over to Valley View to do just that, Grange wasn't there.

No, he was busy slapping handcuffs on the man who'd held Bella at gunpoint, and putting out an APB for a woman driving a white Chevy with Massachusetts plates. She hadn't been hard to locate, waiting in the getaway car just outside the Dale.

The Slaytons' sapphire necklace hadn't been hard to locate, either. Jiffy had produced it from the hidden compartment under a stair tread at Valley View, along with the ugly pink vase from Misty's mantel. He couldn't bear to take her wedding ring or jar of cash, but had correctly assumed Misty wouldn't mind losing the vase.

The stair compartment is a popular spot for necklaces, as Bella's tourmaline pendant had turned up in that very spot last summer. Currently, it's at the jeweler's for a repair on the delicate chain that had broken at some point during Bella's violent struggle with her assailant.

Millicent has since filled her in about Sam's illegitimate half-brother.

'Bella, when that man turned up at my door, I thought for a moment that he was Sam's ghost, just like you did.'

That had been in February last year, when her grief for her son was still fresh. Her shock at seeing his lookalike gave way to the shock of discovering that her late husband had a son just a few years younger than Sam.

'It probably shouldn't have caught me off guard. All Thierry's business trips, the late nights at the office . . . oldest story in the world, isn't it?'

'You never confronted him?'

'About being unfaithful? No. At the time, I don't think I ever allowed myself to suspect the truth. You know what they say – sometimes, we only see what we want to see.'

Oh, yes. Bella knows.

'In any case, even Thierry didn't realize his mistress – one of his mistresses – had had a child. She was married, too. Unhappily, and violently, according to her son. I guess it's no surprise that he turned out the way he did, growing up the way he did. I guess we should pity him, but when I think about what he did to you . . . and the way he acted right from the start, making it clear he wasn't there to find out about his father and brother, or you and Max. I never realized I was putting you in danger, telling him about you. That was in the very beginning, and I thought he was asking about you because he cared.'

What he wanted, Millicent said, was money. She sent him away, only to have him come back from time to time, looking for a handout.

'I stopped answering the door when he buzzed. But he'd sit out there in front of my building, waiting for me to come out. I never thought he was dangerous. Just . . . a nuisance.'

'Why didn't you tell me about him?'

'For one thing, I could never find the right time. You've already been through so many difficult, emotional times. And for another, I was afraid that you might not see him for who he really is. That you might look at him and see Sam.'

As she had. There's no denying the two men shared similar features.

His attempts to get money out of the Jordan family had escalated in the past month, when he began dating his accomplice, the woman using the alias Polly Green.

After seeing Bella and Max getting into that shiny black limo at Millicent's, Sam's brother had assumed he'd discovered a potential new source of cash, and had followed them to the airport, intending to introduce himself as Bella's long-lost brother-in-law and ask her for money.

After the security guard had thwarted that plan, and they'd slipped away, Polly had come up with the idea to go to Lily Dale. She'd checked into Valley View, intending to see what she could uncover about Bella's finances. She'd found not just the whopping check from Millicent, but the bills that had led to the preposterous story about Sam in trouble with loan sharks and faking his death.

As she heads down the stairs, Bella again thinks of the sapphire necklace Jiffy had hidden under the tread. When he'd shown it to

Misty and Odelia, he – and they – had fully intended to tell Lieutenant Grange the full story.

But Misty, hearing that he'd stolen it in a misguided effort to save his parents' marriage, couldn't allow him to go through with it.

'If Jiffy puts it right back where he found it, no one will ever have to know who took it, or how it got back there,' she'd told Odelia, who'd later confided the story in Bella. 'No punishment Grange gives him will hold a candle to what he's going to go through with the divorce.'

Odelia might not approve of that logic, and Bella might not have handled it the same way, but Jiffy is Misty's son, and – as Odelia put it, 'Some tales aren't ours to tell.'

Kevin Beamer won't be sharing any incriminating tales about Jiffy with Grange, either, and not just because the evidence had been deleted from his phone. The day after Odelia had cornered him at the auditorium, he'd had a bad fall while riding Jiffy's scooter in the park, breaking an ankle, his right wrist and his nose in the process.

Max and Jiffy, running through the sprinklers in Valley View's front yard, had witnessed the accident . . . or was it?

'Lizzie pushed him,' Jiffy had informed Bella.

'Who's Lizzie?'

'She's my friend. She likes to swing in the park.'

'There's no swingset in the park,' Bella pointed out.

'It's a tree swing. Lizzie's spirit. I kept telling Kevin she was going to get him for what he did to me, but he didn't believe me. Not even when he got that bad shock from my Playbox.'

'Lizzie did that?'

'Yep. She's electrocuted,' he added matter-of-factly.

A few days later, Jiffy found his scooter, Playbox, Ninja Zombie Battle video game, and phone on the doorstep, and Kevin Beamer hasn't bothered him or Max since.

'Every bully meets his match sooner or later,' Odelia commented when Bella shared the news with her and Pandora. 'All the better if the match is a pretty little girl with corkscrew curls and pink ribbons.'

'It is, isn't it?' Pandora agreed with her – for once. Sort of. 'Oh, and you mean violet ribbons, don't you?'

'I mean pink ribbons.'

'Ah, then you must be thinking of someone else.'

'I'm thinking of Lizzie,' Odelia said. 'From the park.'

'As am I. Lizzie has violet ribbons. But then, you're not much of a gardener, are you?'

'Meaning . . .?'

'Meaning, violets are a flower, as are pinks, and when it comes to flowers, you're rather . . .'

And off they went. Some things, Bella supposes, will never change.

As book club meetings go, last night's had been one of the more argumentative gatherings they've had – mostly, but not entirely, due to Odelia and Pandora's vastly different interpretations of the novel they'd just finished reading. The tension was broken only by Sprout and Twixie, Odelia's newly adopted kittens, chasing a catnip ball around the room.

The book they were discussing was a romance – Bella's pick, courtesy of her mother-in-law's recommendations.

'I just think it was completely unrealistic that the hero and heroine would end up together in the end,' Misty said. 'They have absolutely nothing in common.'

'That's what made it work,' Odelia told her. 'When a couple has everything in common, life is too predictable and boring.'

'Well, when they have nothing in common, they get divorced,' Misty said with a shrug.

'Well, sometimes, people get divorced because the wanker meets a trollop.'

'We're not talking about you and Orville, Pandora.'

'Gammy,' Calla said in a warning tone.

'What do *you* think, Calla?' Bella asked.

'About the book? I don't know. I think it's a lot like every other romance novel I've ever read. Next month is my pick, and I'm going to choose a nonfiction title.'

'Good idea,' Odelia said, and turned to Bella. 'What do *you* think about this one? You haven't said much.'

'I think the message is that true love conquers everything, if you're lucky enough to find it.'

'Most people aren't,' Misty said darkly.

'Sometimes they find it and lose it,' Pandora said.

'Some people find it not just once in one lifetime, but once in several lifetimes,' Odelia said. 'Did I ever tell you that back in the fourteenth century, I was married to—'

'Yes!' they said in unison.

'Well, at least you can all agree on something,' Odelia said dryly, and turned to Bella with a thoughtful smile. 'You know, some people are lucky enough to find true love twice in one lifetime.'

Bella knew that she was talking about Drew. They all did, of course.

But these things are complicated. They take time, and patience, even when two people have a lot in common; when they want the same thing. This isn't a romance novel, where happily ever after is guaranteed. Bella isn't a heroine, and Drew isn't a—

'Hero!' he shouts from the kitchen as she reaches the bottom of the stairs, and she smiles, hurrying to the back of the house.

She can smell coffee brewing, and . . .

'Is that bacon?' she calls, sniffing the telltale scent in the air.

'It is. Well, it was.'

Crossing the threshold, she sees him, dressed for work in his scrubs, clattering about with spatulas and pots and pans.

'I thought I'd surprise you and Max with a nice hot breakfast on a cold morning,' he says, turning to greet her with a quick kiss. 'Eggs, hashbrowns, bacon . . . only *someone* ate the bacon when I wasn't looking, even though he'd already polished off his own food.'

He waves an accusatory hand.

Bella sees the cats, busily eating their breakfast in the usual spot on the mat.

Beside the two small bowls – one that reads Chance in pink lettering, the other that reads Spidey in red – is a much larger bowl. That one bears the name Hero, inscribed in blue. It's also empty.

Sitting beside it, the foxhound regards Bella with those big eyes of his – no longer sad, but perhaps a bit guilty.

Bella laughs and bends to pet his head. 'What did you do, Hero? Did you steal the bacon?'

'Of course, he did.'

'Come on, boy. Let's get you out of the kitchen. You can come with me to get the newspaper from the porch.'

'Good idea,' Drew says. 'I'll fry up some more bacon.'

Bella opens a cabinet and grabs something, slipping it into her sweatshirt pocket.

'Come on, Hero. Let's go.'

'Did you just smuggle dog treats into your pocket?' Drew asks.
She laughs. 'Of course.'

'You're spoiling that dog of yours.'

'He deserves a little treat every now and then. He misses the
puppies.' All three had gone to their permanent homes last week,
while the foxhound remained in his. Right here at Valley View,
with Bella and Max and Chance and Spidey and – occasionally –
Drew.

No, he doesn't live here – *not yet*, as Pandora might say. But
now that the guest rooms are vacant, he's been spending the night
more often than not, helping Bella and Max learn the ropes of dog
ownership.

'Better bundle up,' Drew calls from the kitchen as she heads for
the door. 'It was really cold out when I took him out for his morning
walk.'

'It's still summer!' Bella reminds him, and steps out onto the
porch.

It's summer according to the calendar, for another ten days.

Hero lifts his long nose and sniffs.

'What do you smell?' Bella asks, but she knows. She can smell
it, too.

Just the slightest hint of autumn, wafting in air that will soon be
thick with the scent of ripe fruit and woodsmoke and fallen leaves.

It isn't here yet. No, it's still summer.

Looking up at the big old maple tree beyond the porch, she
confirms that the leaves are indeed still lush and green.

All but one.

Against a deep blue sky, a single, glorious red leaf flutters and
dances toward her, borne on the cool breeze that gently stirs the
wind chimes.

It lands at her feet.

She looks at the sky, and at the delicate blue glass angels, tinkling
softly in the eaves.

'Got it. Thanks, Sam,' she whispers.

She picks up the red leaf, tucks it into her pocket, and wipes her
damp eyes.

Hero is watching her.

'It's OK,' she assures him with a smile. 'It's fine. Come on.'

Back inside, she calls up the stairs, 'Max! Breakfast is ready!'

'Chocolatey Oaty-Os?'

'Something better! Dr Drew made eggs and hashbrowns and bacon!'

'Yes! I love Dr Drew and eggs and hashbrowns and bacon, don't you, Mom?' He bounds down the stairs.

'I do,' Bella says, and she means it with all her heart.